ZERO SUM

Civil Strife Series Book One

By Matthew J O'Connor

D1714202

Find Matthew J O'Connor at his Facebook page and at www.matthewjoconnor.net

A special thanks to my wife, who is both my best friend and biggest supporter

Chapter One: Impetus

Russel Godfrey wheeled his luxury sedan into the right lane, exited off of Interstate 35, and turned right at the next intersection. Coming into view above the snow-covered maple trees and abandoned gas station, was Spencer & Creed Tower. Formerly a multi-purpose office space that was a workplace for the employees of dozens of local companies, Spencer & Creed Tower was now home to the Midwest corporate branch of the 3rd largest bank in the United States, a bank whose total assets rivaled the GDP of Canada and Russia combined.

The building was, in reality, a stout and hulking compound that more closely mirrored the shape of a massive shoebox, than that of a tower. At only 6 stories tall, it made up for the unimpressive height with its expansive footprint. Russel's office was on the 5th floor, and he preferred to use the elevator that went directly from the underground parking lot, where his seniority had afforded him a parking space. Russel nodded to the security guard as he approached the gate that barred entry to the parking lot. Russel deliberately avoided rolling down his window to let in the frigid air outside. The striped gate swung upwards, allowing Russel to roll his sedan down into the subterranean ramp that lay underneath the behemoth of a building.

Knowing he was a part of one of the largest financial institutions in human history brought little pride to Russel. He was several generations removed from when G.H. Spencer and Alfred Creed formed their respective banks in the 1920s. Russel was in diapers when the two banks merged in the 1980s. He held little sway within the corporate structure, a fact that did not bother the middle-aged bachelor. He knew he didn't build this bank, and he knew that he wanted no part in the charades of managing the thousands of tellers, traders, managers, executives, analysts, and more, that Spencer & Creed employed. No, Russel had only one concern this Wednesday morning, and that was making money for the company. Of course, Russel didn't care about the corporation's finances. He did, however, care about making money for his department within Spencer & Creed, which naturally and eventually translated to a larger paycheck and more generous bonuses for himself.

Russel had been on a rough stretch for the last 8 months. Technically, he reminded himself, his department hadn't officially had a losing day in 279 business days. Or was it 280? Regardless, working as an investment manager at one of the largest banks in the world meant that actually losing money was difficult these days. But it took more than not losing money for Russel to set himself apart. Russel was part of a relatively new program the bank had started a few years back, which involved his department investing in a variety of assets, including stocks, commodities, commercial real estate, currencies, and more. He enjoyed the challenge and flexibility of not being relegated to a single asset class.

His phone buzzed as he strolled through the underground ramp. He glanced down to see it was Chris Jenkins, a former colleague and friend from Russel's time at Third Realm Capital, a firm that the two had helped transform from a relatively unknown company, into a well respected and profitable hedge fund. The two men, who had shared an apartment many years ago when they were merely fledgling traders, had since maintained a close friendship, despite their geographic separation and the fact they no longer worked at the same firm.

"What's up, Chris?" Russel said into his earpiece.

"Happy Fed Day!" Chris replied.

"Yeah, happy Fed Day to you too," Russel grunted. "Are we looking at actually making some money this time?"

"Oh come on, is that why I haven't gotten a Christmas card from you yet?" said Chris.

"Chris, upper management was pissed we missed that trade."

"That wasn't my fault, I just give you the leak. I don't tell you how the markets react," Chris said defensively.

"The consensus beforehand was that a rate cut would be good for emerging market stocks," Russel responded, referring to an amalgamation of various analyst's projections of upcoming market moves based on events, such as those that occur on "Fed Day".

"The only consensus that matters is the market, you know that Russ."

Russel was annoyed, but he knew Chris was correct about this. He paused for a moment.

"Ah, sorry man, you're right. That one was on me. I'm not trying to give you a hard time, it's just been rough these past few months."

"Tell me about it, I thought these markets were strange five years ago, but each year they look less and less like markets, and more like a never-ending game of charades," Chris replied.

"Yeah, I know," Russel sighed. "I've been working on something big these last few weeks. Might be nothing, but I want to run it by you later today. This could be big Chris. Really big. Or I'm just seeing something that's not there."

"Come on Russ, why do you have to go and get me all curious about something right before bedtime? I'm not going to be able to sleep now," Chris replied, with a hint of sarcasm.

"It's a little early for a nap, isn't it?" asked Russel.

"Oh, I didn't mention I'm in Singapore? On a trip to meet with some clients out here. Hope you're enjoying that snow up in Minnesota."

Russel chuckled at that; Singapore did sound pretty good right now.

"Alright Chris, so why'd you call me? Or did you just want to brag about your vacation?"

"It's about the Fed meeting."

"What about it?" Russel replied.

Chris was referring to the meeting of the Federal Open Market Committee, often abbreviated to the FOMC, was the title given to a group of policymakers at the Federal Reserve, the United States' central bank. The FOMC was responsible for setting key interest rates, creating new currency, buying financial assets with that currency, and a host of other tasks that fall under the umbrella of monetary policy. "Fed Day" was the term Chris and Russel used to refer to their regularly scheduled meetings that occurred 9 times a year, and were followed by a written statement and often a question and answer session by the chairman of the Federal Reserve. The policy changes, as well as the statements made by the Chairman, were analyzed by the financial world like the paparazzi analyzed the day-to-day life of a movie star. In many respects, the meetings represented 9 of the most important days for markets and the financial community each year.

"I'm not going to have any special information on it for you, this time."

"Then why'd you call?"

"That's the thing," said Chris. "I've been getting leaks about these meetings for, I don't know, 3 years? Sometimes the full release, sometimes just bullet points. But this time? Zilch. Nothing."

"Sounds like a level playing field, buddy, the way it's supposed to be."

"What do either of us know about a level playing field?" said Chris, chuckling.

"We'd have to do some actual research if that was the case. Could you imagine? We'd have to actually work," said Russel, continuing the joke.

"But in all seriousness," said Chris, "I'm staying out of this one. No sense in going for a drive at night without headlights, right?"

"Yeah, makes sense. Well, thanks anyways. I'll give you a call later this week to talk about this big trade I'm working on."

"Still not handing out any hints?" said Chris.

Russel hesitated. "Something fishy in some structured products I'm looking at."

"Corporate debt?" asked Chris.

"How'd you know?" replied Russel.

"You're predictable Russ. Whenever you have a few bad months, you always start looking for that home run trade, and everyone knows the corporate debt bubble popping would be the home run everyone looks for. But, Russel, you know-"

"Yeah, timing is everything," said Russel, finishing Chris' thought. "But, I still have some charts for you to look over."

"Alright, send them over to me and I'll take a look."

"Thanks Chris. Have a good one."

The steel gate creaked as it swung shut. On one side was a large field, half trampled, half-covered in recently fallen snow, filled with roughly 80 half-ton beasts that lumbered about the mostly empty expanse. David Ruiz walked away from the other side of the gate

3

towards his house, 200 yards away. David looked over his shoulder at the field of beef cattle, as he made a mental catalog of the tasks for the rest of the day.

The cattle farmer opened the side door to his house, took off his boots, and walked to the bathroom to clean up. His rough, cracked hands needed time to adjust to the warmer temperatures inside. The hot water from the faucet quickened the process, but also made it mildly painful. He dried his hands and walked to his bedroom to change his clothes, at least for the next few hours. David enjoyed the smell of his farm. This time of year, he considered all the smells of the farm to be warm. Warm manure, warm hay, warm cattle, all in stark contrast to the cool air. However, he had not grown up on a farm, nor had his wife, Alice. Though neither found the smells to be repulsive, they also preferred to keep the smell of the field separate from the smell of his house, as futile a task as it was.

It was almost lunch, and as he exited the bathroom, he heard the footfalls of his two daughters as they ran into the kitchen to greet him.

"Hi daddy!" said Maya.

Maya was the younger of the two. At six years old, David could still easily pick her up, and did so, setting her on the countertop.

Harper walked in next.

"Need help with lunch, Dad?" she asked.

She was eleven years old, and though David still thought of her as a little girl at times, Harper had grown up significantly in the past few years.

"I don't think so. I found some really big worms out in the field, I thought we could try slurping those up," David said, with a smile.

Maya reacted with a giggle, and Harper smirked, more amused by her sister's enjoyment of the joke than the joke itself.

"I'll heat up some leftovers from last night," he said. "How's the homework going this morning?"

"I have a question I'm stuck on with science," replied Harper.

"What's it about?" asked David.

"Well, it's not really a question on the homework. How do cells know what kind of cell that they're supposed to grow into? I know DNA is supposed to tell the cell how to grow, but how do they know what kind?"

"Let me heat this up," David said as he opened the microwave. "We'll talk about it in a minute."

Harper thrived in a homeschooled setting. Always curious, she often was more challenged by her own questions, than the questions in the textbook. So often, her questions extended beyond the scope of the curriculum. This made David proud. He and his wife had decided when they moved to the farm that they would prefer homeschooling. The two could see that public schools had become increasingly inadequate at fulfilling their main purpose, education. Instead, they decided Alice would take on these duties, as education was her major in college prior to switching her focus to marketing.

For some time, this plan had worked. David was able to run the farm, but could still help at home if needed, considering the proximity. The farm grew quickly; it had become profitable far sooner than the two had expected. The demand for grass-fed organic beef was robust early on and continued to rise for the first few years. David even considered buying a neighboring 60 acres to add to his own, which sat vacant at the time.

Then, in 2020, the pandemic happened. In their Southern Indiana farm, they were largely isolated from the virus itself. For around a year, business actually improved. Fears of meat shortages, as well as a new crowd of individuals looking for a healthy and locally sourced food source, sent demand and prices much higher.

For a while, business was great. David eventually did decide to buy the extra land. Then, he expanded his herd another 50%, which was also a large expense, considering the prices of calves had risen in tandem with beef prices. However, within months of this expansion, the local market took a turn for the worse. The nearby town of Columbus, Indiana began seeing industries close up shop or else relocate. This culminated in the bankruptcy and subsequent liquidation of Cummins, the engine manufacturer that had employed a large portion of the surrounding community.

David had lived through the relative decline of the Midwest prior to, during, and after the Great Recession. However, the last several years had been far different. It was no longer just the Detroits and Clevelands of the U.S. that were struggling. David found himself struggling to keep his farm operating during an economic period that was only rivaled in intensity and length by the Great Depression.

"Dad, I asked you something," Maya said sharply.

"Sorry, honey, what was that?" asked David, struggling to take his mind away from the constant replay of what he considered a series of failures on his behalf.

"When does Mom get home from work?"

"Oh, after dinner, I think," he replied, as he poured his daughters two glasses of milk.

The hours she worked only exacerbated his negative image of himself. He had failed his family by not adequately providing for them financially. Of course, he knew that wasn't entirely true. They owned their house outright. and he never had missed a payment on the farm. Food was on the table, the lights were on, and he had two wonderfully bright daughters. David felt he had a marriage as solid as granite, which was a fact he and Alice both credited to their mutual faith in God, the God of the Bible. In fact, his faith was what countered his own feelings of dissatisfaction at times with a reminder of how fortunate he was.

However, the need for Alice to work outside the house was never part of their plan. She had worked for years before they had moved out to the country, and David certainly understood that watching his two girls was as difficult as any job, especially when they were younger. But, Alice loved and cherished those days, even if they left her exhausted and stressed at times. Alice often told David that she doesn't mind working outside the house at a local marketing firm; she had a bachelor's degree in the profession, along with years of experience. They both felt fortunate she was able to land a job in this economy. Still, David often blamed himself for this change of plans.

He felt his phone vibrating in his pocket.

"Hey babe, how's work?" answered David.

"Oh, you know, it's work," said Alice. "I was just checking in on you and the girls."

"We're fine; Maya's just playing with matches, and I think Harper ran away from home, but I'm sure we'll figure it all out," said David, with a grin.

"Sounds about right!" said Alice. "So, I'm running to the store after I get off, do you need anything?"

"Wow, this sounds like something that could have been asked through a text message, or maybe an email."

"Enough with the small talk, David. I don't have time for this."

David paused, unsure if she had misread his joke, or perhaps was in a sour mood.

"I've got to get back to flirting with Tanner from accounting."

"Good one, spend all morning thinking that one up?" David replied. "Um, there's nothing I can think of. Girls, do you need anything from the store?" he asked his daughters in the room next door.

"Candy!" said Maya.

"Chocolate!" replied Harper, simultaneously.

"Yeah, they said they want some toothpaste and a bag of carrots," David said in a volume loud enough for his daughters to hear.

"Alright," Alice said, chuckling. "I'll be back around 6."

"Alright see you then."

"See you later."

Still unsure of who had bested who in the light banter, Neither spouse felt insecure in their current relationship, allowing them to engage in such humor without fear of offending the other. Such phone calls brightened David's day, and often re-centered his thoughts on the positive aspects of his life, the countless ways in which he had been blessed.

David turned to his daughter and returned to the question she had posed. "Let's start by talking about these special cells called stem cells."

Technically, Reid Bowman, was the third most senior employee at Stronghold Capital, when measured based on date of hire. Only the chief financial officer and the director of fixed income investment had been with the firm for a longer period of time. Of course, this was a fact that only Reid was aware of, largely because he was the only employee that cared. He had started with the company over a decade ago as an entry-level IT worker, assisting the IT department and other employees with what he felt were menial tasks, such as implementing software updates, troubleshooting computer problems, and fielding a wide variety of questions from the employees, employees that he viewed as technologically illiterate.

However, through the years, Reid had worked his way up through the IT department. Two years prior, he had been promoted to a position with the title of Information Systems Manager. This position came with the responsibility of supervising a majority of the IT department. In addition to personnel management, he was also responsible for the massive servers that connected the firm to the outside world and, most importantly, the markets themselves.

The fact of the matter was that, though the technology required to sustain firms such as Stronghold Capital had become far more important in recent years, it still played second fiddle to those that actually managed money. Whether it be through trading, managing funds, or even those bright enough to create and manage the algorithmic systems that were crucial to making Stronghold Capital the eighth largest wealth management firm in the United States, the glory, as well as the most generous compensation, went to those that were involved in the markets. Countless other employees, including Reid, were all but forgotten, regardless of their importance to the day-to-day operations of the firm.

It had occurred to Reid in the past that their high level of importance within the company, as well as correspondingly hefty salaries, might be related to vast sums of money that these money managers had made for the firm and its clients.

Who cares how much they make for the company? They'd be nothing without these servers, and the servers would be useless, albeit expensive, hunks of hardware, if it weren't for guys like me.

Algorithms, often referred to as "algos" within the trading community, referred to complex trading strategies that made trades within markets based on intricate mathematical equations. Historically, these algorithms had been created by human minds. In many cases, that continued to be the case, though the creation and modification of the complex trading and hedging strategies increasingly relied on the overwhelming power of artificial intelligence. In many cases, these algorithms were designed to operate with a strategy known as high-frequency trading, a strategy that Stronghold Capital specialized in.

High-frequency trading, as the name suggests, involves a huge amount of trades that would far exceed the amount of trades that a human trader would be able to make with any level of success in securing profits. The profits from these frequent and numerous trades were small, and not every trade was profitable. However, like a casino, these algorithms depended on the law of probabilities in order to create a profit.

Not every financial firm that attempted to implement algorithmic and high-frequency trading had been profitable. Success was dependent on a combination of a variety of factors. A firm needed a strong strategy for trading, as well as state-of-the art technology. Another crucial component of success for such firms was a rapid way in which to communicate with markets. The speed of this communication was a hotly contested competition among high-frequency trading firms. If a trade could be sent a fraction of a second faster by one firm, relative to other high-frequency trading firms, that firm could then benefit from the price movement that occurred due to the latecomers, many of which would have already executed similar trades. Though executed at the same time, these trades would be fulfilled after the trade of the firm with the fastest communication, thus bidding up the price after the fastest firm had already established a position, a position that they may choose to immediately sell, and in turn, make a profit. This process would repeat itself thousands, millions of times in a day, and begin once again on the next trading day.

Firms would often expend a considerable amount of capital in order to minimize this time of communication with markets. Fiber optic cables and dishes sending microwaves were two of the more common modes of transmission chosen to send trades to the desired market, which itself often consisted of a physical location and a series of computers and servers, not entirely unlike those at the various firms. In fact, some firms had paid millions of dollars for land that either allowed a shorter length of cable, or else a more direct path for microwave transmission, in order to improve this transmission time by mere microseconds. Stronghold Capital was a firm that had done just that, with their headquarters in Chicago, only blocks from the Chicago Mercantile Exchange.

The firm had also recognized the importance of superior hardware and had made investments in their technological infrastructure. Of these investments, Reid was most proud of the server room, a room that housed banks of large servers that were responsible for communication between traders' desks and the markets. The room also housed expensive, high-performance computers, computers that were purchased with the same intent of maximizing the speed in which trades could be executed and fulfilled.

These machines created a barely perceptible whirring as Reid walked through the aisles of the room. In half an hour, Reid would clock out for the last time with Stronghold Capital. To others, it would appear he was taking his lunch break. To Reid, it signified an escape from the firm that he had come to both love, and loathe.

He had been a loyal employee for all these years, but in the end, five million dollars in an untraceable, offshore bank account was a deal too hard to pass up, especially considering his already disgruntled attitude. It would be the middle finger he had wanted to give to the executives for so long, but far more impactful. Reid had already booked a flight for this afternoon from O'Hare to LAX, and then from LAX to Bangkok. After he had secured access to his bank account, he then could take his time setting up his new life as a wealthy expatriate in Southeast Asia. To the government and citizens of Thailand, or whatever country he decided to settle down in, he would be nothing more than another American that had chosen to leave the States in favor of the relatively low cost of living of a Southeast Asian country. The dollar went a long way in such a country, and it had been common practice for years.

Reid Bowman was only thirty minutes away from that life. He ensured that this final checkup on the server room went well; no problems with the liquid cooling system, all the servers were up and running, and the temperature and humidity were within the desired range. This was all data he could check remotely in his office, but it was the nostalgia of the room, the sacred room that he had spent countless hours caring for, that had drawn him to walk up and down the aisles of the server room once more. After completing the walkthrough, he ensured the door to the room was closed, and that it locked behind him, before he took the elevator down to the IT offices.

He had ensured that he was the only IT worker available for this stretch of time; most were off tending to tedious and borderline unnecessary projects he had deliberately assigned them to complete on this day. Reid sat down at his computer, opened up a few key programs, and put into motion the plan he had been planning for the last three weeks.

First, he changed settings for the alerts that would be sent out when problems cropped up that required his department's urgent attention. In this case, he wanted to make sure his email address would be the only address receiving such notifications. Next, he altered the upper bound of the temperature range that the computers and servers would be allowed to continue to operate. He altered it to only one degree Celsius above its current temperature. Next, ensured that not only would an alert go out when this temperature was exceeded, but that the servers and computers within the room would shut down. In normal situations, the shutdown temperature was at a far higher level and put in place to prevent permanent damage to the expensive hardware. In this case, the servers would be told to shut down, despite still being at a safe operating temperature. Finally, he shut down the liquid cooling system for the room.

Reid rode the elevator down to the ground floor, walked the two blocks to the parking ramp where his car was parked, and got in the car. Reid was proud of this plan that he had conceived. Though he was fairly sure that this sabotage was not legal, it also wasn't overt. No damage to the hardware would occur, and a start-up of the servers and computers could be completed in time for the remainder of the IT department to make it home in time for dinner. It would take at least until the next day for the company to realize that it may have been Reid that was responsible for the mayhem, and perhaps another few days for them to discuss any legal action with their team of lawyers. By then, he would be in Thailand and would be difficult, if not impossible, to track down.

Reid didn't know who was paying him this five million dollars. He didn't know that he was one of a half-dozen individuals at firms of comparable sizes that were executing similar plans to temporarily halt trading from their respective companies, all on the same day and at the same time. He did not know that this Wednesday afternoon happened to be the date of a Federal Reserve meeting. He did not know that the FOMC had, only minutes ago, surprised most analysts and traders, by raising interest rates, a move that was sure to cause increased volatility in markets.

No, Reid only knew and cared of what his life would be less than 48 hours from the execution of his plan. He planned to be sitting in an upscale Bangkok hotel, without a care in the world, sipping on some fruity alcoholic drink.

However, this future for Reid was not meant to be. Just as he was about to pull his car out of the ramp, his phone buzzed in his pocket. He instinctively reached for it and looked at the screen. It was a bad habit, he knew that, but a habit he had been unable to kick. With his eyes still on the screen, he began to pull out, relying on his peripheral vision for navigation. He didn't see the garbage truck traveling at 35 miles an hour that was barrelling at the driver's side of his compact car. Reid died nearly instantly from the impact. His final conscious thought related to the notification he was viewing on his phone as the garbage collector crumpled his spine and skill. It was an email notification that simply read: *Alert: 13:04 PM - Server temperature warning, shutdown of systems initiated.*

Chapter 2: Liquidity

"I, I just don't get it," said Russel.

"The Fed messed up. They should have gone with the consensus, not try and rock the boat," said Ronald Seehus, a junior analyst at Spencer & Creed, as he sat in Russel's office.

"I get that, but I've never seen the circuit breaker tripped that fast. Not in 2020, not in 2008. And what's with this low volume?" replied Russel.

Within two minutes of the Federal Reserve announcement, the market suddenly plummeted seven percent, triggering the "circuit breaker", a market mechanism that existed on the New York Stock Exchange that halted trading for a full 15 minutes. Russel was surprised by the decision on interest rates within the announcement from the Federal Reserve, but the response by markets seemed overdone. He was also puzzled by the low volume in the markets. Volume is a measure of the number of shares traded over a given period of time that generally rises dramatically during periods of volatility.

"When do they open up again?" asked Russel.

"Thirty seconds," replied the junior analyst.

Russel scoured the headlines from the mainstream financial media. So far, not one news outlet had a good explanation. He watched as trading resumed and the major stock market indices once again plunged. This time, in exactly thirty-five seconds, the markets dropped to the next trigger for the circuit breaker, a drop totaling thirteen percent. The largest stock market in the world was once again closed for fifteen minutes, while market participants, such as Russel, were left reeling. Russel continued to stare at the chart, as though it would tell him why this was happening and how he should respond. Russel's phone buzzed. It was a number he didn't recognize.

"Hello?"

"Russel, I need you in my office in two minutes."

The phone line went dead.

Russel knew the voice, and he now knew why he didn't recognize the number. It was Marcus Avenrow, the head of this regional branch, and an executive that was within the top ten of the most senior individuals with Spencer & Creed. Russel had conversations with Marcus on a semi-regular basis, conversations that generally occurred within Marcus' executive office. The two often saw eye to eye; they were both contrarians at heart. Marcus enjoyed playing devil's advocate to Russel's strategies, strategies that were often unconventional. And yet, he had on several occasions complimented Russel for his ingenuity. He was the man that lobbied corporate headquarters to create what was now Russel's department, and he had handpicked Russel as the head of the department. Despite this history, Russel still saw the man as an enigma; in many ways, Marcus' demeanor and philosophy seemed out of place at a corporate bank. It was an industry in which the range of opinions and philosophies on the market had become increasingly narrow, Marcus was a trailblazer that often made decisions in an unconventional, though deliberate, manner. Russel hustled out of his office and made his way to the top floor.

"Have a seat, Russel," said Marcus, calmly.

"Sir-"

Marcus cut him off. "It's over Russel."

"Excuse me? What's over?"

"Everything. This is it. Pack your things up and head home," replied Marcus, his demeanor having shifted from calm to stern.

"You're firing me? How was I-"

"No, I'm not saying you're fired. I'm saying this whole bank is finished. Hell, maybe this is the end for quite a few other big banks, too."

Russel finally sat down, feeling more confused than angry. "Why are you telling me this? Why me of all people?"

Marcus sighed. "I'll start from the beginning; I've been reading some of your work, your research into the structured products in the corporate debt market. You were onto something, something that you were only scratching the surface of, something that is blowing up in our faces."

"Hang on, you'll have to give me a second here. This is a lot to take in at once. You mean to tell me that what's happening today is related to those structured products?" Russel replied.

"No. Not exactly. To be frank, I'm not entirely sure what's happening today. This stays between you and I, but I have a very high up source that has been telling me that this wasn't an accident. That's their assessment, at least. Multiple different firms have been mentioning hacking, technical difficulties, things like that. Sabotage, even. All within the last hour or two," said Marcus

"What does this have to do with those structured products, though?" asked Russel, missing the point of the conversation.

"Forget the structured products. You were right, Russel. It was a bubble. But it was one of a dozen bubbles across the market. We all knew they were there, we all participated in that. What I'm telling you, is that what happened today? I'm convinced it was no accident."

"And?"

"And? This is the match that is lighting the powderkeg on these proverbial bubbles. You spend enough time in these markets, and you get a gut feeling about these things. This was intentional, I know it."

"Marcus, there's no way we survive this? Why not another bailout?"

"There won't be another bailout. Nationalization, that's what's next."

Zero Sum

Russel dreaded the term. Bank nationalization was something that, in the past, had only happened in Banana Republics, communist states, and the like. But, in the last few years, large banks had been nationalized throughout the European Union, Japan, Canada, and Australia. The wave of nationalization had culminated in the People's Republic of China's decision to nationalize the entirety of its financial system 18 months prior. This had not yet happened in the U.S., but Russel was hardly surprised that the topic would come up in the next crisis, the next crisis that had apparently decided to arrive on this frigid morning.

"But, I've said enough. Russel, I respect you and your work. I called you up here because I wanted to tell you personally. You've done a lot for this branch, and I had hoped you would take my own position one day. So, no, I'm not firing you, I'm just telling you that there's little use in coming back after today. Who knows? Maybe the bank tellers and janitors will keep their jobs, but not you and I. Spare yourself some dignity. Go home, pour yourself a drink, and try to relax. I have a feeling that today is just the first of many dark days to come."

Today was the day. Christie Eckles had received a message on her Preception messaging app during her second to last class of the day. Though she was unaware of the details of what and how the entire operation would be carried out, she had a gut feeling prior to receiving the message, that this was the day that it would all begin. The news of what was happening with markets was her first clue. She didn't understand much about the stock market, other than that it was another tool that the richest in today's society used to get richer. Regardless, she knew enough to realize that the ongoing crash was a departure from the norm. After that, she started seeing much more activity in the online forums that she was a member of. None of the posts, individually, were a dead giveaway. However, Christie was a bright, young woman, and her intuition had proven itself to be correct.

She chose to skip her final class of the day. The professor, she told herself, was liable to be more concerned about the markets, than one student's attendance. Not only was there no time to spare, but there was also no need to attend the class that would have been her final class period, at least for quite some time. Her training that she had received over the previous several months was clear. She understood that timeliness was crucial to success. The sooner and more efficiently she finished her tasks, the better.

Christie walked into her apartment and took off her backpack. She went into a closet in her bedroom and pulled out a different backpack. She changed into a pair of jeans and a dark sweatshirt and put on a pair of nondescript tennis shoes. She gathered a few other items, and then sat on her couch as she awaited more specific instructions

Finally, after several minutes of waiting, they arrived. The message consisted of a nearby address, as well as a code phrase.

151.

She dwelt on this code phrase for a moment, knowing its exact meaning. She, like every other person involved in the day's operations, knew precisely what such codes signified. They represented orders, instructions. The acts signified by the codes ranged from seemingly benign acts, such as organizing protests, to much more serious undertakings, up to and including murder. The orders were not chosen at random; they were decided by leadership on the basis of perceived loyalty, courage, and ability. Christie knew she embodied those qualities, though still found herself grateful that she had not been ordered to take someone's life. The task that she had been assigned, however, still shook her to her core. She was a young college student. She had never committed an act of violence, never so much as stolen a candy bar from a store. However, she knew the cause was worthy.

Pushing aside any doubts, she pulled up the address on her phone and walked out the door. Her heart pounded with both trepidation and excitement. The address she had been given was within walking distance. This turned out to be fortuitous, considering the ride-sharing app she had planned to utilize would require her to use her card or mobile payment app, both of which were rumored to be in the midst of a service disruption. After a brisk 15 minute walk, she arrived at the location that had been provided to her.

"You have got to be kidding me," she murmured to herself under her breath.

What stood directly across the street from Christie was an old-fashioned drug store that looked as if it was pulled straight out of the 1950s. A sign hung over the door that read *TJ's Drug Store*. Christie had never seen the store, but it reminded her of a simpler time, a more wholesome time. She knew that she had to finish what she had set out to complete, but this store stood in front of her, as if fate itself were trying its very hardest to change her mind, to prick her conscience.

She looked up and down the street. Cleveland was as busy as ever, but she could see that many of the people, whether they were in a car, on a bike, or on foot, appeared more distracted than usual. No doubt, much like Christie's college classmates, they were perplexed by what had happened in the markets today.

Suddenly, she heard police sirens blaring. The source of the sound was only blocks away. It took her brain a moment to realize that they were not coming for her. Christie's task was not yet completed, and she was, for the time being, innocent. Still, Christie wondered if that police officer was responding to one of her fellow operative's actions. She didn't know how many others were based in the Cleveland area, though she estimated it to be at least a dozen, considering the size of the city and surrounding communities.

She was stalling, and she knew it. She closed her eyes for a moment, took a deep breath, and began walking across the street. Once she reached the other side, she reached into her backpack and pulled out a bandana that she proceeded to tie behind her neck and pulled up to cover the bottom two-thirds of her face.

Christie entered through the front door of the store and approached the checkout counter. Behind the counter stood an elderly man that appeared to be in his 70s, if she were to make a guess. He was far too young to be the original owner of the shop, but a child of the owner? Grandchild? She was too nervous to do the mental math.

"What can I help you with?" said the man.

Christy hesitated.

"Just so you know, our card reader has been down this afternoon, so we're only able to accept cash."

Chris looked around the store. There were no other customers. Though she was wearing a bandana, it was still not unusual to see some individuals still wearing masks in the years since the COVID-19 pandemic. The man appeared to not be concerned with its presence on her face.

"Hang on a second," she said, as she pulled off her backpack, and reached into the largest compartment, doing her best to hide her shaking hands.

Her hand emerged from the bag, holding a handgun that Christie pointed squarely at the man's face. He immediately raised his hands and put them on the back of his head

"Listen, I don't want any trouble. I keep two hundred in the till. I can't give you any more than that. The safe has a 30-minute delay, and there's no way you'll hang around that long."

"I don't want your money," said Christie, as both her voice and her hand holding the gun, shook with fear.

She realized for a moment that the man behind the counter was calmer than she was.

"Okay, fine. Give me a second. And I'll find the key for the tobacco shelves," referring to the large display box, fully stocked with various brands of cigarettes, cigars, and electronic cigarettes.

"That's not what I'm here for. I, I want you to lead me to your backroom."

"Why?" said the man, with a confused expression.

"Listen," she said, raising her voice, "I don't think you're in a position to ask questions. I said, show me your backroom!"

The man obliged and began walking towards a door behind the counter with a sign that read *Employees Only*.

"Wait!" shouted Christie, in a stern voice. She kept the gun pointed at him as she grabbed a broom that sat behind the counter. She walked backwards towards the front of the store, not taking her eyes off the man. She placed the broom through the two door handles, securing the door from being opened from the outside.

"Okay, let's go," said Christie, as she gestured to the door leading to the back of the store.

The man began walking, and Christie followed, keeping the gun pointed at his back the entire time while also maintaining a distance of several feet. The back of the store was small, and much of the space was dominated by a large cooler in one corner and a desk in another.

"Stand in the corner, hands behind your back," said Christie, gesturing to a corner of the store that was clear of any furniture or merchandise.

Christie used her free hand to grab a set of zip-tie wrist restraints from her back pocket. She had practiced applying these several times in the past, but completing the task with a gun in one hand was a difficult task. She knew that, for a moment, the need for two unencumbered hands would leave her vulnerable, because she needed one hand to clasp his wrists together, and the other to pull the restraints tight. She tucked the handgun between her elbow and right hip and leaned in. As soon as she did this, the man attempted to pull his hands apart, while simultaneously stepping backwards. Christie was thrown off balance. She tripped over a box on the floor, falling on her back. The gun clattered on the floor, only a foot away from her hand. Before she had hit the ground, the man had already begun making his way towards the door to the front of the store.

Realizing her mistake, Christie panicked. She fumbled with the gun as she attempted to pick it up. While still laying on the ground, she aimed at the man's back as he fled. Of all the training she had completed, she only spent a short amount of time training with handguns. For lower-level operatives, such as Christie, it was never part of the plan to actually use the gun. Even in the mission that had been assigned to her, the instruction was not to kill employees or civilians unless certain criteria had been met. Any physical resistance or attempts to flee prior to the task being completed met that criteria.

She let fly a single round out of the nine-millimeter gun. It was not well aimed; she was still sitting on the floor with her legs stretched out, and she only was given a few seconds to line up the shot. At a range of fifteen feet, and to her complete surprise, she managed to place the round in the back of the man's neck. He fell immediately, and lay on the floor, his body having been rendered incapable of voluntary movement. Her ears rang from the shot in a small, enclosed space, and she winced in pain as she clasped her ears.

She stood up. Within twenty seconds, the ringing was no longer painful, but a high-pitched whine could still be heard. She breathed heavily as she slowly approached the man. A pool of blood had formed around his body. He lay on his stomach, with his head turned to the side. His eyes were wide open, and his face was frozen in fear.

A wave of nausea swept over Christie. She bent over a large washbasin, as her body attempted to vomit. She was unable to produce more than a dry heave, no doubt a result of the fact that she had not eaten since breakfast. She fought back tears and panic, as she tried to remember her purpose in this store.

She closed her eyes, took a deep breath, and walked through the door leading to the front of the store. The store was empty, and it appeared as though life was continuing on the street outside. Much to her relief, it was evident that the lone gunshot had not been heard on the street outside, or had else been dismissed as yet another non-descript noise that contributed to the clamor of the modern-day city.

She reached into her backpack and removed a pair of road flares, as well as a large can of lighter fluid. She unscrewed the cap and began spraying the fluid throughout the inside of the store, taking care to spray extra amounts on the old wallpapered walls, walls that she felt would be far more flammable a form of construction than much of the more modern construction that could be found in other parts of the store. Once the bottle was empty, she grabbed a road flare and struck the end against the cap. It immediately began burning with a bright red glow. She tossed the flare against a wall that stood twenty feet away. The flames rapidly spread both laterally and vertically across the wallpaper.

Christie had begun walking to the exit when she heard a loud ringing. She immediately recognized the noise and braced herself to be soaked with water. The water, however, did not rain on her. She looked back at the corner in which she started the fire. There were two sprinklers that were spraying water on the flames, which had already begun to subside. Another sprinkler near the other two began spraying water. Christie kicked over a shelf in anger. The entire reason for leading the employee to the back of the store was to locate and disable the sprinkler system, a key part of the plan she had forgotten in her panic after shooting the man. Already, she could see someone peering through the window, watching the scene unfold. She didn't have much time, and she

15

wouldn't let her efforts, as well as the unexpected death of the man, to have been completed in vain.

She again walked to the back of the building, entering through the door, and taking care not to slip on the wet floor. She stepped over the man's body. Christie quickly located the cluster of pipes, one of which had a sprinkler shut-off valve that was labeled as such. She turned it ninety degrees. She briskly walked to the front of the building. The fire was only barely burning but had begun to give off thick, black smoke. She coughed and tried to use her bandana to filter the air she was inhaling. She walked down three different aisles, before finding what she was looking for. She grabbed a can of lighter fluid, this one smaller than the one she had brought in her backpack. She quickly unscrewed the cap and sprayed it all around the small flames on the wall. This revived the dying flames, which subsequently spread to a shelf full of baby diapers that was up against the wall. In another direction, it followed the stream of lighter fluid onto a clothing rack that held a small collection of adult clothing. The smoke filled the store and first accumulated around the ceiling, but slowly made its way down towards the ground. She was almost finished. A small crowd had gathered outside the store. Several of them aimed their phones at the store, filming the blaze. Another one had his phone up to his ear and appeared to be calling 911. Two women tried to push open the door, though were unable to overcome the broom that barred their entrance.

Christie was planning to escape through the back of the store but remembered one more part of her training. The store had begun to grow dark with the smoke, and the fire had begun to be choked out by the lack of fresh air. She found a large glass bottle that held some form of shampoo or makeup, she wasn't sure. She was about to throw it at the window at the front of the store, shattering the thin glass and allowing the blaze to burn with no limitation on fresh air. However, before she could get in position to make the throw, she saw a man outside throw a metal garbage can through the window, accomplishing the task before she was able. The smoke flowed out through this new exit, and she quickly felt the building, which was already hot, grow warmer. Still shrouded in smoke, she took this opportunity to run towards the back of the store. She was coughing violently at this point, but she knew her job was complete. The back of the store was hazy, but the door had done an adequate job of halting the spread of the smoke for the time being. She halted and took several seconds to cough, as she struggled to take in the relatively clean air.

Once the coughing had subsided temporarily, Christie pulled down her bandana and took off her sweatshirt in order to quickly alter her appearance. She opened up the back door. Before leaving, she looked back at the man's body that lay on the floor. Shrugging the guilt and hesitation aside, she walked out into the alleyway. She was alone. At both ends of the alley, she could see the busy city streets. Off in the distance, she could hear a blaring siren, a siren that possibly belonged to an approaching fire truck. As casually as possible, she turned to her left and walked down the alley. Once at the end of the alley, she turned to her right and joined the foot traffic on the street.

Christie found herself wanting to sit in a dark corner of her apartment and cry. She wasn't sure why that was the case; was it guilt over what she had done? Or, was it the stress of what had happened combined with the effects of the adrenaline now leaving her body? Before she could linger on such thoughts and emotions, her phone buzzed in her

pocket. She looked at the screen. It was a new address, an address that was once again within walking distance. At the end of the message was the same code phrase as before.
151.

"You won't believe what I just saw, David," Alice said over the phone, with shock in her voice.

"What?" David replied, concerned.

"Milk is on sale for six dollars a gallon," said Alice, with exactly the same distressed tone.

"Alice, you have to stop doing that to me," said David.

Alice giggled at her own triumph and David's exasperation. "I'm just trying to keep you on your toes."

"Congrats, you've succeeded."

"By the way, I'm at the store now. Did something happen today?"

"What do you mean?" replied David.

"I'm not sure. There's a line at the gas station down the street, maybe 10 or 15 cars lined up behind the pumps. I thought that was, I don't know, unusual? Then, I walked into the store. Some of the people here are trying to push around two fully loaded carts of groceries like they're panic buying, or something."

"Hm. That is a little strange. I haven't had a chance to check the news or anything, I just got in from outside. I think I saw something earlier about the-"

"The thing about the stock market, right. Some of the people at the office were talking about it. They made it sound like the sky was falling."

The two did not own a considerable amount of equities; keeping the farm afloat had taken precedence over the contribution to a retirement fund. Alice tended to not worry as much about the stock market or other financial matters that were well outside of her control. "Don't make financial stability your idol" Alice had told David on many occasions. David, on the other hand, did concern himself with such variables. The oscillation of the stock market, real estate market, and cattle markets had caused him considerable stress in the past.

"Do you think that would cause something like this?" asked Alice.

"It hasn't in the past. It's hard to say."

"Hm. Alright. I'll pick up a few extra things, just to be safe. I'll be home in a little while," said Alice.

They exchanged their goodbyes as she walked through the supermarket. It was certainly busier than usual; many shoppers appeared to be buying as though they were stockpiling. Some filled their carts with canned foods and boxes of pasta, while others stacked large packs of toilet paper on top of their other groceries. A concern grew within her as she pushed her cart down the aisle containing coffee, breads, and condiments, noticing that many shelves had begun to grow bare. If she was unable to obtain some food items to fill her own cart, it would not be catastrophic. She and David maintained a moderately sized stockpile of foods that they regularly rotated through, foods that largely consisted of the very foods they usually consumed on a daily basis. However, the mentality that drove these other shoppers to become hoarders, seemingly in a manner of hours, brought Alice to question what had or was expected to occur that elicited this response.

Her thoughts were interrupted by shouting near the front of the store. She walked one aisle over, giving her a clear view of part of the line of checkout booths. Two men were shouting over something. She could only understand portions of it, both because of her distance and the ambient noise within the busier than usual store. The younger of the two men gestured to the man's cart, though it was unclear what had upset him; the older man repeatedly referred to his adversary as a snowflake, as he tried to drown out the man's voice with his own. Such confrontations were uncommon in an otherwise sleepy midwestern town. *What changed?* Alice asked herself.

Alice pushed her cart to a checkout line that appeared shorter than the rest, her cart still largely empty with only a few, non-food=related items she had planned to purchase prior to witnessing the frantic atmosphere of the store. The verbal confrontation between the two men ended; the younger man stormed off, leaving his cart in the middle of an aisle.

"Ma'am, do you have another card we could try?" said a cashier to the woman at the head of the line of the aisle Alice had selected.

"Try it again," the customer replied, tersely.

"Sometimes cards wear out, or our scanner gets picky," the cashier replied, as the error message continued to appear on his terminal.

Alice could practically hear the customer roll her eyes at this.

"There was enough in the account this morning."

The cashier didn't reply, trying desperately to not escalate the situation.

"Try this one," said the customer as she handed the cashier a separate card from her purse.

The alternate card returned the same error message. The cashier pressed a button near her computer, indicating she needed help from a supervisor. Alice's first instinct had been to offer up her own card; if the woman was in a bind, she would not mind helping her, assuming the other woman would have the humility to allow her to help. As she rifled through her purse for her wallet, she was halted by another woman's offer.

"Ma'am, if you'd like, you can use my card. It's no problem, I don't mind helping," said a voice next to Alice.

She realized the woman she had heard was in a checkout lane two rows to her left and was talking to a woman in her own line. Alice paused and took a moment to scan the growing checkout lines. At first, it was hardly noticeable. However, after a full thirty seconds, she noticed the lines hadn't moved at all; customers weren't exiting the doors, and the lines themselves kept getting longer. Nearby cashiers were completing the same sequence as the one in her own line. First, try the card several times, then ask if a different card is available. Next, ask if they are able to pay cash. If the answer is no, they depress the button next to their computer and wait for the supervisor to arrive. Alice watched as this played out in over a dozen lines. The self-checkout lines had also come to a standstill. As the lines grew, some abandoned their carts and walked out of the store.

Alice looked behind herself. A young man stood behind her. On his face was a stressed expression. He stood in front of a cart containing, among other things, a large box of diapers, five cans of baby formula, and a car seat that was bundled up to protect the child inside from the cold winter winds.

Alice could see the look in his eyes seconds before it happened, as if she could read his thoughts. He was desperate. The young man casually, but briskly, walked behind the lines of carts towards an exit. However, unlike many other customers that had chosen to give up their spot in the queues, this man pushed his cart as he approached the exit. An employee, who under normal circumstances was tasked with offering a "have a nice day" to departing customers, though was also tasked with identifying possible shoplifters, stood between the man and the door.

"Sir, did you pay for these items?" asked the employee, knowing full well what the answer was.

The approaching man stopped in front of the employee but did not answer the question.

"I'm going to have to ask you to be patient and get back in line. Otherwise, you can leave the cart and merchandise, and come back at a different time."

Alice's eyes were fixed on the two men. Half of the checkout lines, already at a standstill, quieted themselves to observe the confrontation. It reminded Alice of a crowd at a golf tournament that silenced themselves before a crucial putt. The customer stared at the employee for what seemed to be an eternity. 5 seconds. 15 seconds. 25 seconds.

Finally, the silence was interrupted by the employee, "Sir-."

The employee, who appeared to be only a few years short of retirement age, didn't get a chance to finish the sentence, as the young father turned his cart to the side, brought both arms back, and delivered a forceful shove directly to the other man's chest. He fell backward, catching himself with his two arms outstretched behind him, though they were insufficient to fully blunt the impact with the floor. The young man maneuvered his cart around him and exited out the sliding doors.

The crowd of customers began to slowly murmur amongst themselves. Another shopper, this one closer to the exit, peeled out of her line and exited the store, still pushing her cart. One by one, others began to follow suit. Some, including Alice, continued to wait in line. The assaulted employee had recovered from the fall and was now standing, though he made no attempt to stop the growing line of those choosing to commit theft. Alice was not conflicted on her own decision. As far as she was concerned, there was no decision to make. It was wrong, and that was that. Still, the scene filled her with unease. This was mob mentality, playing out in her own town. No aide had been rendered to the employee that had been pushed aside. No one had questioned the actions of so many to leave the store with carts full of unpurchased merchandise. She had seen these scenarios play out before on the TV or on news reports, usually in the wake of a riot or natural disaster. *But in rural Indiana?* What had caused this change in mentality? Alice left her cart and followed the stream of people that left the store. She watched briefly as several other individuals entered through the entrance doors, no doubt glad to take advantage of the seemingly free merchandise.

Some, such as those that proceeded to ransack the store, could perhaps be labeled as thugs. But the rest? They were not much different from herself. Alice knew something had to have occurred to elicit such desperation. She wanted answers.

Chapter 3: Fissures

David waited anxiously for Alice to pull into the driveway. He had already called her phone a handful of times after she had hung up, in order to ensure she was safe, though he had another excuse planned out as the reason for the phone call in order to avoid causing her any distress. In any event, she had not answered. Finally, he saw her headlights approaching from the end of the driveway. She walked into the house, with the usual ecstatic greeting from Maya, and a more subdued reaction from Harper.

"Girls, do me a favor and go upstairs to put on your pajamas," said Alice, now turning to her husband. "David, what's happening?"

"Things are getting bad, Alice. I was worried about you tonight," he said, as he wrapped his arms around her.

"I heard sirens the whole way home. People were looting the stores, too. It's not like those riots a few years ago in Minneapolis or Portland. I saw parents, people we know, leaving with carts full of groceries they didn't pay for."

David sighed. "They're talking about it on the TV. Some banks are thinking about not opening tomorrow. Something about an irregularity in their payment system."

"Irregularity?" said Alice, skeptically.

"I have my doubts too."

The two sat in silence for a moment, both contemplating the ramifications of the developments.

"I don't like it," said David.

Alice furrowed her brow. "Maybe I should stay home from work tomorrow, you know, just to see if it blows over."

"I won't argue with that. Besides, the girls will be happy to have you home," said David, as he took her coat to hang it on a hook. "Alice, what if this-"

Alice looked at him as he turned to face her.

"Nevermind. We can talk later, after the girls are asleep.

The two did their best to enjoy the evening, to treat it as they would any other evening. To be present in the moment was a challenge they had faced in the past, and the unspoken agreement for the evening was to strive to remain focused on the valuable time with their daughters, rather than get wrapped up emotionally in other affairs.

However, they both knew that there was not wisdom in pretending the all was well in the world. After the girls went to bed, the two stayed awake watching the news. All across the country, similar acts of lawlessness were occurring. More worrying for David was the multiple experts being interviewed, many of whom were being interviewed via phone call or through video call, given the urgency of the situation, sounded less confident than the relatively scant statements being released by the government. David's knowledge of these financial and economic matters was limited. However, like most Americans, he knew the information conveyed by the government did not always correspond with reality. One such individual that presented a pessimistic outlook on the situation was a hedge fund manager that had previously worked within the U.S. Treasury and had maintained close ties to politicians on both sides of the aisles in the years since.

"Look, here's the deal. I don't know what happened to these markets today. I have my theories, and there's been plenty of rumors circulating. But, that's not what's important right now. What's important is that there was a major liquidity event, which led to an insolvency event. These banks we're talking about? First Bank of the U.S., Wagner's, Spencer & Creed? Those are three of the largest banks in the world. And that's just today. Give it until tomorrow or the next day, and I promise you that more will follow. Like it or not, but nationalization is next. These banks will be bought out by the government."

"Wait a second, nationalization? On what basis?" the host replied.

"What's the alternative? We all know the phrase 'Too big to fail,' and we're going to see if that holds true," said the fund manager.

"This would have to be an act of congress, right? With a deeply divided House and Senate, do you foresee them running into problems?"

"I certainly hope not. My understanding is that the Senate leadership is already drafting legislation, and my hope is that it will be passed by the end of the workweek. If not, well, the longer this is allowed to run its course, the more damage will be done to our economy. The more unhinged things will become in some of these towns and cities."

The host took a pause, as she contemplated herself what she was hearing. As she asked a follow-up question, David's mind wandered. *What if this guy on the TV was right?* More chillingly, David contemplated what would happen if the man was wrong. What if the government couldn't fix this problem? What if today was the beginning of something much more prolonged? David pulled Alice closer, as the two continued to watch the endless stream of interviews and analysis. Though he was worried about his own business, worried about their finances, worried about their safety, he was grateful for the family he had. For the first time in several years, the two nodded off on the couch. Though the circumstances were not as tranquil as in the past, it was the comfort of this relationship that helped the two overcome their unease and uncertainty, and allow sleep to take the place of their restless consciousness. The two curled up on the couch together, TV still casting a glow on them, as the world outside began to crumble.

Chris Jenkins rolled over in bed and reached for his phone on the hotel nightstand. He fumbled with it as it continued to emit a chime, a chime that was chosen by Chris because of its annoying nature. He muted the morning alarm, set for 10:30 AM, Singapore time. His vision was blurry from a hard night's sleep, a sleep that was aided by a few drinks he had consumed after returning to his room but hampered by the jet lag that had followed him on the flight to the city three days ago. Chris had allowed himself to sleep later into the morning, on account of the late dinner he had shared with a few clients the night before, a meeting that had stretched into the early hours of the morning. His itinerary for the day was relatively empty, which had allowed for the late alarm. In fact, the only task he was obligated to complete for the day was to fill out and email a few forms back to the States, leaving the rest of the day to do as he pleased.

As Chris's vision and mind cleared, he noticed the screen of his phone flooded with notifications. He read through the first three messages, before deciding that the cryptic but plainly serious nature of the messages required him to gain some context before continuing.

Chris flipped on the TV and turned it to the financial news network, which, though based in the U.S., often had live segments focused on Asia and the rest of the world. These segments generally would air when the U.S. audience was fast asleep. It was on a commercial break. As it came off of the commercial break, a female host with a British accent was on the screen.

"Welcome back. If you're just joining us, we're continuing to follow developments from markets across Asia, as the turmoil from U.S. markets continue to spread across the globe. The Nikkei is frozen today, as are the major markets and indices in South Korea, Singapore, Australia, and China, as nearly the entire Asian market has elected to not open their markets today, for fear of experiencing similar levels of volatility as the U.S. markets. The New York Stock Exchange, of course, closed early yesterday, following a surprise rate hike from the Federal Reserve, which sparked a rapid 20 percent drop in all three major U.S. indices.

"In related news, most Asian and European countries have declared today a bank holiday, and U.S. officials have already done the same for tomorrow. This is after widespread reports of outages across the banking system, leaving much of the public unable to access bank accounts or purchase goods with wireless methods, as well as through the use of credit and debit cards. To discuss this, we welcome a returning guest, the chief financial officer of..." the host trailed off, as Chris tried to comprehend what he had just slept through.

Chris Jenkins noticed a drumming in his head. *I didn't drink that much, did I? A few beers shouldn't leave me with a hangover.* He muted the TV and noticed the drumming was growing more intense. Chris quickly came to the realization that the noise was not in his head, but rather, external to himself. He walked over to the window and lifted the shades; he was assaulted by the bright morning sunshine. The bright light induced a mild headache, but he willed himself to gaze out on the cityscape of the historic city.

Silhouetted against the bright, blue sky was a dark object. Chris squinted and found he was looking at a helicopter. It was not a helicopter that he might expect to see over a U.S. city, like the type used by local news agencies, complete with a traffic reporter inside. No, this helicopter was distinctly military in its outline. Chris knew little about military helicopters but guessed it was a Blackhawk helicopter, or something similar. He didn't fully understand why such a helicopter would be present over Singapore, especially at such a low altitude. He looked down at the streets, a full 8 stories below, and found a sight that differed from his expectations.

The city streets, generally clogged with vehicles and pedestrians alike, were scarcely populated for what should be a busy Thursday morning. The streets contained only a fraction of the normal amount of traffic. Upon closer inspection, Chris noticed that those strolling on the sidewalk were interspersed with pairs of men wearing military garb that wielded assault rifles slung over their shoulders. At one large intersection, an armored vehicle topped with a large machine gun that was manned by another soldier had parked on one corner of the intersection and sat as a sentinel that watched the light traffic passing by. From the opposite direction came another armored vehicle, nearly identical to the first, though the machine gun turret was replaced with a much larger bank of loudspeakers. These loudspeakers, which Chris could hear more clearly as they approached the street below his room, emitted a statement, alternating between three languages. The first two were languages Chris could not positively identify, though he guessed one was likely Malay. The third language was English, which Chris listened to intently.

"Please stay calm. Remain in your residence. Approved workers in critical infrastructure will be allowed to go to work after showing the appropriate credentials. All others will be detained."

Chris didn't recall the news network mentioning anything about a mobilization of the Singapore armed forces. This was practically martial law. Then again, Singapore was just one city-state in an entire hemisphere waking up to bad news, and the news network no doubt was unable to field, verify, and report on every aspect of what appeared to be a busy morning for media outlets.

Chris did not hesitate, knowing that his decision to sleep in already had wasted him valuable time. He now knew what should be his first course of action. He picked up his phone and looked up the number to the U.S. Embassy on a search engine. He typed the number in and called their line that had been designated for U.S. nationals. The phone rang for a full minute but yielded no answer. He found himself unable to reach anyone at the Embassy, regardless of where he directed his call. Undeterred, Chris still wanted answers. He surmised that most, if not all hotlines on the mainland U.S. would either be closed at this hour or else overwhelmed with callers. His next choice was a natural one.

"Russ, how's it going?" said Chris, as though the world wasn't falling apart around them.

"Oh, I don't know, besides the financial system falling apart, and essentially losing my job today, not that bad for a Wednesday evening," joked Russel.

"I need you to help catch me up to speed on this."

"Oh, right, Singapore. Just wake up?" asked Russel.

"Truthfully? It feels like I haven't woken up yet, like I'm in some crazy dream."

"Ok, where should I start? The Fed hikes rates, and the markets go berserk."

"That's it? Are you buying that? This isn't just a market crash. I've worked through enough of those, and I've never seen banks close up shop like this. If the network on TV is right, here in Singapore, bank accounts are basically frozen. No one, not even companies, can buy a thing. How does a run-of-the-mill market crash make that happen?" replied Chris.

24

"That's the big question," said Russel, as he thought back to his conversation with Marcus. "Do you remember our last phone call? I mentioned I had something big I was working on. I think this might be related. Or at least that's what I'm being told."

"Told by who?" asked Chris.

Russel further hesitated, "Marcus Avenrow, the-"

"Yeah, I know the guy, what does he know about this?" interrupted Chris, growing more curious.

"He gave the impression that it was an open secret among some, that there was a bubble waiting to be burst."

"That's no surprise, people have been calling it a bubble since before the Great Recession," replied Chris.

"Yeah. But, this sounds different. Sounds like it goes deeper than my own research in the corporate debt markets. This bubble, I'm thinking that it could have been something the regulators, maybe even the Treasury or the Fed was aware of, but had turned a blind eye to. They probably chose to ignore it on on the basis of the banks involved being, well-"

"Too big to fail," Chris said, finishing his thought. "Looks like that strategy backfired," said Chris.

"It had to happen eventually. They keep trying to hold back a big crash for long enough, and one comes along that they can't stop," Russel said. He took a deep breath, and continued, this time in a lower voice. " Chris, there's more to this."

"What do you mean?"

"I don't know, call it a gut feeling. I think there was some sort of an attack, maybe a cyberattack, a hack, or something along those lines. I've spent some time looking at the data form the equity exchanges, forex, commodities, you name it. It all looks, well, wrong."

"How so?" asked Chris.

"Around one o'clock, here in the States, the liquidity in the markets evaporated. I mean, it just disappeared. As soon as the announcement comes out, the market plummets, but the shares? They aren't trading hands, at least not as fast as they usually do. It was like the volume was for a sleepy Tuesday afternoon. And I know what you're thinking, what if it was just a glitch? Maybe, but the timing? It's all too convenient."

"You think it was deliberate? Like, terrorism?" asked Chris.

"No clue. But if it was intentional, I can't think of a worse outcome than the mess we're in."

Charlotte Yates bit at her fingernails as she watched the president on the television, seated in the Oval Office, speaking to the camera in his usual calm and collected tone. Charlotte was anything but calm. Sleep had not come last night, and she gave up trying after a half-hour of tossing and turning. She instead chose to catch a taxi back to the Congressional Offices near the Capitol Building in Washington, D.C., the same building she had left only a few hours earlier but took care to make a stop along the way at a gas station for a pair of energy drinks. Charlotte counted herself as fortunate to have enough cash and coin on hand for both the taxi and the beverages, though she had needed to dig through her purse and a kitchen drawer in order to scrape together adequate funds.

Despite the fact she had arrived hours earlier than usual, she had no meaningful work to complete, instead waiting for her boss to arrive while she watched a variety of news networks. Charlotte had worked for Emily Tomkins since Emily's early days in politics, first as state senator in Maryland, later as Maryland's Attorney General, and now as a U.S. senator to the state of Maryland. This ascent through the political ranks had not come easily. It was due in large part to Emily's deft political maneuvering and questionable ethics, that she had been elected eight years prior at the relatively young age of forty-four. Charlotte's political acumen had undoubtedly also played a key role, a fact both knew to be true, though Emily often was reluctant to admit this out loud, instead praising Charlotte for her assistance in clerical and administrative matters and ignoring her adept discernment in political matters.

For Charlotte, there was no ill will towards Emily for this omission. She had no desire to be in the spotlight, and she knew that her personality lacked many of the key traits of successful politicians. Though she could manipulate others and leverage influence as well as any career politician, she did not possess the charisma that so often was a prerequisite in American politics. Simply put, she felt she was not compelling enough of an individual to the average U.S. voter, despite her belief that she would be an effective public servant, given the opportunity.

However, she had accepted the fact that such an opportunity was unlikely to present itself. For that reason, she instead chose to work behind the scenes. To an observer, her dedication and passion may have appeared as though it stemmed from a commitment to a political ideology, a zeal to change the world for the better. Such an assumption would not be entirely incorrect. Charlotte did care about her work, the issues, and her party's ideology. Like so many in the world, she did believe her perspective was the closest to the correct view on the issues. However, hidden behind this truthful desire to change the world, was a hunger for power. She enjoyed the feeling of knowing her boss, Senator Tomkins, continued to be so successful in large part to her own counsel. To the outsider, it would appear Emily was riding on her coattails as she ascended through the ranks of U.S. politics. In reality, Emily was unlikely to have made it this far without Charlotte.

This week, however, had revealed a side of Charlotte that was rarely on display for others. Charlotte's normally confident, cunning self had been replaced by a woman plagued by trepidation and indecision. The market crash that began less than 24 hours prior, had come as no surprise to Charlotte. She did not know all of the details behind how it was carried out, simply the desired result and a rough timetable. It wasn't this information, or even the widespread chaos and eventual destruction that could occur due to such an event, that bothered Charlotte, it was her own connection to the planned disturbance that had kept her awake at night. This fear and guilt was what had kept Charlotte awake through the night, and she once again began to internally panic. She envisioned her own arrest, the questioning by some intelligence agency, and finally, her confession on display for the world to behold.

"Can you believe it's finally happening?" said Emily, as she walked into the office.

Charlotte nearly jumped out of her chair in surprise.

"Everything okay?" asked Emily, with a calming smile.

"Yeah, sorry. It was a long night," said Charlotte, as she arranged some files for Emily to review.

"Sorry to hear that," said Emily.

Can she tell? It's like she can see right through me, that she can see the hesitation and guilt on my face, though Charlotte.

"I've already set up a meeting at Senator Fremont's office later this morning for yourself, Fremont, Hillstein, Logan, and Willard."

"I assume the four of them are still on board with the plan?" replied Emily.

"We have no reason to believe that they aren't. The White House and Treasury have already floated the nationalization plan, and I'd expect a response from the opposition later this morning. I don't have any indication they'll do anything other than oppose the President, even if he is from their own party," replied Charlotte.

"And if they go along with it?" replied Emily.

"They won't, or at least not more than a few. Not enough to sway the majority, especially after the five of you come out against the plan. Maybe with a few more days, maybe a week of people losing their jobs and not being able to buy food, maybe then it'd become unpopular enough to sway them into supporting the President. Regardless, we're not at that point yet and we shouldn't need their votes anyways," said Charlotte.

Emily walked around in order to gain a better view of the TV screen.

"I didn't expect this much violence and unrest," said Charlotte, as the two watch scenes of large crowds clashing with police while smoke and tear gas filled the air.

"Yeah, that's really something," replied Emily, as the hint of a grin spread across her face.

David took stock of their situation. He had already driven to the houses of his nearest neighbors. During these brief visits, he tried to get an idea of their own perspective of the situation. As expected, their view on the events of the last 24 hours varied, but all shared the common theme of uncertainty.

With his evening tasks finished, for the time being, he was left with his own thoughts. David Ruiz prided himself in his ability to harness technology to grow his customer base. Farmers in the 21st century were far more tech-savvy than popular stereotypes would suggest. David, with Alice's expertise in marketing, had taken it to a new level. However, with this increased presence online, came a closer relationship with his phone. In light of the recent events, David has begun to see this online visibility and market penetration as more of a curse than a blessing. His phone had been vibrating intermittently throughout the day, as a steady stream of messages and emails slowly overwhelmed him. Some correspondences were from customers, distributors, and suppliers; others were from friends and acquaintances in the Southern Indiana livestock business. The one commonality among the messages was that they painted a dire picture of how damaging the past day had been for his customers, and in turn, his own industry. He was stunned by how quickly even the most loyal customers and local distributors reneged on what were often informal agreements.

The truth of the matter was that grass-fed cattle were nothing more than a luxury for most consumers, a fact David was well aware of. David believed in his beef, and he knew it was far superior to any similar product you could get at the supermarket, though he also knew it to be far more expensive. Similar to how consumers traded oversized SUVs for compacts when gas prices soared, Americans were more than willing to make substitutions when they felt a squeeze on their wallets and purses. Many appeared to be making those substitutions, and others in the industry and supply chain complex were anticipating others to make that decision in the near term.

Eventually, David resorted to silencing his phone, allowing himself a moment to process this crisis, a crisis that was both personal and international. His thoughts were interrupted by the soft touch of Alice's hand on his back. She had managed to approach him undetected, no doubt a result of his stressed and distracted mind.

"Dinner's ready," said Alice, with concern displayed on her face.

David let out a sigh. "It's bad, Alice."

"It's big," Alice replied.

"Huh?" said David, expecting his wife to be the calmer, more rational voice.

"It's big, bigger than you and I, bigger than this farm. This is bigger than the last recession, or the one before that, or before that. I know we both don't want to admit it, but the sooner we face reality, the better. But, it's also something that's well outside our control."

"Hang on a second, you're supposed to be making me feel better," said David, knowing there was more to follow.

"Focus on what you can control, be faithful with that, and trust God in the rest. Besides, you're lucky," said Alice, with a smile on her face.

David returned a quizzical expression.

"You have a farm to fall back on. I work in marketing. I think we can be pretty sure who has more job security."

"This farm is just as much yours as it is ours," said David, returning the smile.

They stared into each other's eyes for a moment.

"Yeah, you sort of are screwed," said David, as he chuckled.

Alice laughed as they embraced each other. These pep talks from Alice were nothing new; the two often encouraged each other in areas of weakness or worry. David had struggled with similar fears before. He knew what it was to fear not making a payment on the farm. They could both recall what it felt like to borrow dollars from a friend, a parent, or even a co-worker, in order to pay for gas.

David had little understanding of what the talking heads on TV were saying about the faltering economy, the crashing stock market, and banks deciding to not open on the following day. The topics were not his forte, which contributed to his level of uncertainty.

However, David knew he had skills and knowledge that were both uncommon and valuable. He understood raising cattle and how to run a successful farm. Though it was a set of skills that could be summed up in a single sentence, it was the culmination of years of experience, dozens of very specific skills, and thousands of pieces of data that were all but impossible to learn from anything other than doing. He knew there was truth to what

Alice said. He did have both a farm and set of skills that would help him weather whatever storm lay in wait. But, more importantly, David Ruiz knew that his hope ultimately was found in God, and not himself.

Maya opened the front door, interrupting their moment together. "Mom! Dad! We're waiting for you!"

David and Alice shared another smile, before walking to the house, hand in hand, confident that they would weather this storm together.

Chapter Four: Advance

Spencer & Creed had wasted no time contacting Russel. They confirmed exactly what Marcus Avenrow had already told him. Technically, he was still an employee of Spencer & Creed. Officially, he was only "laid off". He had received several emails from worried employees of Spencer & Creed, many of which he had rubbed elbows with on a daily basis, hopefully suggesting that the layoffs would only span a matter of days, perhaps a week at most. Following his conversation with Marcus, Russel was not so optimistic.

Following the previous day's events, Russel did not bother going to the office. Instead, he spent the day at home, watching the network news channels, especially those that focused on the markets. He had also taken the time to place a handful of phone calls to several former co-workers and associates from the financial world. He made these calls primarily out of curiosity; he knew that such phone calls would not change his employment situation, but he did know these individuals to be both bright and insightful. The spirit of competition that had once existed between himself and the others had evaporated, giving way to cooperation and commiseration.

Unlike so many others in the newly crippled U.S. economy, Russel was not concerned about his finances. He had saved his money responsibly, taking care to divide his excess income between savings, which were primarily held in U.S. Dollars, and in a retirement fund, which consisted of the same assets that constituted the retirement accounts of countless other Americans: a healthy mixture of equities, bonds, commodities, and some exposure to other markets, including real estate. He knew his investments would take a hit, but the thought of those funds no longer being available to him for a span of time that extended beyond the next few days was inconceivable. Furthermore, his success within the financial world spoke for itself. Regardless of Spencer & Creed's future or the prospect of widespread nationalization of banks, he knew his value to any prospective future employer.

Despite this relaxed and confident internal dialogue, he found himself on his fourth drink this evening. He rarely had more than a single drink when alone at home. It was only during social events, such as an occasional night out at a bar, that he would have more than a single drink. He had not bothered with such restraint on this night; he had no duties the following day, though it was also a sense of nostalgia as he reflected on his time with the bank, as well as a more subconscious consternation over his future, that had driven him to take his mental state to a more pronounced buzz.

In front of him glowed the television. He watched a local news station report, as Minneapolis, St. Paul, and surrounding communities delved into chaos as the evening progressed. Along some of the highways and other busier roadways stood crowds of thousands of protesters. Some carried signs with social justice slogans, others bellowed out chants against the financial and political elite. Within these crowds were also the armed protesters. Though it was a practice that, in the last decade, had originally been more prominent in conservative circles, many on this side of the spectrum had followed suit. Many could be seen wearing body armor, wielding rifles, and moving in coordinated groups interspersed throughout the crowds that numbered in the thousands. The local news stations focused on these sprawling crowds but also documented the mayhem that occurred along the periphery of these crowds. The air was choked with not only the tear gas from the outnumbered law enforcement personnel, but also by the burning of cars, tires, and even some buildings. Russel even spotted the abandoned gas station that he drove by every day on his way to work, engulfed in white-hot flames. Gunfire had been reported in many areas. In many respects, it called to memory the events that had begun in the Twin Cities many years prior and had occurred several times since, though no occurrences matched the magnitude of what Russel viewed on the TV.

Though he was not in a drunken stupor, his mind was dulled, and Russel had to remind himself that he was a mere 10 miles from the epicenter of this mayhem. This sneaking sense of paranoia compelled him to stand up and look out the windows on his quiet suburban street. It appeared the same as always. In summer, he would be seeing school-aged children outside at this hour. Of course, during the cold winters, most were inside by sunset, an event which occurred several hours prior.

As Russel walked back to the kitchen to pour himself another drink, he heard a loud knocking on the front door. Having been just reassured by his brief surveying of the neighborhood, he felt no apprehension about what lay on the other side of the door. He walked up to it, whiskey glass in hand, and opened the door. He found that there was no one and no thing on the other side of the door. Puzzled, he looked back and forth across his yard, briefly taking a few barefoot steps out on the old porch. Not locating anything of interest, Russel turned around and re-entered the house, closing the door behind him. *Must be some kids*, Russel thought to himself.

A moment after the door slammed shut, an intense pain shot up his body as he felt a blunt object assault his abdomen just below his rib cage. Russel let out an involuntary gasp, as he saw a masked figure standing in front of him. The intruder held a metal baseball bat in his gloved hands. Beside him were two other individuals that quickly advanced on Russel. Though they all were wearing masks, all three had the build of muscular men of an average height. Russel was on his knees now, still gasping for air, as the other two rushed at him. One took a black hood and slipped it over his head, as the other grabbed his barely resisting arms, placed his wrist together behind his back, and secured them using zip-tie handcuffs. The whole affair lasted all of 5 seconds, with little to no resistance from Russel, who had already been impaired by the alcohol, only to be rendered defenseless following the stunning and excruciating pain inflicted on his abdomen.

Zero Sum

The two men that had secured him, grasped him by each arm and led him out the front door. Their muscular frames lifted him by his shoulders and carried him down the three steps to the sidewalk, before dropping him back on his feet. They forced him into a jog for a few steps, before shoving him into what Russel perceived as only a dark void. He felt his legs taken out from under him by a firm metal surface, before he sprawled out onto the rough carpet of what his senses immediately identified as some type of vehicle, on account of the context of its location, as well as the light rumble he felt upon being thrown inside. His legs were lifted out of the way of the door, and he felt as they applied a strap around his ankles, restricting the movement of his legs. He heard the door slide shut behind him. Russel Godfrey was in darkness. He heard two loud knocks against the side of the vehicle and felt the vehicle begin to accelerate down the road.

"What do you mean compartmentalization, Carter? That's something you do when you're trying to keep private life and work-life separate. That's something they teach you in therapy or some leadership workshop. This? This is keeping me in the dark!" said Senator Tompkins.

Charlotte sat nearby. She couldn't hear the words on the other end of the conversation, only the rough outline of words and sentences. She could, however, discern that it was a man. His volume and cadence also told her that he was far calmer than Emily.

"You've been keeping me in the dark since day one! How am I supposed to trust that you don't have something more planned? What's next? Are you going to assassinate the president? How about starting a nuclear war with Russia? I don't think you understand what you've done."

The man replied from the other end. Charlotte watched as the Senator's posture and facial expression relaxed somewhat.

"I know, I know. In for a penny, in for a pound, or something like that, right? All I'm saying is that with what happened with markets, and then with the, what was the name you gave me? Operation Foundation? Those were different. But what if this gets picked up by the FBI? You and I both know they aren't too friendly with our party right now. Frankly, nevermind politics. I don't think politics would even matter with this. We're talking…" Emily paused, and looked at Charlotte, before continuing. "They won't care, they'll go after us all."

Charlotte listened, as the muffled voice spoke into the Senator's ear.

"What do you want me to do?" replied Emily.

The man's response lasted a full 20 seconds.

"Okay, talk to you soon."

Emily turned in her leather-bound office chair to face Charlotte. "You and I, we've known each other for a long time. I wouldn't be where I am without your help. We're in this together. Let's not kid ourselves about how serious this is. But, I know you believe in the cause. Right now, I need to know how serious you are."

Behind her quizzical expression, was a clear understanding of the loyalty test Emily had just given to her, a test disguised as a heartfelt and considerate statement.

Charlotte attempted to feign the same concern. "Of course, Emily. I'm on board. What is it?"

Chris hit send on his smartphone's email application and continued to play the waiting game. This was something that had become all too familiar in the past 24 hours. He never was able to get through to the US Embassy via their phone lines, instead repeatedly receiving a busy signal. However, he was able to find an email address and had been in correspondence since with a mid-level employee at the embassy. This individual, Rahim was his name, informed Chris there were no plans for widespread evacuation of U.S. nationals, but that some smaller flights were still taking place, flights that had largely been reserved for government officials and corporate executives. Of all the information he had been given, he found to be most curious, was the use of the word "evacuation" to describe the exodus of Americans from the small city-state.

Of course, Rahim would not have given Chris this privileged information if it weren't for Chris inflating his own resume. Chris had convinced him that he was a high-level executive for a hedge fund and that his presence in the United States was crucial in this volatile time.

As Chris opened the curtains once more to view the largely abandoned street below, his phone buzzed. Rahim stated that a flight was departing for the United States later that evening. Evidently, Rahim's boss was fooled by the inflated title Chris had supplied and agreed to allow him on the flight. The Embassy was sending Chris a vehicle to transport Chris the ten miles to the airport. Chris replied with a simple acknowledgment of the arrangement, and that he would be in the lobby at that time, taking care to omit any expression of gratitude, as he felt it would not fit his image of an important executive. For the time being, he had a new persona.

Chapter Five: Collaboration

Warren Carlyle was a simple man. At 55 years of age, his face displayed a maturity that exceeded his years, complete with deep, permanent wrinkles across his face, and weathered skin from the long hours outside. Despite the rugged and aged exterior, he had not yet lost much of the strength and endurance of his youth. Warren was every bit the stereotypical Midwestern farmer, just as his father was before him. His life story stood in stark contrast to that of David's, who was entirely inexperienced when he and Alice had first bought their farm. True to form, the local farmers had been every bit Midwestern as David thought they would be, though none were as helpful as Warren. His house stood across the road, a full quarter-mile to the west.

Like David, he raised cattle, a fact that tied the two together more closely. In many ways, David had begun to see him as a father figure. Warren not only freely shared his knowledge about farming but also cared deeply for David and his family. David's relationship with Warren had been cemented some years ago when David was pondering expanding his farm. The sentiment of the vast majority of local farmers at the time was that such an expansion was foolhardy. Despite the boom in business at the time, many doubted the durability of the business model for the small to mid-sized family farm. The lone dissenting voice to this popular opinion was Warren, who encouraged David to expand, and even offered to loan him the money to do so. This was a loan David ultimately did not take, instead opting for a bank loan that was far simpler, and also did not complicate their friendship. However, the offer, which would have undoubtedly been backed up by action, spoke volumes about the man's character, as well as his genuine caring nature towards Alice and David. Rarely did a week go by in which David didn't find himself flagging down Warren as he walked to one of the multiple structures on his property in order to ask Warren a question, or to simply chat. Warren's wife, Caroline, was cut from the same cloth as Warren; she too had taken Alice under her wing, despite the generational difference. It helped that the two couples shared a common faith in God, though their differing Christian denominations made for what could be lively theological discussions, at times.

Over the years, the two couples had shared many meals, which were always accompanied by lively discussions and banter. The mood for this meal, however, was far weightier than usual. The ongoing crisis dominated the conversation among the four. It was Warren that reminded David that, in such a capital-intensive industry, cash and credit were crucial to keeping a farm operating. Not unlike farmers who grew corn or soybeans, cattle farmers made a bulk of their profit in a relatively short amount of time. In theory, this cash then covered the following year's expenses, and credit from the bank could cover the rest, were there to be any shortfall. However, with banks essentially boarded up, both literally and in the digital sense, the two farms were left dangerously low on financial resources.

Larger family farms and sprawling commercial farms could take advantage of futures markets when selling their products, which gave them the ability to smooth out their cash flow throughout the year. This assisted with the cyclical nature of revenue and expenses in the farming business, and also served to protect against price volatility. This was a luxury that was not afforded to their comparably smaller farms. An added complication for Warren and David was the fact that they both raised grass-finished cattle. This meant that the animals were allowed to graze on grass during the summer, leaving them at their largest in the fall. They were then slaughtered, usually during the months of October to December. This meat fetched a premium compared to grain-finished cattle but could leave their two farms at a disadvantage to the larger farms when hard times struck.

However, economic downturns varied from each other, and if the financial system remained seized up, then large farms would be in the same boat as David and Warren. They would have no access to cash or credit to purchase feed, fuel, veterinarian care, repair of machines and tractors, or any of the other miscellaneous expenses that comprised a farm's typical budget.

"I think we have to move fast. I know it's not an easy decision, but the longer we wait, the sooner it is before there's nothing left for us," said Warren.

"I've never bartered before. I'll be honest, I don't know where I would start," replied David.

Warren sat back in his chair at the dinner table. "I've put some thought into this. See, we could start at the feed mill, and ask around. After that, we could go door-to-door. We could make a list. Maybe, if we get enough local guys on board, we could set up our own market. We can trade based on what we have and what we need. Of course, we'll be short on some things, regardless. Fuel, feed, parts, those will be shortest in supply," said Warren.

"I could set up a ledger. We could even have an exchange rate that I could update periodically," chimed in Caroline, who managed the finances for the farm she and Warren owned and was savvy with both numbers and business.

"I like this. Let's make it happen," said David.

The four of them compiled a list of individuals they wanted to talk to. This list was primarily local farms, both big and small, but also contained the names of veterinarians, local businesses, and anyone other locals that had a skill, service, or resource that would be helpful. Some they knew on a first-name basis, while others were known only by an address on a map or a name on a mailbox. It was a lengthy process. But, in the end, they were pleased with the plan and its prospects.

"I have to get back home and finish some things up, but I think that there's one more thing we need to talk about," said Warren, soberly.

"What's that?" asked David.

Warren glanced between Alice and David and continued. "I think we need to be realistic about what's happening in the world right now. This could all blow over, but I'm not so sure. Things might get much worse before it gets any better. I'd prefer to prepare for the worst-case scenario and hope for the best. There's a myriad of bad outcomes we could see in the coming weeks. The dollar could crash, we could get involved in some war, who knows? What if the internet goes dark, or the power grid goes down? Imagine what that'll do to everyone's psyche, especially with spring still over a month away.

"What I'm saying is that we need to think about our safety. Before we know it, there will be hordes of hungry and scared people. I'm not only talking about people out of the big cities, but I'm talking about people that live in our own town. People with hungry stomachs. People that will be desperate, angry, and armed. This is Indiana, there's plenty of guns and ammo to go around, plenty of people that know how to use them, too. We need to start acting and thinking like we have a target on our back."

"What do you mean?" asked Alice.

"We might look at our herds and see the financial future for our farms. To all of those hungry people, those herds are nothing more than a meal. Maybe it's a bit of a cliche question, but if you're watching Maya and Harper starve in front of your own eyes, would you steal food to keep them alive? And if your answer is yes, would you make sure that you also brought a weapon, so that those daughters would still have a father at the end of the day? Those people exist, and they're not so different from you and I. Give it a few weeks, and anyone could turn into a killer, concerned only for the survival of themselves and their loved ones."

David felt his pulse quicken, as he imagined not only the potential for such a threat but also the thought that Warren had evoked of his own daughters being in such a position.

Warren continued. "Now, just because there are people out there that will kill over a can of beans, doesn't mean we need to do the same. The Bible talks about helping the needy and feeding the poor. But, we need to remember that at some point, those in need will be in line for the very food you need to feed your daughters. For the next few months, I think it's in our best interest for us to be generous with what God has given us, but there will be others that are willing to kill you to take what you have."

David saw where this conversation was going. Several years ago, Warren and he had discussed gun ownership and self-protection. Both of them owned hunting rifles at the time, but Warren decided to purchase both a handgun and a pair of AR-15s at the time. David did not disagree with him at the time. Given the rise in local crime and the use and trade of illicit drugs, as well as the rising commonplace of riots in major cities, he did find himself concerned about the safety of his family. Despite this concern, David repeatedly found himself prioritizing other things, and had never followed through in purchasing a new gun himself. Since that time, roughly once a month, David would hear Warren fire several hundred shots at the makeshift firing range he had constructed in one of his fields, complete with an earthen backstop. David had joined him on a few occasions and found that his abilities from his hunting rifle did not fully carry over to the semiautomatic rifle.

Warren continued, going the direction David had predicted, "You have a family to protect here; I want you to take one of my rifles. I'll teach you how to disassemble it and clean it. You already know how to handle a rifle; I've seen you shoot, and you're more than serviceable. I'm not implying we could fend off an army. But, if anyone ever wanted to take your things or raid your herd, I have no doubt that they might go so far as to hurt you or your family to accomplish just that. The hunting rifle might work fine to take down a deer or a hog, but might not cut it against something that shoots back."

Warren looked at the others at the table, as his words set in.

"I take it you've been giving this some thought for a while," said Alice.

"Long before any of these more current events started. What's the old saying? Luck favors the prepared? I don't buy into the idea of good luck or bad luck, but I know it's true that preparation and prudence pay off."

Warren paused once more. David could tell Warren had more on his mind that he wanted to discuss.

"Come on, old man. I can tell you're still holding back something from us," said David, with a grin.

Warren nodded, knowing David was correct. "Look, there's a limit to firepower. Let's be realistic; suppose all four of us were armed. We're still at a disadvantage. We're defending. That means we have the advantage of being familiar with the location. Beyond that, we're at a disadvantage in almost every other category. We have no choice on the time or circumstances of any encounter. The four of us don't have the time to keep watch over these farms around the clock. It's too much time and area to cover, and not enough of us. We need more than just four. I want to make a network, of sorts. Let's say, 2 miles. Each direction. We get as many houses and people on board with the idea of looking out for each other. Maybe market it as a neighborhood watch on steroids. My guess would be that the potential for some of these scenarios hasn't crossed their minds. I don't want to wait until it's too late." Warren paused once more and began to stand up. "Speaking of late, I think it's time we head out. I hope I've given the two of you plenty to think and talk about. I'd like to talk more about this tomorrow," said Warren.

As Alice and Caroline said their goodbyes, Warren walked to the door to grab his coat while he talked with David. "You're a good man, David. It's times like this that I'm glad to call you a friend and a neighbor. I can tell you're stressed; we all are. But, I want you to remember two things. First, your greatest asset is your faith. Don't find your security in your farm, a gun, a pantry full of food, head knowledge, or even a good plan, find that in God. Second, well, your second greatest asset is your community now. I meant what I said about strength in numbers. No man is an island, and no house, farm, or man should stand alone. That's never how it's been around here, and I don't think it's time we start."

Russel lay on his side in a fetal position, though with his arms secured behind his back. He was alert but was struggling to focus on anything other than the intense aching that emanated from his abdomen. With the world appearing to be no more than darkness on account of the dark hood that had been slipped over his head, he had begun to imagine the pain being similar to the abandoned gas station that he had seen burning down only hours previous, the same gas station that he remembered driving by every day for work. The same gas station he could vaguely remember stopping at for fuel, years ago.

For long stretches, this fire in his midsection would seem to be slowly dying down. Then, the vehicle he was riding in would hit a bump in the road, and it would feel as though a propane canister had been tossed onto the fire and suddenly exploded. He had an irresistible urge to place his hands on the area of his abdomen in order to brace it. He imagined doing so would be akin to spraying water on the fire within, or like a helicopter draping an enormous blanket over the blaze, snuffing out the flames. But, in his current, detained state, this comfort was denied to him.

Russel was not alone in the van, or, at least he had surmised at this point that it likely was a large van's rear cargo space that he was within. There was another detained individual beside him. The van had made one additional stop after he had been snatched. With this stop, he had first heard the door slide open, before then feeling the suspension of the van rebound for a brief moment with the thud of a large figure landing on the floor of the van. He could still sense the figure beside him. After the van had continued down the road, Russel had attempted to converse with the individual, but no reply was offered. Russel could not be sure of whether the body was dead or alive; the ambient noise of the van on the road masked the noise of any breathing. Russel had considered maneuvering himself in such a way to feel for the silent passenger's pulse, but something within himself felt fearful of doing so, partially because he feared the potential of discovering the man to be nothing more than a corpse.

The van was now making a second stop, a stop that would yield no additional passengers. Russel could hear the driver exit the van and then open the rear doors of the van.

"Hey, what are you doing?! Who are you?!" said Russel, suddenly panicking as he considered the prospect of the driver of this vehicle picking this location to end his life and subsequently dump his body.

"Go ahead and make some noise. We're in the middle of nowhere. No one will hear a thing," said the driver.

Russel heard the loud noise of the action of a gun, maybe a rifle. Russel wasn't sure.

The man let out a belly laugh at Russel's sudden panic. "If we wanted you dead, we would have left you on the front step of your house. You have nothing to, well, no, that's not true. You have plenty to worry about, just not dying, not yet."

Russel stilled his body. He had considered yelling in a desperate bid to attract attention but decided to take the man at his word. Through the open rear door several feet away, he heard no cars, voices, or other sounds that would give him a clue to their whereabouts. Most likely, the man was telling the truth. No one would hear the yells. In the relative silence of the night, Russel did hear the man twisting off the gas tank cap and pouring gas into the tank for a few minutes, before returning to the rear door. This process repeated itself two additional times. Russel picked up on the faint smell of gasoline through his hood. The discrete refueling made sense to Russel; there was no sense in a criminal going to a gas station, allowing his face and vehicle to be easily seen on surveillance cameras. What Russel failed to recall was the ongoing economic crisis which left most gas stations overwhelmed, ransacked, or closed altogether, eliminating that option regardless. Russel briefly considered attempting to slide his way to the back of the van, but the restraints quickly put such an idea to rest. He was unable to come to a seated position, which made the plan to attempt a sprint for freedom not only foolhardy but near impossible.

The driver returned to the driver's seat after closing the rear doors and continued once more down the road. Initially, the driver made several stops and turns, each spaced out by anywhere from thirty seconds to three minutes. After this last turn, Russel sensed they were likely on a freeway or similar roadway. There were no stops, fewer bumps, and the turns were long and gentle.

Russel found it difficult to stay focused during this long, uneventful part of the journey. The initial fear he had felt after first being thrown into the van had subsided somewhat, but he was still apprehensive about what lay in wait for him at his destination and was still unsure why someone would abduct him. He had seen enough TV shows and heard enough real-life stories about abductions to know that just because you weren't killed right away, doesn't mean you will survive the ordeal, though he did find some comfort in his abductor's comments about how easy it would have been to leave him dead in his house. It was not much comfort, but it was something. It was the unknown that Russel feared the most. The unknown of the seemingly lifeless figure only feet away did not help his unease.

The van continued for what Russel guessed was approximately an hour before he felt the van slow down and turn, much as though it was exiting a freeway. It then began driving with short periods of acceleration and stopping. The bumps in the road had returned as well, once again aggravating the pain that had continued to smolder just below his ribcage while on the relatively smooth freeway.

After a few minutes of driving that felt as though it was in a city or residential area, he felt the van slow to a stop. However, unlike the previous stop signs and red lights, this time he heard the transmission shift into park. This was followed by the driver opening the driver's side door. He then slid open the side door. The driver returned to his seat, closing the door behind him. Though he still could see only darkness, Russel could see an opportunity to potentially attract the attention of anyone nearby. He ignored the pain within and began to inhale as he prepared to let out a shout.

Before he released his bellow, he paused. He heard the shouts of a woman. The shouts were a moderate distance from the van but sounded as though she was moving closer to the van. She was yelling obscenities as she ordered the figures escorting her to let her go. With the considerable noise the woman was making, as well as the potential for punishment from those detaining him, Russel decided against shouting. The voice neared. He heard the loud thud of the woman's legs side of the van, and the van rebounded as she was tossed beside Russel. He heard the van door slam shut once more. As the van began to accelerate, the nearby woman continued to scream and struggle against her restraints. Russel attempted to calm her, but he found himself struggling to match her volume.

"Hey! Calm down! No one can hear you!" shouted Russel. He struggled to find more calming words but found his own thoughts to be both scattered and frustrated.

The woman grew quiet and responded with a shaky voice. "Who are you, and what do you want with me?"

"You're asking the wrong person. I'm not one of those men that threw you into this van. They gave me the same treatment," replied Russel.

"What? Why?"

"I don't know. All I know is that I was sitting at home. One minute someone knocked on my door, and the next they took a baseball bat stomach. After that, it's been, I don't know, 2 hours in here? It's hard to say," Russel paused before continuing. "They picked up another person. I don't think they made it."

"You mean they're dead?" she asked.

"I can't say for sure, but they haven't moved since they were tossed in here," said Russel.

"Have you checked their pulse?" the woman asked.

"No."

"Are you going to?"

A pause.

"They're dead, aren't they?" said the woman.

"Probably. To tell the truth, I'd rather not know the truth right about now."

Russel wanted to change the subject from his fear of death. He could hear the woman struggling against the van's floor. He guessed she was trying to remove her mask as he had tried as well.

"It's no use. These hoods are secured at the bottom. They won't come off unless we get our hands-free, or they decide to take them off."

He heard her continue to struggle against her hood and restraints, ignoring his advice.

"Where are we?" asked Russel.

"Eau Claire. Well, to the west of Eau Claire."

Russel did the mental math of the total mileage between his own home and the western Wisconsin town. His estimate of how long he had been in the van was a reasonable estimate but depended on the location of the second stop.

"Do you live alone? Would anyone have seen you or seen the men go into your house? How long before someone realizes you are missing?" asked Russel in a flurry of questions. He wanted to keep her distracted, as he could tell she was still panicking internally, not unlike himself.

"That wasn't my house, it was just a rental. I had it rented out for two weeks. My parents and sister live in Eau Claire, and I was taking some time off to visit. You know how it is, what thirty-five year old wants to stay with their mom and dad?"

Russel was glad that the questions were helping her stay distracted. Still, there was a purpose to the questions. The entire situation didn't add up. Why would they first abduct him, and then do the same with a second individual who lived presumably 30 minutes away from Russel's house, based on the driving time, before driving all the way to Eau Claire? It didn't make sense to Russel. Then again, when did these things ever make sense, in the moment?

"You said you were just staying in Eau Claire. Where are you from?" asked Russel.

"Chicago. I left about a week ago. Talk about bad timing for someone that works in finance to go on vacation. Or really good timing, depending on your perspective. I thought about heading back sooner, but-"

Russel cut her off. "Wait a second, you work in finance? Where do you work? What do you do?" he asked.

"What is this, a first date? You're full of questions," she said, chuckling.

"I'm asking because I work for Spencer & Creed. I worked in cross-asset management in their Minneapolis branch. Until yesterday, that is."

"I work at Superior Bank and Trust. VP of the fixed income division," replied the woman, seeming to realize the strange coincidence. "Wait, so you're saying-"

"It is a bit strange, isn't it? What are the odds that the two of us both work in finance, get thrown in the same van on the same night, all while the entire financial system teeters on the brink of collapse?" said Russel.

"What would they want with us?" said the woman.

"Good question. I wish I could say we need to get to the bottom of this, but-"

"Yeah, bigger fish to fry," said the woman, finishing his thought.

The two of them both noticed that with the most recent turn, the van had transitioned to a rougher surface like that of a dirt road or driveway. Russel sensed they could be nearing their destination, and not a moment too soon. The conversation had distracted him from his pain for the time being, but his concern had shifted to his bladder. There was only so much conversation that could distract him from this, and much like with pain, the bumpy road only worsened this problem. The several alcoholic drinks, which had worn off, but had served as a diuretic while in his system also contributed to this.

As the van rolled to a stop, Russel glanced at the nearby woman, though his eyesight was still limited to only darkness.

"I think this is our stop," she said.

"Let's hope this isn't another stop for a new passenger," said Russel.

"No, I don't think so. I hear voices."

Russel listened closely. She was right. He couldn't make out what they were saying, but he could hear the voices of multiple men. They both listened as the voices grew closer.

"I think this is it," she said.

"I think you're right. Whatever happens, we'll get out of this. Try to stay alive," replied Russel, surprised by this sudden sense of camaraderie.

Russel noticed that her breathing rate had once again increased, though he did not notice that the same was true for himself. He could make out three distinct male voices that were conversing outside the van. He could make out occasional words, which were in English, but nothing more. Russel's heart was racing now, with a thumping that he was sure the woman next to him could hear as well.

"I never got your name," said Russel.

"Kate."

"I'm Russel. Nice to meet you."

"Same to you. When this is all over, we'll have to-"

She was cut off mid-sentence as the door slid open.

Chris settled into his seat. The plane that the U.S. government had sent to Singapore was a Boeing 777, a twin jet passenger airliner that was commonly used for long-distance flights, including those that transited the Pacific Ocean. Allegedly, the U.S. government had borrowed the plane from a major domestic airline. Chris had learned this information while listening to a few members of the flight crew conversing amongst themselves. Their conversation had suggested that this practice was occurring more widely with various domestic airlines.

Though there were many individuals displaced during the current crisis, few had access to physical cash to pay for an airline ticket, leaving the vast majority stranded. The U.S. government evidently was not concerned about those individuals, or at least not concerned to the same extent as they were about government employees, diplomats, and those with VIP status, such as was attributed to Chris under his current persona. This status had earned him a first-class seat; he rarely sat first class and was initially indifferent, given the circumstances, but found himself increasingly grateful as scores of additional passengers continued to board the plane, and was glad he would have some additional space to relax.

A woman wearing a dark blue pantsuit sat beside Chris. She appeared to be in her early 50s, a fact betrayed by her mildly wrinkled face, though her hair did not yet have a hint of gray.

"Hey."

"Hello," she replied.

"Glad to be leaving?" asked Chris, trying to make small talk.

"To be honest, I wouldn't have minded staying a little while longer. I only flew in yesterday. But, you know how it is working for Uncle Sam."

"I don't, actually," Chris replied.

"Oh, that's right. They did say they were widening the criteria to fly out. So, let me guess, you're a wealthy tech executive? Or maybe a lobbyist from an oil company?" she asked.

"Nope, try banking."

"Not much better. I'm guessing they decided you were desperately needed at home? Your presence must be that vital to that God-forsaken industry," she said as she cracked a thin smile.

"Hey now, take it easy on me. We all have our deficiencies. How about you? What makes you so important to be needed back in the States?" replied Chris.

At that moment, the woman's phone rang. She looked at the number, and without so much as a glance in Chris's direction, stood up and walked to the front of the first-class area. Chris was puzzled but thought nothing of it. Besides, he knew he should be more worried about blowing his cover than making small talk. If anything, he should be feigning a nap with a large pair of headphones on.

Chris checked his phone. Russel had yet to reply to Chris's last message, though this was not surprising, given the distractions he likely also faced during the ongoing financial crisis. He took the time to update himself on the events in the financial world, though it had only been a matter of minutes since he had last scrolled through updates on all manner of social media and news outlets. Markets were closed, banks were closed, and the value of every stock, bond, derivative, and even the dollar, was entirely unknown. The current value of each asset was impossible to determine until markets opened. Some thinly traded markets, most of which were fairly obscure, were open. Many media outlets had used the change in asset values on these obscure markets, some of which existed on cryptocurrency blockchains and others on small exchanges throughout the world, to write sensationalist headlines that told of massive price swings in what Chris, along with every other financial professional, knew to be thinly traded markets that should not be used to assess true changes in the value of assets.

Chris found it reasonable to think that many assets would be worth a mere fraction of their previous value once markets opened up again, but this fact didn't make him uncomfortable. In fact, he had been positioning funds in order to make a profit on any correction in the U.S. stock market for the past few weeks. The bet against the broader equities markets was based on both a hunch and a considerable amount of research. The firm would have profited significantly if the stock market had dropped from five to ten percent. This event, on the other hand, could leave a major index such as the S&P 500 down far more than he had expected. 50%? 70%? Maybe more? By dumb luck, the trade might end up being one of the best of his career.

In the back of his mind, another possibility tugged at Chris' perception of the state of the financial system. There was a possibility that the very derivatives he had used to bet on a move to the downside would itself cease to exist because of some unforeseen consequence of this crisis. Even worse, there was the small, but distinct possibility that the broader financial system would never fully recover from the event. Such a scenario would see the financial system not in the midst of a crash, but a full-blown collapse.

The woman in the pantsuit returned to her seat beside Chris. She had a serious looking face to begin, but it had now taken on a more stern appearance.

"Who is it you said you worked for?" she asked.

"I didn't mention that, actually. I'm the head of portfolio management at WhiteWater," said Chris, without hesitation.

Her eyes narrowed somewhat, as she reached into the side pocket of her pants, and pulled out a badge which she flashed at Chris.

"FBI. Before we go any further, I'd like to remind you that lying to a federal officer is a crime."

Chris's heart felt as though it skipped a beat. His face went pale.

"Well-," Chris stammered.

She interrupted. "Dana Covington, I investigate white-collar crime. So, let's start over, and I'll give you another chance with this. Who do you work for?"

"You got me. I don't work for WhiteWater. I'm a senior analyst at-"

"Right, a firm called Third Realm Capital. A hedge fund," she said, once more cutting him off. "Let me guess, you lied to get a seat on this plane."

"Look, I said you got me," said Chris as he placed his wrists together in front of him as though he was waiting to be cuffed. This attempt at humor, however, was only being used to mask his internal panic. He genuinely feared that he had made a mistake that would cost him dearly.

Dana glanced around to the nearby seats. No one appeared to have noticed the discussion or returned a glance in their direction. However, there were several passengers that appeared alert and well within earshot.

"Follow me," she said.

Chris saw an opportunity.

"No."

The reply stopped her as she was in the process of standing up. She sat back down.

"Excuse me?"

"No. I want a lawyer."

"A lawyer? This isn't about you lying so you could get back home," she said in a harsh, hushed voice.

Internally, Chris remained petrified by fear, but he did his best to maintain a cool exterior. He stared into her eyes.

"You're bluffing," he said.

Her eyes narrowed further.

"Bluffing? This isn't bluffing. Your life is in danger."

"What are you talking about?"

Dana glanced around once more, and further lowered her voice.

"A few hours ago, your house was destroyed by a bomb blast."

"What do you mean, a bomb blast?" replied Chris.

"What I mean is that it was standing, and now it's not. Their best guess based on the preliminary reports is that some type of small explosive was likely used. Here's the thing, your house wasn't the only one."

Chris struggled to formulate a sentence.

Dana discretely gestured to those in nearby seats. "That's all I'm willing to say here. I need to speak to you privately."

Chris nodded and rose from his seat to follow her as they made their way to the front of the first-class compartment. They found a small food service room that was occupied by an attendant, but a quick glance at Dana's badge was all it took to have the space to themselves. Dana closed the door behind them.

"I'd like to record this interview," she said as she pulled out her phone.

Chris nodded.

Before she was able to ask any questions, Chris asked one first. "What do you mean that my house was not the only one?"

"In the last twelve hours, the FBI has noticed a large number of violent crimes that don't fit the pattern of the ongoing crime and unrest that has swept the country," said Dana.

"What do you mean?"

"You haven't been home in the States, but I'm sure you've seen plenty in the news or on social media about unrest and crime. The truth is even worse. Murder, rape, arson, robbery, you name it. It's bad. Worse than it's been, well, maybe ever. In the midst of that, some analysts noticed a pattern. My guess is that, even in this crisis, houses exploding is not all that common. Once they found that pattern, it was a matter of identifying any commonalities between the victims."

"How many are we talking here? 3 or 4?" asked Chris.

"9, so far. But, that's not all. From the information provided to me, it would appear that there is a coordinated targeting of individuals that are closely tied to the financial system in one way or another."

"So, you're telling me that there's some group of terrorists that are leveling houses that belong to bankers?" said Chris incredulously.

"That's part of it. It appears that explosives were only used in a small minority of cases. We only have a few reports localized to the Northeast, including your own house, and a few in Florida. As if that's not bad enough, the bombings are part of a wider pattern. We've seen a number of individuals targeted. Some were beaten to death, others shot. A large number have been reported as potential missing persons. My guess would be that with the strain on local law enforcement as well as federal agencies, we're only scratching the surface."

"What do you consider scratching the surface?" asked Chris.

"When I spoke on the phone, the number stood at 72 potential cases. The timing on these all appear to be coordinated fairly well; they all occurred in the last 24 hours. 72 cases identified in 24 hours during a time in which law enforcement has many other crises to deal with is, well, alarming. Like I said, only scratching the surface."

Chris was shocked. Not only was there an attempt on his life, but 72 other people in the same situation as him. *No, that's not right. They aren't in the same situation. I survived without a scratch. I'm halfway across the world*, Chris thought to himself.

Those people were just that, people. Sure, finance work sometimes deserved a bad rap. There were many that he knew that fulfilled the stereotype of the greedy, heartless, egocentric individual that operated in the gray area of ethics and morals or ignored such guidelines altogether. The criticism the industry had faced following the Great Financial Crisis and since was certainly valid, a fact he conceded on many occasions when talking with friends and family on the matter.

But, many of those men and women he worked with were smart, determined individuals. Many had families of their own. Some emphasized philanthropy and charity. They were not the monsters and sociopaths that they were so often portrayed as. Only a small minority belonged in those categories, and that was true for nearly any profession. The difference was that, just like with politics, a sociopath in finance was able to do far more damage than a fast-food worker, a real estate agent, or even a police officer. Unfortunately, it was those that sought power over others that tended to rise through the ranks the most rapidly. Such power could then be used to amass more power, wealth, and influence, often at the expense of the lower and middle classes.

This history of the financial system, a tainted history that mirrored the tainted system of the present, was something that Chris had pondered often. It was a history that he had struggled to come to grips with. To some extent, he was not surprised by the information this FBI agent was sharing with him, though the scale of the crimes left Chris astounded.

"I need to ask you some questions. First, who was aware that you would be traveling to Singapore?"

Chris paused as he considered this. "It was last minute, really. An assistant to the CIO, Rick was his name, gave me a phone call the day before and told me when I would be leaving, and who I would be meeting with. Jeff, the CIO, knew I was always more than willing to travel. He knew I was flexible since I don't have a wife or kids of my own."

Dana paused for a moment, then began jotting down notes on a small notepad.

"How well did you and Jeff Gillis know each other?"

"We went back a few years. We get along. He respects me for my talent, and I respect him for his management abilities. What can I say, he's a good boss."

"Ok, you said he may have known you-"

"Hang on a second," said Russel, interrupting. "How did you know his last name was Gillis? You guys at the FBI are good, but why would they have passed that information along to you?"

Dana didn't respond.

"They got him, didn't they?"

She nodded. "It was the same M.O., with explosives used to destroy the house."

"What about his wife and kids?" Chris asked.

Dana shook her head. "I'm sure it was the same group that did this to your house. Like I said, the Northeast and Florida were the two main areas we identified using this method."

"How did they know Jeff would be home, but not know I was halfway across the world?" asked Chris, trying to keep himself focused despite an overwhelming sense of anger and frustration.

"That's what I'm trying to figure out. My assumption would be that they only had limited intel. They most likely only had access to some of your communications, such as your company or personal email and similar accounts, but there's a big jump between gaining access to emails or social media, and wiretapping. The impromptu trip to Singapore is likely what saved your life," said Dana.

"So, where does that leave us?" asked Chris.

"Please understand that the Bureau shared a bulk of their intel with me during that brief phone call and in a subsequent email. What I mean is that we know very little about what is happening due to the recent timing of these crimes, but also because we're short-staffed. Other pressing matters that have cropped up in recent days are taking priority over this for the time being. That should tell you something, this has the potential to be one of the largest acts of domestic terror in U.S. history, and it's not even at the top of the list of the FBI.

"With that being said, it's not safe for you to go back to your hometown or to Third Realm Capital. My hunch is that the organization responsible for these acts tends to operate within individual cells across the country. This means a group in, let's say, Southern Louisiana, will care very little and have very limited intel on you. They certainly could coordinate with other cells to receive that intel, and clearly some coordination has already occurred since these crimes appear to roughly coincide with each other, but it makes it unlikely and far more difficult.

"You have another factor working in your favor, as well. This was a widespread operation. For all we know, there could have been hundreds of targets. I would expect there would not be one-hundred percent success in the task of reaching every target, and this is likely something that these people, whoever they are, expected while in the planning stages. Whatever their goal is, failing to kill one single target likely won't impact their ability to reach that goal. For that reason, there is a good chance that they have no desire or need to go after you again unless an opportunity presents itself that they see as low effort and low risk. What I'm trying to say is that they will likely see the overall operation as a success, regardless of if they were able to kill you."

Chris nodded, as he followed along.

"But, I'd prefer we not give them that opportunity. For the time being, I'd like for you to return with me to Richmond. I'm sure they would like to interview you further, as you may have some information important to the case."

"Would you be working the case?" asked Chris.

"Under normal circumstances, absolutely not. I generally stick to cases involving white-collar crime. I've worked on several fraud cases that you probably have heard of in the past. Money laundering, securities fraud, that type of stuff. It's my wheelhouse and it's the type of crime that I've fought for most of my career. Domestic terror is not my strong suit. Still, it would appear there is likely a connection to the financial system, considering each of the victims is employed by one financial firm or another. If anything, that seems to be the common thread and one of the few leads we have so far. We have an intel analyst to thank for picking up on that pattern."

Chris's mind suddenly went back to the thoughts of those targeted that also had families. "Back home, do you have a family? I mean a husband or kids?" he asked.

"No."

The manner in which she gave the answer made it clear to Chris that she didn't want to discuss the topic further. He didn't know why he asked the question. He had no family of his own. He had a brother that he was still close friends with, and Chris still talked to his parents regularly, but had never settled down and started a family of his own, despite nearing the latter half of his 30s.

Despite having only met Dana a short while ago, Chris already knew the most likely answer as to why she did not have a husband or children of her own. Put simply, she was married to her work. The cases she worked on replaced both the challenges and rewards of a marriage, and no doubt her underlings were viewed by her as children in need of her guidance. It was a reality that he struggled with himself in his own line of work; Chris had been in a number of serious relationships over the years, but never was able to commit himself in the same way he was able to commit to his work.

Likewise, before him sat a woman that was as committed as he, though each to a different profession. Unlike so many others in the United States and around the world that would soon or had already decided that their own personal wellbeing was higher than that of their employer or profession, Dana had made the conscious decision to forge onward, no matter the price. She had admitted herself that the agency was already significantly short-staffed, despite the recency of the market crash and the beginning of the unrest. He admired her for her determination and dependability. In fact, Chris found himself thankful to be in the same room with such a capable and focused individual. He didn't know why, but Chris found himself feeling very strongly that the two would not part ways anytime soon, as there was something important for them to accomplish.

Charlotte drank her coffee that she grabbed at the Russell Senate Office Building's cafeteria. She felt the quality was subpar, but local coffee shops she frequented were all closed. Additionally, Charlotte was limiting her trips out of the newly established perimeter, as leaving and entering was a lengthy process for all but the highest ranking politicians. The entire area surrounding Charlotte's office was on lockdown, a zone that included the White House, Capitol Building, Pentagon, and every major government building or memorial in that area. This included the nearby congressional office buildings. The perimeter was maintained by hundreds of US Army soldiers, peppered with a few Capitol and DC police officers. Outside of this perimeter, Washington, DC was experiencing the same lawlessness and violence that continued to be common in most major U.S. cities. In the past day, this looting, rioting, and widespread protests had become increasingly intense and unpredictable. For that reason, the House of Representatives and the Senate had remained within the perimeter as they attempted to carry on business as they were best able.

Charlotte sat in Emily's office, though the Senator was not present, as she was slated to address the Senate in person within the next few minutes. In the last several days, the members of Congress had, on an individual basis, done their very best to capitalize politically on the ongoing financial crisis. The narratives differed slightly, but Charlotte could see that some of the most powerful and influential senators and representatives within each party had coalesced around a unified message. Emboldened by the desperation many Americans were expressing, this coalition had come together and written a nine-hundred page bill that was planned to be officially presented in the Senate by Emily. Along with this presentation was a bipartisan proposal to skip some of the usual procedural steps required to finish in order for a bill to be voted upon, including skipping its time in committee. Of course, ninety-nine percent of this bill existed in written form well before the events of the past days. Many of the items had been on each party's wishlist for some time, whether in the form of spending or policy changes. The bill was also packed with earmarks, a practice that included provisions for specific members of congress and their constituency. It was a practice that had ceased long ago but was ripe for a comeback in the current, frenzied political climate. Charlotte, along with every other member of Congress, knew that the contents of the bill would put anyone who would oppose it in a politically vulnerable position. There were many from the other party that opposed this bill, but Charlotte and Emily did not expect them to have the votes to make a difference.

Like so many other pieces of legislation, this massive bill contained the fingerprints of Charlotte, as well as other high-level aides, who had spent hours upon hours drafting the language of the bill and its contents. However, it was not these aides writing it entirely or without direction. Rather, direction was provided to the aides, with a limited amount of leeway in terms of specific language. The elected officials contributed very little to the nitty-gritty of the vast majority of such bills, instead only asking for items to be included on a less specific and more broad basis. The creation of the framework for the bill was also contributed to by special interest groups, political action committees, lobbyists, and the other interested and influential parties. It was up to Charlotte, along with the help of others, to stitch such tomes of legislative action into cohesive bills. In the end, it was a process that Charlotte herself only supervised for quality and content, delegating much of the grunt work to lower-level aides within both parties.

As Charlotte sat in front of the TV, the cable news network returned from a commercial break. The existence of advertisements, given the current national climate, was surprising to Charlotte, though she did feel they conveyed a much needed sense of normalcy. The camera cut to the Senate chambers rostrum, the large raised platform that the whole of the Senate's chairs and desks faced. Emily adjusted the microphone after setting down her written speech.

"In the past several days, this great country of ours has been shaken to its core. This bastion of economic and financial prosperity has been gravely wounded. In our streets, chaos violence, and anarchy prevail. With financial institutions being unable to conduct even the most basic of transactions, desperation has set in. Parents are unable to buy food for their children, businesses are unable to be reimbursed for their goods and services, and employers are unable to pay their employees. Those that are the most vulnerable, including children, the elderly, and those in poverty, find themselves in a dire situation. Today, I am introducing a bill that is designed to augment the President's recent executive actions in response to these exceptionally difficult circumstances. This seeks to facilitate the distribution of goods and services to those that need them the most, and also seeks to bring order to our cities and the countryside. What we need right now are the necessities: food, water, a warm place to live, and protection from those that seek to cause harm to others. That is what this bill is designed to provide.

"The American people are a resilient people. We will rise from this present crisis. However, make no mistake. This crisis was both predictable and preventable, and I am not content with only fixing the consequences of this crisis without also addressing its root causes. We have seen the abject failure of the heart of our financial system, and they have found themselves in a position in which even the Federal Reserve is unable to extricate them from, with the powers currently available to them. But, as I said, this was both predictable and preventable. For too long, large banks and other financial institutions have gambled with our financial and economic future. For generations, they have been rewarded with enormous payouts, whether in the form of profits or bailouts. They gambled but were never allowed to lose. Whenever faced with a potential of major losses, the executives and their cronies cried to the American people and to Congress, saying 'we're too big to fail!' Today, we see that they were not wrong in such an assertion. They are too big to fail. However, while expedient over the short-term, bailing them out has only led to higher wealth disparity, and in turn, has encouraged more of the same behavior.

"Today, despite the uncertainty of the future in the great country that we call home, we have an opportunity to change this long-standing policy of throwing a lifeline to those that are least deserving of a rescue. Let's not try to fix this present situation by their rules. They don't get to dictate the terms of their own rescue. It's time to put a stop to this once and for all. In addition to the relief within this bill, there is also a proposal to effectively and expediently nationalize our financial system. For the bank account holder, they will notice little change. However, the key difference will be that the entire system will have the benefit of being formally backed by both the Treasury and the Federal Reserve, eliminating the risk of this happening ever again.

"At the heart of the unrest and violence in past days is not only desperation, but also anger, a just anger, an anger directed at those who have so irresponsibly put our future at risk. Today, I am calling on my fellow Senators and members of Congress to listen to this anger, and use it for good. I am calling for each of you to support the passage of this legislation. Let's ensure that such an avoidable tragedy never occurs again."

As the senator walked off the raised platform, there was no applause in the chambers. In fact, very few senators were physically present for the speech. However, the effects were noted and well covered by the media. The cable news network continued their coverage following the speech. Predictably, the pundits were supportive of the proposal contained within the new legislation. Nationalizing the financial system had long been a goal of one party and had more recently been gaining the support of the other major party. Still, in such a fluid situation, it was unknown to either party whether they would have the votes necessary to pass the bill. They had linked the relief bill to the bank nationalization for a reason. Doing so placed the legislators and the President in a difficult position, should they choose to not support the bill. The momentum of the crisis and the urgency of some form of relief by the government would likely seal the deal.

As the discussion between the pundits and guests on the network continued, Charlotte's thoughts wandered to her own involvement in the present situation. Charlotte found herself becoming more uncomfortable with the clandestine operations that she had been made aware of in the past twenty-four hours. As with the initial stages of the operation that sought to throw the financial system into disarray, she remained entirely convinced that what they had done was for the greater good. Still, the extent of the chaos and carnage was undeniable, and the risk posed by the targeting of those that had worked within the financial system was very real. Charlotte had begun to grow concerned that the anarchy that gripped the streets would take on a momentum of its own that could not be stopped by more conventional measures, such as those being proposed today. She had not yet shared these concerns with Emily but planned to do so as soon as the two had some time alone.

Privately, both she and Emily held some resentment at the fact that they had not been privy to the involvement of the United Workers Front, a group often referred to as the UWF. The partisan group supported Emily and her party, but their methods made it difficult for much of the party to publicly support them. They were a useful ally, and by all accounts, they had shown a high rate of success in their widespread operation against hundreds of those within the financial system. Their intent was that such a bold act would serve as a rallying cry for millions of desperate Americans that were growing angrier by the day. It would be an act privately or publicly celebrated by the masses. In theory, it would spark a revolution of sorts that would ultimately carry far too much momentum to devolve into the far bloodier revolutions that had been witnessed and documented throughout human history. Regardless, the operation was risky and could very well lead to partisan violence.

And yet, there was another facet of her own mind that reminded her that trailblazing moments in history were often only seen as well-conceived and inevitable in retrospect. The current ordeal was messy, but so was the French Revolution, the American Revolution, the Civil War, the Civil Rights movement, and a host of other historical battles, both bloody and otherwise, that were waged for the greater good.

Regardless of the wisdom behind the seemingly unchangeable trajectory the country was on, Charlotte was surprised that the abductions, and in some cases, murders, had not yet been reported by the mainstream media. There was no doubt that the overall atmosphere of unrest and violence may have hindered law enforcement in making the correct moves and connecting the dots. However, the plan was for these acts to be made public. If the mainstream media had not picked up on the story in the next 24 hours, the plan was for the story to be leaked. The identity of the man that Emily had spoken to on the phone was still a mystery to Charlotte. However, she got the sense that he was not the mastermind of the abductions and killings, but only a co-conspirator. He expressed that his desire was for the media to uncover the story on their own, in order to give additional legitimacy to the UWF. The intent was to use the story, in all of its grisly details, as propaganda.

Emily had explained the reasoning to Charlotte. The operation was intended to not only leave the current financial system without some key mid-level employees and executives when they were needed the most, but also to strike fear into the hearts of high-level executives, CEOs, board members, and other leaders of what the UWF had termed the financial corporatocracy. Such a successful and widespread act was also designed to rally support from other more extreme groups and individuals within the party. As Charlotte contemplated this, as if on cue, the topic of conversation on the news network suddenly changed.

"To add to this busy news day, we have additional, disturbing headline news to report on."

Chapter Six: Acclimation

It had been a successful day. David and Warren had begun their marketing campaign by seeking out those within the local business and farming community that they predicted would be the most easily persuaded into joining their proposed makeshift market. David had thought that choosing people on the basis of geography, essentially going house to house, was the simplest solution. Instead, it had been Alice's idea to begin with what she had defined as 'easy wins'. The strategy made perfect sense. They could build both confidence and momentum, while also scaling up the size of their community market, by first targeting those that would be most easily swayed. They could then present it to the others as an inevitably successful program that would be well established, based on the participation from a large base of the so-called early adopters, another phrase Alice had used frequently.

Likewise, they had taken the same approach when discussing Warren's concerns about safety and security. Warren felt that these discussions were something to begin with at a slow pace, and present over a greater amount of time to those in their defined two-mile radius. On the first day, he and Warren had only identified a single household, which was near both of their houses, that would be most receptive to the idea. The rest of these nearby farms and houses were allowed some time to come to their own realization of their diminished safety and need for a community-based approach.

At the end of the day, David and Alice sat in the living room. This was his first opportunity to relax for the day. David was accustomed to busy, long days, but the volume of work tended to decrease during winter months, as there was less he was able to do because of the weather and the season. One of the benefits of having been kept busy for the entire day was that David had not been given the opportunity to follow current events. This was a positive for David's mental health, as he felt it was all too easy for him to get sucked into the same cycle of catastrophe that the mainstream media had been mired in over the past number of days. David had recently found himself growing more concerned about his family's financial future, as well as their safety. In the absence of the constant updates, these were still concerns of his. But, they were concerns that he spent the day acting upon in a proactive way. Aware of his own vulnerability to the media and its negative effect on himself, David was intentional about how he could best avoid it. He even went so far as to keep the radio in his pickup truck tuned to a classic rock station, which had continued to play its regular songs, though the DJs did spend some time remarking upon current events.

Now, at the end of the day, he allowed himself to soak in the events of the day. Prior to the ongoing crisis, David knew that he did not live in a vacuum that was separate from the rest of the world, and that certainly was not the case now. He felt there was prudence in maintaining an awareness of current events, just so long as they didn't consume his thought lift. As he watched on his television a summary of the day's events, he found himself encouraged, though also skeptical of Congress's relief plan which had been paired with a plan to nationalize the nation's financial system. He did not hold a particularly strong opinion on such a move, but he did find himself frustrated by the political gamesmanship during such a crisis. A simple relief bill likely would have passed already, given the urgent nature of the crisis, but the added weight of the plan for nationalization could add days or weeks onto the timeline for the passage of the bill in a best-case scenario. Alternatively, it could prevent the passage of the bill altogether.

The network continued, now changing topics to the ongoing widespread violence. David was thankful that he and Alice no longer lived in Indianapolis, as most major cities continued to languish in a state of chaos and, in some cases, outright anarchy. He saw the images of major interstates leading out of cities that were clogged with traffic. This was compounded by a snowstorm on the Eastern Seaboard, as well as fuel shortages which had led to a high percentage of cars left abandoned on the freeway. He saw images of people, even entire families, walking alongside the road in the freezing temperatures and blowing snow. David tried his best to not imagine Alice, Maya, and Harper in such a situation.

However, what he found to be the most concerning were the reports from overseas. The media appeared to gloss over the details, as these were stories halfway across the world, but the shock of the collapse of the financial system was felt worldwide, often in countries that were not as well prepared as the United States. One story in particular that he found concerning was the loss of electricity across a majority of India, Bangladesh, and Myanmar. It was a simple thirty-second story, but it represented over a billion people that were now without power, a population equivalent to three times the population of the U.S.

David had a suspicion that the path that second and third world countries were taking would be the same path the U.S. would soon follow, should the crisis not be remedied. Already, in the last 24 hours, rolling blackouts had begun on the East Coast. The majority of the nation's power grid was dependent on consistent delivery of fossil fuels, including coal, oil, and natural gas. The delivery of these fuels, as well as the operation of the power plants, were also heavily dependent on the skill and experience of thousands of workers, many of which reportedly had not been at work over the several days, thus leaving power plants dangerously low on manpower. This concern over the power grid's reliability was compounded by the fact that Indiana was in the dead of winter. The furnace in his house was an older model and still ran on fuel oil. In most houses, such models had been replaced by more modern furnaces that ran on natural gas. The large tank in his basement was three-quarters of the way full, which, if conserved, would last through the next few months and into spring. However, for those gallons of fuel to be meaningful, he needed electricity to power the furnace. He had a gasoline powered generator, but relying on the generator would mean relying on a steady supply of gasoline, which was yet another variable he did not want to be dependent upon. If nothing else, he had a wood stove that he often used to supplement the heat from the furnace on the coldest of the winter days, but it would be inadequate for heating the entirety of the house. David made a mental note to consider this further, and discuss it with Warren at some point.

As if on cue, the screen that the cable news network was streaming on suddenly went dark. His first assumption was that the very blackouts he had been worrying about had arrived. But, he quickly realized the overhead light was still shining. Behind him, in the entrance to the living room, stood Alice with the TV remote in her hand. The two shared a smile.

"The world will go on, with or without you," she said with a grin.

David knew what she was getting at.

"Maya, Harper, come here for a minute," said Alice, as she pulled a box out from behind her back.

It was a board game.

Maya came running into the room. "Yeah! Candy World!" said the youngest daughter.

The game was most age-appropriate for Maya, but the older daughter enjoyed it as well.

"Clear the table off," said Alice, as she handed them the box.

The girls ran into the dining room to set up the game. David stood up from the couch. He walked towards Alice, arms wide, pretending to prepare to give her a hug, before throwing an arm behind her back and another behind her legs, swooping her into his arms, as though he was a groom carrying his bride over the threshold of their first house. Alice giggled as he did so. David kissed her on the lips and allowed his lips to linger, barely touching her lips, as he opened his eyes and gazed into her eyes. She wrapped her arms around him.

"You're always keeping me grounded. You and the girls both. Life can move so fast, and sometimes it feels like the world and its problems are too big for me," said David.

"Small is good. Small is what keeps you grounded. We can handle the small things, and let someone else worry about tackling the big problems."

Russel had been expecting to be thrown into a cold, concrete cell with steel bars. Instead, he found himself in a bedroom. He knew the room was a second-story bedroom. There was a window on one side of the room that was a full 15 feet above the ground outside. The window was complete with rebar spanning its width and secured into the window's frame. Beyond the window lay a grass field that spanned roughly one hundred yards, before meeting a forest. The room had a bed. It was an unremarkable, solid metal frame. Atop the frame sat a full-size mattress and large blanket. Next to the bed was a small, wooden nightstand. The room was otherwise devoid of furniture. Off to one side of the room was a small bathroom that was connected to the bedroom, though the door had been removed. The bathroom was complete with a shower, sink, and toilet. The door separating the bedroom from the outside hallway had clearly been recently installed. It was a metal door equipped with both a traditional lock and a deadbolt, though the locks could only be manipulated from outside of the room.

The room was far from being a prison cell, but Russel still found himself treating it as such. The man that had deposited him in the room had also left without so much as a word, though he did take the time to first remove his restraints. Since then, Russel had spent much of the time pondering ways in which he could escape the house. He had considered escaping the house on his own, but he knew he wouldn't be able to live with himself if he didn't also include his fellow captive, Kate, in the plans. Presumably, she was also in this house, though Russel did not know where. He stood at the window. The sun had risen a short time ago, and it shone through the window, nearly blinding him as it also reflected off the bright white snow in the field.

Russel heard the door unlock. The door swung open. Standing in the doorway were three men. He was not certain, but suspected they may have been the same men that had grabbed him from his house. All three were caucasian, and had a muscular, lean build, with clean-shaven faces. What caught Russel's attention was that the two men flanking the man in the center both held AR-15 style rifles, one of which was pointed directly at him. The man aiming at his chest stood with an otherwise relaxed posture and did not appear as though he was going to fire the rifle, though this brought little comfort to Russel, who was entirely unaccustomed to firearms aimed in his direction.

The man in the center grinned as he spoke. "I hope you're enjoying your stay at our B&B. It's a cozy, little place, don't you think?"

Russel did not return the grin and remained silent.

"Oh, come on, relax! The sooner we get along, the better your stay will be."

Russel remained stone-faced.

"All right, suit yourself. Let's talk about ground rules. You have a bed, a working sink, shower, and toilet, and we will be providing three square meals a day. I want you to know that any and all of that can be taken away if you choose not to comply. Let's start by getting rid of the holier-than-thou, I'm a martyr, attitude. You're not. You're the scum of the Earth. No, you're worse than that. If I had it my way, you'd be dead already. But, for now, we have a purpose for you.

"So, here's the plan. A couple times a day, me and my friends here will be stopping by. We're going to spend some quality time together. Enhanced interrogation, I think that's what I've heard it been called before? Then again, you don't have any information we're trying to get from you. So, maybe torture would be the most appropriate term. I won't spoil any more of the surprise of what we have in store for you. Let's just say we're a creative bunch, and leave it at that. At the end of each session, we leave you alone. You keep your bathroom, your bed, your meals, and we keep the heat vent to your room open. Life goes on. And then, we'll come again when we feel like it. Once a day, three times a day, who knows? That's part of the fun of it. Each day, wash, rinse, repeat. What's the saying? The beatings will continue until morale improves? Something like that. Oh, and I didn't mention this, but each of these sessions will be filmed."

Caught off guard by the last statement, Russel broke his silence. "Filmed?"

"Yeah, filmed. That's the orders I received. It's for the whole world to see. That way, everyone will know what happens when you dedicate your life's work to lying, cheating, stealing, hoarding unimaginable riches, and leaving the rest of us the crumbs. I want every CEO, executive, board member, trustee, and anyone that's ever been a part of this criminal enterprise you're in, to witness what happens when the 99% fight back."

The man had been walking in Russel's direction, taking a step every few seconds. He continued but now switched to a lower, angrier voice, as he stared into Russel's eyes. "I want you to remember two things: First off, you are not important. There are hundreds that are in the exact same situation. No one cares about you, and no one is coming to save you. The second thing you need to know is that you won't escape. You can try, but you won't. You'll end up as dead as your friend in the back of that van."

"Kate?" asked Russel, with concern evident in his voice.

The man let out a hearty laugh. "Wait a second. Are you two hearing this?" he said as he looked back at his men standing near the doorway. "You care about her, don't you? I think Russel has a crush on the lady downstairs," he looked back at Russel. "I think we could have some fun with this," said the man, with a devious smile on his face. "No, she isn't dead. But, since you care about her so much, I'll let you in on a little secret. She'll be getting the same treatment as you.

"I was talking about the body lying next to you in the van. I actually forgot that you have no idea who that was! Said the man, laughing to himself. "I am glad we didn't go cheap with those hoods. That body belonged to your old buddy Marcus. We were planning to keep him alive, but he tried putting up a fight. He drew a gun on me, but this gunslinger over here put a round through his forehead before he knew what was coming," said the man, gesturing to one of the men in the doorway.

At this, Russel felt his composure break momentarily. His anger was clearly displayed on his face, but he resisted the urge to lash out verbally or physically.

The man's smile remained on his face. "I'll see you after breakfast, Russel," said the man as he began walking towards the door to the hallway outside. He paused, and looked back, "One more thing, Russel. Remember this: We're not the bad guys, you are."

"We had a deal!"

"You're right, we did have a deal, Emily. Then, you had to go and tack on spending for NASA."

"NASA? Who cares? This is a multi-trillion dollar bill. Who cares if we add a few billion? It's sort of like adding a few dollars as a tip for a high-class call girl," retorted Emily.

Senator Forsyth's eyes narrowed. Emily was referring to her colleague's not yet publicized scandal that they both knew she had knowledge of. It was only by chance that she had come to know of the secret affair the senator had been having with an expensive prostitute, but she had taken full advantage of the illicit behavior and had since used it as leverage. It would be a damaging scandal, should it go public. Forsythe was a high-ranking senator with a reputation as a family man that prioritized both morals and integrity.

"Look, I don't care. We had a deal, and you changed that deal. I'm not supporting the bill, and neither is Mike," said the senator, referring to the freshman senator from his own state that he had taken under his wing over the past three years. The support of the two senators was vital to the bill's passage, and without it, Emily feared additional senators would jump ship.

Emily regrouped herself. "Let's be serious. This is NASA we're talking about. NASA is not unpopular with the voters. I don't care if they never got around to that Mars mission. For whatever reason, the average voter still loves it when they dangle that carrot in front of them, decade after decade."

"Ok, you got me," said Senator Forsyth, wryly. "Between you and me, it's not about NASA. You and I both know that."

"What is it, then?" asked Emily.

"Principles."

"What do you know about principles?"

"I'm saying that, on the basis of principles, I don't agree with the plan for nationalization. Remember, I have another five years until re-election. Mike has three. I think we can handle bad press now, and still be in good shape, come election time," said Senator Forsyth.

"What I think you're forgetting-"

"You don't need to finish that sentence, I know where you're going with this. You're singing the same tune you've been singing for the last six months. Well, guess what senator? Go ahead and leak that story. Better yet, hold a press conference. Maybe I'll even give you the girl's number, and you can invite her. I would love to see what the American people think of you throwing mud at your political opponents at a time like this. The story would flop. That gun you've been holding to my head? You'd find out it was loaded with blanks."

Emily was taken aback at this and was frustrated. She needed these votes.

Senator Forsyth continued. "Besides, I can't put my finger on it, but something tells me that is more than just you being an opportunist."

"What are you implying?" said Emily.

"I'm not implying anything. It's just that, if I didn't know better, I might find myself thinking that this was planned out ahead of time. Now look, I'm not saying you're in on it, I'm just saying it looks all too convenient to be just a coincidence. First, there's these finance guys that got whacked or thrown in the back of the van. I mean, I get it. People are mad at big banks. But, how do you organize something like that in the span of a couple days, and still manage to not get caught? That takes planning, clout, money, not to mention quite a few people involved. I'd guess it would take at least a few hundred to make it happen, maybe a few thousand.

Emily maintained a blank face. "What does that have to do with this bill?"

"Don't play stupid. There has to be a connection between the two," said Senator Forsyth.

"Or, as bad as those attacks were, maybe we have bigger fish to fry right now. That will all be investigated in due time. In the meantime, we're all going to be judged by how we react to this. I'm talking about your legacy, senator."

"I'm not budging, Emily. My mind is made up. Maybe you'll still pass the deal without me, but remember, future generations will judge you for that as well."

"I think we'll have no trouble getting the votes, with or without you," said Emily.

"We'll see about that."

Chapter Seven: Allegiances

"Hi, Sandy."

"Hey, Josh, how ya doing tonight?"

"It'll be a rough one, that's for sure."

"Let me take a guess, you haven't slept since I saw you last night?"

"Nope. I doubt there'll be any chance I'll get any sleep tonight, either," he said, as he looked about the convenience store.

"Now Sheriff, don't make me lecture you about driving when you're sleep-deprived," said Sandy, as she stood behind the counter.

"I know, I know, that driving tired is as bad as driving drunk. How have things been here?" he asked, deliberately changing the subject.

"Quiet."

"Good."

"There's still been a few out-of-towners that I've had to turn away. Otherwise, compared to what we're seeing on TV, this feels pretty tame."

"I know. I wish I could guarantee that would continue to be the case."

He walked up to the counter and looked the clerk in the eyes.

"It's just me and one other deputy covering the whole county. If anyone gives you trouble, I don't know how much help we'll be," said Josh Edgerton, Sheriff of Jackson County, Wisconsin.

He was referring to the fact that several of his deputies, as well as all but one guard at the county jail, had not reported to work over the past few days. That left the county sheriff's department stretched thin. Tonight, a few of those deputies that had pledged to continue to fulfill their duties were at home catching up on some much-needed sleep, but Josh knew he was needed, though he knew he was only able to last at least a few more hours before a reprieve. The number of calls and incidents they responded to were higher than usual, but not extraordinarily high. He was thankful for that; he knew that nearly every police department in the U.S. was swamped, and in some cases, in a purely defensive posture in response to the violence and unrest. Thus far, the last several days in Jackson County had been dominated by much of the usual domestic disputes, drunk driving, cases of drug abuse, and only a few cases of vandalism and shoplifting.

He took a more serious tone. "I don't want you to be afraid to close up shop. You know, we've been pretty lucky around here. I guarantee you that if this gas station was in Madison, or even Eau Claire, those windows would be shattered, and the pumps would be dry. I'm not trying to scare you, I'm just saying there's nothing wrong about trying to protect yourself and what's yours."

"Thanks, Josh. I've thought about it, but this is all I have. I already told Trevor and Emma to stay home for a while, and I'll hold down the fort as long as I can," replied Sandy.

"Suit yourself. Hey, about the gas-"

"Don't worry about it, pump whatever you need," said Sandy. "Oh, and take these for the road."

She handed him a pair of energy drinks.

"I appreciate it. Give us a call if you need anything," said Josh, before walking out the door to begin the long night.

Chris slipped on his shoes and began to tie them. Dana hadn't given him a specific time that she would arrive to pick him up, but he had her pegged as an early morning type. After two nights back in the United States, he was already beginning to return to his normal sleep schedule, as the few days overseas limited how much his normal circadian cycle had shifted. Dana had been able to find a motel for Chris to stay in, a task which took a considerable effort. Most hotel and motel chains had closed their doors to new reservations in the last few days. The motel that they were able to eventually locate was a family-owned motel that was surprisingly well kept but appeared to be running on a skeleton crew. Dana paid for five nights upfront, in cash. Chris had only seen one other customer at this motel since arriving; a family of two boys and their parents. They only stayed one night before embarking in their SUV, a vehicle that was filled to the brim and had several containers strapped to its roof. It was obvious they were leaving their home, wherever that was, in search of somewhere safer.

Chris grabbed his winter coat and walked out the front door. Sitting in the parking lot was a black, government-issue sedan. He climbed into the passenger seat.

"Coffee?" asked Dana.

"Thanks," said Chris, as he picked up the travel mug.

"It's homemade," said Dana.

They drove in silence for the first several minutes, as Chris sipped his coffee. This was the same routine that had played out yesterday, though she had not had coffee to share yesterday morning. Chris had accompanied Dana to the Richmond FBI field office where they spent the day. Chris participated in two brief interviews, each lasting about 10 minutes. The rest of the day, Chris had sat in Dana's office as she alternated between short meetings and spending time on her computer gathering information about the case. As Dana had warned, the field office was sparsely populated, and no one had taken notice of Chris, with the exception of the two agents that had met with him. As Chris sat in the car, once again on their way to the field office, he felt unsure of his purpose in assisting Dana and was not looking forward to another day of what he considered tagging along and being babysat.

"Are there any more interviews today?" asked Chris.

"No, I don't think so," she replied.

"Then what's the plan?

"That depends."

"Depends on what?" asked Chris.

"It depends on how much you want to help."

"I already told you everything I know," said Chris.

"That's not what I'm saying. Look, you're between a rock and a hard place. You don't have a home to go home to, and even if you stayed with a friend in town, you're still risking a lot by returning home. On the other hand, we can't keep you in that motel forever. Honestly, I'm surprised that it's still open. What you need to understand right now is that the information you know so far about this investigation extends far beyond what we generally share with those without some form of security clearance. I'm putting my career at risk when I allow you to get involved. Frankly, I don't care. As someone who has made a point to live by principles and follow procedure to the letter, I can say that I doubt procedure matters much right now. To be honest, I'm not convinced that my work matters much right now. There's a reason three-quarters of the agency haven't reported for duty over the last few days. For them, what matters is their family. For you and I, we don't have a family to worry about."

She paused, taking a deep breath. Chris looked on, unsure of what to say, but knowing she had more to say in this monologue that she likely had rehearsed multiple times in her head before picking him up from the motel.

"Look, I'm sorry if I'm not making complete sense. What I'm trying to say is that this is one of the most important cases I've ever worked on, and the Bureau needs me now more than ever. And besides, I don't know what else I'd do right now. I'm not the type to sit at home and twiddle my thumbs while also neglecting my responsibilities.

"I'm asking you if you're willing to help me as, let's say, a consultant. I can expedite you receiving some level of security clearance. Chris, you're a smart guy. I've been looking into some files on you. How you helped the SEC take down Cryolax? That was tremendous investigative work."

"You found out about that?"

Dana was referring to a biotech company that he had discovered was reporting fraudulent scientific information in research that they had been funding. He had handed over his research to the SEC, which conducted an investigation. The company ended up worthless, and Chris's firm made millions by betting against their stock.

Dana responded with a knowing look. "What does that have to do with this? That was a case of scientific and financial fraud, not domestic terrorism," replied Chris.

"Whether we're dealing with a case of either terrorism or organized crime. Financials are incredibly important to an investigation into either type of organization. And, believe me, if you had access to the information we're willing to provide to you, you could be exceptional at this. I can honestly say that we need you and your abilities right now. Under normal circumstances, that may not be the case. The Bureau is full of experts, and we have literal binders full of potential consultants, all with their own individual areas of expertise. But right now, well, you know how short-staffed we are. That applies to expert consultants as well."

The car continued down the road as Chris considered this. Richmond and its suburbs had also endured a difficult few days, and there was evidence of this all about. Chris could see shattered store windows, trash littering the sidewalks, numerous burned-out cars, some of which were police cruisers, and the occasional house or storefront that had burnt down, leaving still-smoldering ruins. For the time being, the Richmond Police Department and the Virginia State Police had managed to keep some of the main arteries clear, allowing traffic and emergency vehicles to navigate some portions of the city.

Chris knew that even though his house had been leveled, there would be a spot on the couch of his parent's house or even his brother's apartment, should he need it. If he moved fast, he might be able to reach upstate New York, where they resided, before the unrest made travel too difficult or dangerous.

And yet, Chris found himself yearning to agree to Dana's proposal. He was still angry about the attempt on his life, but it wasn't personal revenge that drove him to feel this way. Much to the surprise of Chris, he found a sense of injustice driving this desire to help Dana. A travesty had been committed, and he wanted to bring those responsible to justice. This was surprising; Chris had never seen himself as an especially upstanding citizen. He never felt compelled to serve his country, had never had a desire to become a lawyer or police officer, and knew that his own firm at times had operated in the grey area of legality. Paired with this desire to help right a wrong, Chris also found part of himself looking for adventure. He enjoyed what he did for work. However, he also knew that many that he worked with were primarily motivated by money and status. He was once that way, but a small voice inside him had been growing more recently, even before his time in Singapore and the ensuing crisis. He wanted to be a part of something bigger, and this could be his opportunity.

"OK. I'm on board. Point me in the right direction, and I'll do what I can to help."

Much to his dismay, Russel had found that the man that had come into his room and talked to him, Mitch was his name, was a man of his word. Just as promised, his needs were being met. They had provided three square meals, all of which were of above-average quality. The sink and shower still had running water. The bed was exactly where it was when he had arrived, and the vents continued to allow the warm air from the furnace into his room.

Additionally, as promised, he also had suffered through two separate visits from Mitch and his two accomplices, though the two men that accompanied him appeared to rotate, and Russel had now committed five separate faces to his memory. The visits consisted of varying forms of torture. Yesterday, the first session had been waterboarding, and the second involved electricity that ran through powerful electrodes. Russel thought about this as he choked down a plate of eggs, which, under other circumstances, he would have enjoyed immensely. Mitch had instructed him yesterday that his plate was to be clean upon their return, or else.

The pain of the torture sessions was still fresh in Russel's mind. Fear caused his fork to shake somewhat, as he shoveled the food into his mouth. It was perspective that Russel clung to the most. He remembered the stories he had heard of those that suffered in POW camps during the Vietnam War. It was not only the severity of the torture and neglect that chipped away the men's psyche but the longevity of their imprisonment. He had only been at the house for slightly more than a day.

Someone knocked at the door, and the door swung open as Mitch, along with two other men, strolled into the room. Russel placed his plate on the end table as he turned to face the men. Once again, one man had a rifle aimed at Russel, and the other held a pair of zip ties, not unlike the pair that were used when he was originally captured.

"Get up, stand in the corner, face the wall, and put your hands together behind your back," said Mitch in a stern voice.

Russel stood up in a slower than usual manner, as if doing so was a meaningful way to resist, and walked to the corner of the room opposite the door.

"We're going on a field trip today," said Mitch.

One of the other men secured Russel's wrists behind his back. Like before, Russel's world once again went dark, as a black hood was pulled over his head.

"Let's go," said one of the men, as he pulled, and then pushed Russel by his wrists, and maneuvered him out of the room and down the hallway.

He was instructed to carefully walk down a flight of stairs, before once again walking on level ground for several steps. He heard a door creak open, and he was led down another flight of stairs. Russel knew immediately he was now in a basement, not only because he had descended two flights of stairs, but also because he could feel the cool, damp air on his skin. It also smelled musty and reminded him of his basement in his childhood home. He continued for several paces more, as one of them then pushed him forward, before they pulled off his hood. His wrists, however, remained tightly bound behind his back. In front of him was a metal door identical to the one leading into his own bedroom. Mitch opened the door, this time without the courtesy of knocking.

"Lead the way," said Mitch, as he lightly pushed him through the doorway.

On the opposite side of the room was Kate, sitting on the floor with a blanket wrapped around herself, and her knees pulled up to her chest. She flinched as she looked towards the men, but appeared confused by Russel's presence and appearance. Despite having not seen her face before, he immediately sensed this was Kate. Her dirty blonde hair was a mess and was matted with some dried blood on one side. On her face, he could see a large bruise on her left cheek. Her eyes were filled with fear initially, but Russel could see a realization behind her eyes as he approached her.

"Russel?" she asked.

"Yeah, it's me," he said, as he walked over and crouched at her side, with his hands still bound behind his back.

"You look terrible," she said.

"Look who's talking," said Russel, as the two shared a grin.

Russel began to ask her a question, but the man pulled Russel backwards from his crouched position into a seated position on the floor. Another man stepped in to help drag him across the room. Russel heard a chair being dragged into the room, and the two men hoisted him up onto the chair. They tied legs to the chair, and a rope was tied around his torso, securing his trunk against the back of the chair as well. The fear returned to Kate's face as she saw this happening.

"That was such a heartwarming moment, but I didn't bring him down here for a heart-to-heart discussion between the two of you. No, Russel is just here to watch today," said Mitch, with a wide smile on his face.

At this, Russel felt the anger burn inside of him, and it took every ounce of his strength to maintain his stoic expression. After Russel was secured in the chair, another chair was brought into the room. The men repeated the same process, lifting Kate into the other chair. As they attempted to secure her hands behind her back, she struggled as they tried to secure the restraints around her wrists. One of the men became frustrated and slapped her across the face with the back of his hand. Russel's anger erupted, and he let out a shout as he struggled against his own restraints. He tried to push through his legs but soon found his resistance was in vain, as the only motion he would be able to achieve would be to tip his chair.

"Russel, relax," said Mitch, as he put a hand on Russel's shoulder.

Russel shrugged his shoulders but was unable to remove the man's hand. "You bastards."

Mitch knelt in front of Russel, and the two men stared into each other's eyes. Mitch's serious face turned to a smile.

"Let me guess, next you're going to tell me about how you'll make me pay. Let me remind you what I said when you arrived. We're not the villains here. See, I know you two don't believe me when I say that, so I want to tell you a little story before we get started.

"When I was twelve, my life was great. My parents loved each other, and they loved my brother and I. That fall, I joined the junior high football team at my school. I was so excited to finally play. My mom, she always said it wasn't safe, but she finally gave in. I wanted to be just like my big brother. He was all-state his senior year in football, and I always thought it wasn't fair that I couldn't join a team when I was younger. When she changed her mind, I felt like I was on cloud nine. I knew exactly what position I wanted to play. I was going to work so hard. I wanted to make that my life, and I wasn't going to let anything stop me from reaching my dreams.

"I remember the day just like it was yesterday. It was the second week of practice. School wasn't in session yet, so we were having practices in the morning. That day was the hardest practice yet. I was exhausted, but I was proud of how hard I had worked. I knew the coaches were watching me, and I was hoping they'd give me a starting position."

Mitch stood up and slowly paced across the room, staring at a blank wall, as though imagining a distant past.

"My mom picked me up that day. As soon as I got in the car, I knew something wasn't right. She was acting too nice. She always did that whenever something was wrong. Whenever she and Dad were fighting, or when her mother was in the hospital. That was her defense mechanism, or something like that. She'd bottle it all up and act like everything was great. We pulled into the driveway, and I noticed my father's truck was in the driveway. It wasn't even noon yet, and he never came home early, and never called in sick. I didn't say anything, but I knew. Too many of my friends had already gone through the same thing."

Across the room, Mitch turned to face Russel.

"I saw my dad go to work every day, and he'd always work his hardest. But it didn't matter. No job was safe. Losing his job like that, it crushed him. Of course, just like with my mom, he tried to act like it wasn't a big deal. But, the longer he was out of work, the worse things got at home. I watched my dad change. He wasn't the same dad.

"My mom, she picked up a job at a gas station to try and help out, but it wasn't enough. Within a few months, we lost the house. A few weeks later, after we moved into an apartment across town, he took up drinking. There was no hiding the pit that he was in at that point, partly because he didn't have the money to go out to the bar, so he drank at home. He wasn't an angry drunk, it wasn't in his nature. He was too gentle for that. But he was depressed, and it only made things worse. My mom loved him so much. She never stopped loving him, but she didn't know what to do. None of us did. I was just a kid. A year later, almost to the day, I came home from football practice again. They had saved enough for me to join the team."

Mitch's voice began to break, and Russel could see his eyes were welling up with tears.

"I walked in the door. Dad was sitting in that same chair he always was in when he got off work, after dinner. It was the same chair he was in when I had first seen him after he had lost his job. The same chair I found him passed out drunk almost every night. This time, I found him in that chair with a hole in his head and his revolver on the ground next to himself."

Mitch gazed past Russel as he recounted this as if he could see his father in the room with them. He shook his head as he appeared to pull himself back into reality.

"So, like I said, I'm not the bad guy here. This isn't about you, Russel, and it's not about you, Kate," he said, as he turned towards her momentarily, before facing Russel again. "This is about every family broken up, every mother and father that lost their job, every person that lost their life because of what people like you did. My dad is gone, because of what people like you did. And, do you know what really pisses me off? Not one of you paid the price you should have for what happened. I know, I know, the both of you were still in college during the Great Recession. So, like I said, this isn't about you. But, in a way, it's all about you.

"This is about an entire class of people that have lived without consequences for far too long. You've wiped away too many livelihoods, you've destroyed too many lives, and you deserve to pay a price for that. Every one of you. I want to make you feel pain. I want to see those liars on Wall Street squirm, as they see videos of you and a few hundred other puppets that are complicit in this crime, begging me to stop, begging me to put them out of their misery. If I have things my way, we'll come after them too, eventually, but they have a purpose in this regime change, too. In the meantime, I'm content with the fear I see in your eyes because I know they'll feel that same fear, one day," said Mitch, with a snarl across his face. "Just remember, Russel. This might hurt, but you don't know pain like I do."

Chapter Eight: Suspicions

"Why didn't you say anything sooner?" asked Dana, as they walked into her office after lunch at the field office's cafeteria.

"I don't know. I thought about trying to get a hold of him, but I just assumed he was busy. When things were normal, we'd go weeks, or even months without talking, and then pick up right where we left off. That's just how it was between us. We were both busy."

"It's fine, I understand," said Dana, as she sat at her desk and focused on the screen, nearly acting as though Chris wasn't present in the room.

Chris could see that she was determined.

"What are you doing?" asked Chris, after several minutes of near silence, with the exception of the click of the mouse and sound of her typing.

"I'm trying to find any case files they have. Here we go, this is from the Edina PD, right outside of Minneapolis. Looks like a neighbor called it in, said he saw a large gray van parked across the street before driving away. Apparently, the van blocked his vision of the front of the house, I suppose he was right across the street. But, after it drove off, an SUV pulled up, and he saw three men get inside before it followed the van down the road. Apparently, the door to the house was left wide open, which is why he decided to call it in since it's the middle of winter."

"That's it? asked Chris.

"That's it. Are you OK?" asked Dana.

"Yeah, I'll be fine. As soon as I realized he hadn't gotten back to me, I had a feeling. At least-"

"He's not dead?"

"Right."

In truth, Russel was one of Chris' closer friends, which was not saying much. Much as was the case with romantic partners, his occupation limited the depth of the friendships he had. It was no coincidence that most of his friends were also employed in the world of finance, and also had been similarly engrossed in his work.

On the other hand, there was a part of Chris, a part he cared to not reveal to Dana, that was genuinely worried for Russel. Just as he had realized earlier in the day, Chris knew there was more important things in life than his work, and that he was made for bigger things. *Maybe my friendship with Russel is one of those things?* Chris thought to himself. He couldn't rationalize why, but it was this sense of purpose that was the driving force behind his next statement.

"This is it."

"What's that?" asked Dana.

"This is the case we're going to work on. We're going to find him, and we're going to get to the bottom of this."

"Ok."

"Wait, I get to make that kind of decision?"

"I'll let you pretend that you're the one making that decision. In all seriousness, I like the idea. I always work harder on a case that means more to me, personally. Let's follow it as far as we can. Maybe we run into a brick wall, maybe I get reassigned, but Chris, I have a good feeling we can figure this out and find Russel."

"Alright, what else do we have on this case?"

"A single officer answered the call, did a quick sweep of the house, and didn't find a lick of evidence. He took down the account of the 911 caller, but that's it. Chris, I've read the summary on a few dozen of these cases by now. That seems to be par for the course. Most of these cases have little more than a single witness, or else a family member that noticed their loved one wasn't answering the phone or wasn't at home when they usually would be.

"And with the local law enforcement stretched so thin, who can blame them? They have bigger concerns right now. The only cases that have been elaborated upon with forensic data or a search for other information, like traffic cameras, are the ones that the ATF or FBI has sent agents to investigate. But, obviously our resources are limited, and such visits have been reserved for the cases that involve explosives or…"

"Or what?" said Chris, after a moment of hesitation on Dana's part.

"The cases in which the person targeted was deemed higher profile. I know it sounds bad, but it's not my call," said Dana.

"I get it, that's the way the world works. Dana, you brought up something interesting. I've been looking at some of these cases today. If this was some sort of coordinated attack, and if they wanted to make a point with this attack, then why is it that everyone targeted was so-"

"Low value?" said Dana, as she finished his sentence.

"Hey, you're talking about Russ and I. How about you show some respect?" said Chris, as he smirked.

"You're not exactly a C-suite exec, are you?" quipped Dana.

"That's big talk from someone that's probably in the same position she was 20 years ago."

"Touché," said Dana, as she returned a smile. "I see what you're saying, though. They went after some smaller firms, but they also went after some of the largest banks in the world, too. Take Spencer & Creed for example. Their entire board and executives, including the CEO, CFO, CIO, etc. are all safe and accounted for. Why would they leave them alone, but go after yourself and Russel?"

"Does it have something to do with security? I know those executives sometimes have bodyguards, sometimes even around-the-clock security for the wealthiest of the bunch that can afford it," said Chris.

"That's a good guess. Still, they clearly did their homework ahead of time. Just because some have armed security, doesn't mean that they all do. There had to have been some other reason they chose to go after people like you or Russel."

"Since they keep getting brought up, who is the 'they' that we keep referring to? A foreign government? A cartel? Terrorist group?" said Chris.

"Nobody knows for sure, yet. I talked to some of the other agents. You know, the ones that are accustomed to running these types of investigations. So far, we have one piece of information that might tell us who 'they' are, but it's tenuous at best."

Dana pulled up a file on her computer.

"Outside of San Francisco, they found a girl at one of these scenes. 21-year-old Angela Sanders was found at the home of Danny Ebright, a mid-level employee at a financial firm out west. He wasn't at the scene when officers arrived, following a 911 call from a neighbor that thought they heard gunshots and saw a large van outside. They found Ms. Sanders in a pool of her own blood."

"So, what's the clue they found?" said Chris.

"I'll get to that. But listen to this. Ebright, the house's resident, had a handgun that it looks like he tried to use to defend himself. They found a bullet lodged in her abdomen that matched his gun. But, that's not what killed her. The cause of death was a gunshot in the side of her head, but the bullet, or at least the bullet fragments, didn't match the caliber or bullet type of Danny Ebright's handgun."

"And?" asked Chris.

"Their theory is that one of the other subjects delivered the kill shot. Either they saw her as dead weight and didn't want to wait for her, or else they got into some kind of an argument. Who knows? She already had left a trail of blood, so maybe they figured she would already be identified, regardless of if she escaped with the rest of them."

"That's ruthless," said Chris.

"And lazy. Even if she was in the DNA database, it would have taken a while to positively identify her. But, officers found an ID and some credit cards in her pocket, belonging to her. We ran a check on her name. She's young and doesn't have much of a record, but she was listed on some dismissed charges from three years ago at a UWF protest."

"The United Worker's Front?"

"Yep."

"Huh, didn't ever think they'd be capable of something like this. If we were to believe the media, they're nothing more than a bunch of unemployed college kids throwing a fit."

"A few years ago, that probably was accurate. But, according to some agents that have been following them in the last half-decade, they've become much more organized, and nearly impossible to infiltrate. Before any of this happened, we already had reason to believe they were becoming increasingly militaristic. What little information we have suggests that they were working on anything from firearms training, to explosive manufacturing, and other forms of asymmetric, guerilla-like activity. But, they've also been very effective in using Preception."

Dana was referring to the encrypted messaging platform that exceeded the privacy of any previous platforms but was entirely decentralized, devoid of a company that could be strong-armed by government agencies for information. It was a platform that had become ubiquitous within society among everyday citizens, though critics had often pointed out its potential to be used for unsavory purposes.

"You haven't cracked Preception yet?" asked Chris, referring to the U.S. government as a whole.

"That's above my pay grade, but I think we can assume that it hasn't been compromised. The UWF has been excellent in using it, and also show a unique ability to remain compartmentalized and relatively decentralized, making infiltration less fruitful than, say, infiltrating a far-right militia. Also, there's reason to believe that such infiltration operations were themselves compromised."

"The Bureau doesn't have anyone on the inside, do they?"

Dana shook her head. "Not that I'm aware of. The way some of the other agents talk, those who are more familiar with the UWF, would suggest that we have no valuable intel from infiltrated agents."

"So we have a loose connection, and that's about it?"

"That's about it."

Dana turned to her screen. Her face suddenly changed from a look of frustration to instead showing an intense interest in her screen.

"I take that back, Chris. Take a look at this."

"We have breaking news at this hour. In the past day, there have been some rumors of a larger scale targeting of certain individuals within, all of which had one thing in common: they worked at a bank, hedge fund, or other similar financial firm. Anonymous individuals had confirmed these rumors, though we felt we did not have enough information to definitively report on the story. That, however, just changed. A short time ago, a series of videos were anonymously posted in an online forum, videos which appear to have each been filmed in unique locations. However, what they all have in common, is they depict dozens of different men and women undergoing physical and verbal abuse.

"Law enforcement agencies have declined to comment on these videos at this time, but it is apparent from the text that accompanied these posts, that the individuals in the videos are some of the same persons that went missing over the past few days. Many had expressed that those disappearances, which accompanied multiple murders as well, appeared to be organized in nature. Today, some of our independent sources have confirmed that they have been able to match the identities of those that went missing, to the victims in these videos.

"We'd like to share some short clips from these videos. They have been blurred to protect the identity of the victims, and we have removed some of the more graphic portions of the videos. However, keep in mind that, as we show you these videos, some viewers may find the circumstances, as well as the language used, to be both disturbing and frightening."

The clip the news agency chose to show first depicted a pair of men with hoods over their heads sitting back to back in what would appear to be dining room chairs. They were each secured to their chair and wore only a pair of boxer underwear.

One of the other men in the room walked off camera for a short moment, before returning with a red hot metal rod in his hand. Before he had a chance to use it, the feed switched to another video. This time, it depicted another man, secured in a similar manner. Another man, off-camera, shouted at him. The news network was careful to censor any unsavory language.

"You mother******s did this. You screwed over the rest of us for too long, and now, you're going to burn."

Charlotte was unprepared for this. She was aware that these individuals would be abducted. However, she was not privy to the fact that they would be treated in this manner. She immediately felt a sense of shock and disgust at the videos. Emily looked at Charlotte's expression. Seeing her discomfort, she did her best to assuage Charlotte's concerns.

"I know this looks bad. Believe me, if I had created this plan, I would have left this part out. But, I didn't. I'm not the one in charge here. I'd never do something like this," said Emily.

"I'm not so sure anymore," said Charlotte, with doubt in her voice.

"Excuse me? You seemed comfortable with abductions and murder, but now you can't stomach some torture of these lowlifes? Charlotte, you and I both need to trust that this is being handled. I've talked to Carter about this. He doesn't make the call on this either, but he knows it's not his job to question the plan."

"Like a good soldier, right?" quipped Charlotte.

"Charlotte-"

"Because good soldiers don't question orders, right?"

"Nobody is ordering you to do anything. You're doing this on your own accord, and that has always been the case. Besides, no one has asked you to even so much as say a harsh word towards someone," said Emily.

"Right, and I next you'll tell me the guard at a Nazi concentration camp should have a clean conscience because he wasn't the one pulling the trigger."

"I'm sorry, I didn't know we were in a high school debate class. That's a garbage argument, and you know it Charlotte. This is different. They were on the wrong side of history. You and I, we're fighting for something that will change this country for the better."

Charlotte sighed. "I'm sorry, Emily. It's a lot to stomach. And, there's a part of me that is terrified this will all go south."

"Carter has assured me that we're isolated from all of this. And the UWF, they operate in a very sophisticated way. Each cell is decentralized, meaning infiltration would only be effective in taking down a single group, leaving the rest of the organization intact. And, let me remind you, they have plenty of friends in government."

"It's not that, I'm worried about us being implicated in this, Emily. Don't get me wrong, that's something we should be worried about. But, what I'm more worried about, is how bad things are getting. I've been thinking a lot about this, Emily. Let's say we do pass that bill. Maybe we'd even be on track to win some extra seats, maybe the White

House next election season. What if we don't make it to the next election? What if the government loses control and can't get it back?" said Charlotte.

"We'll come out the other end of this as a changed country. But, I have all the confidence in the world that this plan will work, and that we will have changed for the better."

"I understand your concern, Mrs. Johnson. No, really. Okay. You have my word. I'll stop by there later today and make sure everything's on the up and up. Okay. Okay. Take care."

Josh hung up his cell phone. A call from Clarice Johnson had ended his four-hour stint of sleep. Mrs. Johnson was a frequent caller. He had made the mistake several years ago of giving his work number out to some of those in the community. He was new to his position and felt it would help build rapport with the community. The vast majority never used the number, but Mrs. Johnson was an exception.

Josh checked his phone. He had only been asleep for about five hours, but it would have to suffice. His body was still exhausted and begged him to rest more, but his mind was alert. All too often, he had received calls from the department in the middle of the night while sleeping, and he had become accustomed to transitioning from sleep to a fully alert state in a matter of moments.

He put on his uniform, grabbed a few granola bars, and headed out the door. The house that Mrs. Johnson had called about was on the way to the department, so he decided to stop there first. Before leaving his driveway, he called the office.

"Good morning, Sharon. Ugh, right, afternoon. Can you do me a favor? I'm texting you an address. Could you run it through the system real quick? Yeah, just ownership records, anything else relevant about the owners. Yeah, that'll be all. Yeah, I'll be there within an hour. Thanks, see you then."

Under normal circumstances, Josh would have the luxury of an additional deputy to accompany him on such calls. The vast majority ended up being nothing more than a misunderstanding, or, at most, a disagreement within a family that would best be settled in court. However, every now and then, he would hear stories of officers that would take such calls and find themselves at the front door of a meth lab, a gang or cartel safe house, and even cases of the residence being connected to human trafficking. Of course, those stories were few and far between, and he didn't have the manpower to prepare for such a low likelihood event.

After a brief 10 minute drive, he arrived at the address. Sharon had not yet sent him any information on the house. He could have looked it up himself prior to leaving, but found his computer in his squad car to be clunky at times, and knew that she tended to do a more thorough search. He decided to proceed anyway.

The driveway had been plowed since the last snowfall, roughly one week prior. But, no vehicle was present. This wasn't unusual. The garage door was closed, so the vehicle could be parked in there, or else the residents could be gone for the day.

Josh had not driven down this specific road in many months, and he couldn't recall who had lived at this address. As his car sat motionless on the dirt road, having not yet turned onto the driveway, Josh considered waiting a half-mile down the road, in hopes Sharon would fill him in on any details. But, he knew time was precious on a day like this, and he couldn't afford an extra five or ten minutes of his day sitting at the end of rural dirt road.

He pulled into the driveway and parked his squad card at an angle in front of the garage. The curtains prevented him from seeing in the windows, but it looked as if there were at least one or two lights on inside, but the midday sun and the glare from the snow prevented him from saying so with any certainty. The sidewalk was shoveled, but he could make out some footprints in the thin layer of snow that had not been moved by the shovel.

He exited his squad car and slowly walked to the front door. Josh tried ringing the doorbell but didn't hear a ding on the other side. Like most older houses, the doorbell on this house probably had failed at some point, and the owner had never taken the time to repair it. He opened the screen door and knocked on the solid metal door in front of him. Josh briefly thought to himself that the sturdy, plain door looked out of place relative to the rest of the house.

After a few moments, he saw the curtain on the window next to the door move as someone looked out. However, the individual didn't open the door immediately. He knocked again after waiting a few seconds.

"Jackson County Sheriff's Department, do you have a minute?" Josh said, with a raised voice.

He announced his affiliation merely as a formality; he was sure that whoever had looked out the window had recognized him as law enforcement. After several more seconds, the door opened. Before him stood a man that appeared to be in his late 20s. He was a clean-shaven man with a short haircut and a muscular build.

Unlike much of the public that he worked with, who often appeared nervous regardless of why he was talking to them, this man appeared cool and confident.

"What can I do for you, officer?"

"Hey there, I got a call this morning about some new residents in the house, just making sure everything is on the up and up."

"Let me guess, someone wants to know who suddenly moved into the house?" said the man, in a calm and disarming manner.

"That about sums it up."

"This is my grandfather's house. He moved into a nursing home a while back. It's been sitting here since then. His daughter, well, my mom, she's the one that takes care of it now. With all this craziness going on in some of the big cities, I figured it'd be a good place for me to hang out for a while."

"Are you here alone?" asked Josh.

"I have a few buddies of mine that tagged along."

"Do you have any ID on you?"

"Yep, no problem at all," said the man.

"I didn't happen to catch your name," said Josh.

"Mitchell Jenkins ."

71

Mitch reached into his back pocket, pulled out his wallet, and handed the officer an ID from the state of Minnesota.

"I'll be right back," said Josh.

He walked back to his squad car and ran the ID through the database. It showed a few traffic violations, but nothing more. He brought it back to the man.

"There you go," said Josh, as he handed him back his ID. "Sorry about the inconvenience, just doing my due diligence."

"No worries, you can't be too careful these days. Have a good day officer," said Mitch with a smile on his face.

"You too."

Josh walked back to his squad car. Before driving back to the office, he checked his phone. Sharon has sent him some screenshots. The house belonged to Jill Jenkins. Before that, it belonged to Ronald Jenkins. The man's story appeared to match up.

As he drove to the sheriff's office. He couldn't shake a feeling about that house. The man's story about who owned the house matched up, but he wasn't naive enough to think that such information meant there wasn't more to the story. His excuse of leaving the big city for safety didn't quite make sense; the man's ID was from Glencoe, MN, which was well outside the Minneapolis-St. Paul area. But, the man may have moved to the city recently. Or, maybe he still considered it his home and hadn't taken the time to change his address. Such instances were not uncommon.

That alone wasn't enough to arouse Josh's suspicion. There was a look in the man's eyes that Josh had seen before, though he couldn't put his finger where he had seen it before. The man he saw at the house, he was a complete stranger to Josh. And yet, there was something all too familiar, something that Josh feared.

Chapter Nine: Opportunities

"Alice, grab the kids and go to the basement!" yelled David as he burst in the back door.

Alice ran from the living room to meet him.

"What is it, David?" she asked in a frantic voice.

"There's some men outside with guns. I need you to hide, now."

Alice's face flashed fear before she turned to go find the girls. David briskly walked over to a closet near the living room. He opened it up and reached along the top of the inside of the door frame. Resting on several hooks was the AR-15 that Warren had given him. He hadn't had a chance to even so much as practice dry firing the weapon and hoped to himself that he wouldn't ever need the practice in the first place.

David was taking these actions because, as he walked back to the house from the field, he spotted a pickup truck that was driving down his road. It was an unfamiliar truck to David. It turned down his long driveway, and he had seen that it contained two men in the cab. This alone would not have alarmed David. However, for a brief moment, he saw an outline of what appeared to be the barrel of a rifle, a rifle not unlike the one Warren had given him. Once he was out of the line of sight of the truck, he had taken off running for the house. It was not uncommon, from time to time, to see a pickup truck with a gun draped inside its back window. These ranged from simple bolt-action rifles, to shotguns, to rifles with a more tactical appearance. However, the fact that this rifle was beside the man in the cab, and given the widespread violence of the past number of days, sent David into a panic.

David chambered a round and turned on the red dot sight mounted on the rifle. He walked to the front of the house in a half crouched position as he heard the door of the truck close. His heart pounded. His hands began to feel numb, and his mouth began to feel dry. He peered out the window, taking care not to disturb the curtains. The two men had nearly reached the steps to his porch. Both were dressed in drab-colored cargo pants and similarly colored jackets. Neither man carried a rifle. They walked to the front door and knocked. David was unsure what to do. Because they had not carried the rifle while walking to the door, and otherwise were moving in a casual manner, David felt less threatened. He considered not answering the door but reminded himself that they almost certainly had spotted him as they were driving down the driveway. He leaned the rifle on a wall near the hinges of the door, and opened the door as casually as possible, trying to mask this recent surge of adrenaline.

"Can I help you?" asked David.

One man, with a full, red beard stepped forward.

"Let me introduce myself. I'm Rick, and this is Kyle."

The other man nodded his head and tipped his beige baseball cap as a non-verbal greeting.

The red-bearded man continued. "We're with the Libertas, Indiana division. Libertas is a group of freedom loving patriots that are dedicated to protecting this great country of ours from any threat, domestic or abroad."

David could tell he had practiced this sales pitch. The man's cadence, tone, and straightforward speech were a giveaway that he likely had been in the military. David had heard of this group before. They had found themselves in the news on multiple occasions in recent years.

"You're a militia," responded David.

"So you've heard of us? Great! Look, I'll keep this short, because I respect your time, and the Lord knows we have a thousand other houses to get to today. We're stopping by houses for two reasons. First, we want to let you all know that we are holding ourselves responsible for the safety of the entirety of this state, and we will do whatever we can to protect the average citizen from any threat, whether it is a lawbreaker, federal agents, or even those far-left revolutionaries. Second, we're opening up our ranks to anyone between the ages of eighteen and sixty, with preference for those that have useful skills, including former and current law enforcement, former military, small arms, hunting, and medical skills. The only other requirements will be a willingness to serve, and a pledge to uphold our values and policies. We'll be having a meeting at this address, next Wednesday, at 7 PM."

Rick handed David a slip of paper, with an address printed out. It also included contact information, including phone numbers, email, and a series of radio frequencies that were not the usual FM/AM format, and thus meant little to David.

"Now, if you'll excuse us, we'll be on our way. I appreciate your time, and we hope to see you tomorrow."

The man extended his hand for a handshake, which David met with his own hand.

"Take care," said Rick.

"You too," replied David.

The two men turned and walked back to their truck. David had barely gotten in a few words in the entire exchange. These were men of action, David thought to himself. Warren and David, while planning their own safety network, had briefly discussed militia groups. They both were aware of their existence, but David was surprised to find Libertas, which may have been the largest militia in the nation, to be organized to this extent at the state level, especially in an area like southern Indiana.

David took a deep breath. He realized he felt weak, and his muscles ached, as he came down from his brief but intense adrenaline fueled high. David looked out the window. The pickup truck had turned down the road in the direction of Warren's house, no doubt to make the same pitch. He turned to see Alice standing in the hallway next to the front door. Her face showed relief.

"What was that all about?" she asked.

"We have some decisions to make."

Russel was shaken awake. He gasped, as his dream world struggled to transition to reality. The room was dark. A dark figure knelt beside him. His mind was at first confused as to why a mysterious figure was in his house. As he began to sit up in bed, a wave of pain was sent from his nerve endings. The pain instantly oriented him to his situation and the events of the past several days. His confusion turned to dread, as he was able to faintly make out the features of the face that was before him. It was Mitch.

"Rise and shine, buddy! Hope I didn't interrupt any sweet dreams."

Russel groaned.

"Hey, cheer up! I have some good news. Check this out, you're famous!" said Mitch, in a cheery, nearly maniacal voice.

Mitch held up a tablet. The bright screen blinded him, as his eyes attempted to adjust. On the screen was a video on a website belonging to one of the larger news agencies in the United States. Mitch pressed the play button. The video contained the voice of a reporter, as the video itself scrolled through images and brief video clips. Each one depicted captives in a similar setting as his own. Some were sitting, nearly naked, with hoods over their heads. The voiceover explained that the news outlet had, on their discretion, to cut out any acts of violence or torture, but the wounds were evident, both in the bruises, burns, and abrasions, as well as in the faces of those men and women. They looked defeated, each and every one.

"Did you see it? Here, I'll rewind it."

Mitch touched the screen, rewinding the screen several seconds. For a brief moment, Russel recognized himself. He couldn't tell what session the picture depicted, but he recognized it as being in his current room. His own face looked pale, bruised, and dejected.

"Why are you showing me this?"

"Because Russel," began Mitch, with a defensive tone, "this represents years of hard work. This represents the sacrifice of thousands of men and women just like me. This represents some semblance of justice, even if-"

"You mean revenge," said Russel, interrupting Mitch.

"What's that?" asked Mitch, with anger in his voice.

"You could care less about justice, you're just looking for revenge. Well guess what, you're looking in the wrong place. What happened to your father and your family, it sucks. But, I didn't do that to you, and neither did Kate," said Russel, with defiance in his voice.

"You know what? You're right, it is revenge! They were taken from me, and I want someone to pay!"

He struck Russel in his abdomen with the last word. Russel felt pain shudder through his body. The area no longer hurt throughout the day but was still tender. The blow sent him onto his back, and Mitch jumped on him, kneeling over him on the bed. He delivered blow after blow, as he screamed at Russel.

"It's not fair! You did this!"

The punches delivered to his face rocked his brain. With each hit, he could feel his head rocking backwards, and was thankful for the pillow under his head, which made the hits more bearable. Finally, Mitch grew fatigued. He continued to sit on Russel, panting, as he attempted to catch his breath. Russel's vision was filled with stars, stars which were contrasted by the darkness that filled the room. Then, just as abruptly as had arrived, Mitch left. He didn't say a word and calmly closed the door behind him.

Russel himself tried to catch his breath and calm down. Despite the beating, he felt a small level of satisfaction. He had accomplished something by driving Mitch to such anger, and in doing so, had taken advantage of Mitch's weakness. Russel had seen Mitch as being capable of being cool and effective. However, what would happen if Mitch was no longer able to keep his sanity intact? Russel had given this some thought. He knew that he and Kate's prospects of survival were low. But, for the time being, they were an asset for Mitch, which meant Russel had a window in which he could act, with the knowledge that he had a certain level of immunity. There was the risk that Mitch's instability could cause him to act outside of these boundaries in an irrational manner. Doing so could lead to a sooner death for Russel and Kate.

Russel was willing to take such a risk. He had spent years in finance, and he had seen what happened to traders and investors when they lost their rationality. Inevitably, they would make a trade or investment that was far too risky. These mistakes occurred due to their impaired judgment that was a result of their emotional state. Every now and then, those risky calls would turn out well for the investor or client, but only over the short term. Those successes did not punish their emotional and irrational decisions and inevitably led to them taking similar gambles in the future, often with far worse outcomes.

Russel could see that Mitch was now moving into such a state. Rationally speaking, if Russel were in his shoes, he would lie low, do his best to work towards the goals they set out to achieve, and in the end, dispose of the captives after ending their lives. But, Russel knew men like Mitch, and as far as Russel knew, Mitch had no one inside this house to keep his power in check.

Russel's face hurt, but this pain had become a constant companion. His fear was still present, though it was more so related to the severity of future pain, as well as the health and wellbeing of Kate than it was his own fate. To some extent, he had come to accept that his fate was likely to be death unless he should act to alter such a fate. Russel still had his mind, and he knew that would be his intellect and creativity to have any chance of survival.

Finally, Russel had his resolve. This surprised Russel more than anything else about his condition. He knew that few people in the first world experienced suffering that rivaled what he was experiencing, and he himself had never experienced any extraordinary difficulty in life, though he also knew that his suffering was a far cry from what others had experienced, including the POWs that he had recalled often in past 24 hours. And yet, he had found within himself a flame that he did not know existed, a resolve that had prodded him to drive Mitch into a rage rather than submit in fear. Though his future was bleak, this was a flame that Russel had confidence would not be extinguished as long as he drew breath in his lungs.

"You're positive?"

"I'd bet my life on it. That's Russel in that picture."

"Chris, I'm sorry you have to see this," said Dana.

"Don't be. I'm honestly just glad to see he's alive."

The two had spent the better part of the last hour hunting down the specific footage that had been uploaded of Russel. They had initially seen it mixed in with a news report, and after asking around, Dana was able to quickly get the specific forums in which these videos and images were posted. Next, it was a matter of sifting through the hundreds of posts, before finally finding the one of Russel. The forum user that had posted the videos of Russel had also shared several videos of a woman undergoing similar acts of torture. In one clip, both she and Russel could be seen in the same room. In every video they found on the forum, the voices of the captors were altered. The voices of the hostages could be heard but were occasionally censored. Dana found that other agents working the case had determined this was done whenever the individuals said anything that would give away the identity of the captors or the location they were being held. Those that edited the videos went so far as to blur their mouths when being censored in order to prevent their lips from being read. As a further testament to their desire to protect the locations and identities of the captors, on occasion, the faces of the captors would be blurred at any time they were in the field of view of the camera.

"After how many people have died so far… I mean, they didn't find his body at his house, that's good. But knowing Russel, he's a stubborn guy. Part of me worried that he'd done something to get himself killed along the way. So, we're going to find him, right?"

Dana sighed.

"I'm not sure, Chris. This is sophisticated work. As far as I can tell, this offers no new data on his whereabouts."

"Well, then we can start looking harder. The data is there Dana, it's just a matter of finding it. You said so yourself, we have traffic camera footage. We have financials to look through. We have witnesses to talk to. Somewhere in that pile of data, there's a clue. How about this woman in that video of Russel, what about her? Can't we figure out who she is?"

"Ok Chris, we can do this. But, I need you to agree to something first. If we find a piece of information that leads in a different direction than Russel, but still leads us to someone else involved in this, then we need to follow that trail. Each of the men and women have a family and a story, and none of them deserve what they're going through. I know you want to help Russel, but we need to be impartial."

"You have my word."

"Good. I hope you slept well last night because we're not leaving this building anytime soon."

Josh woke up in a cold sweat. His planned nap on a cot at the Sheriff's Office had been cut short by a troubling dream that brought back memories of a case he didn't care to remember. It was during his first year as a police officer. He was working in a Madison, Wisconsin suburb. He was working on a case involving a local elementary school teacher that had sexually assaulted several of his students over a 20-year time span.

The teacher was well-respected in the community. He was friendly, approachable, and had mastered a demeanor that struck a balance between professional and personable. Josh's perception changed entirely after finding out about the man's secret. It was as if a switch flipped in Josh's mind. He wondered how he, or anyone else, was ever able to see him as a normal human being. How were all of those parents, faculty, and even kids, so easily fooled?

Josh was inexperienced at the time and thus was not given a major role in the investigation. He did, however, have a chance to see a fair amount of the evidence. What he had seen disturbed him to this day. After the trial, Josh had taken the time to go to the man's sentencing. He maintained his innocence throughout the entire trial, but the evidence was overwhelming, and the jury had only deliberated for a mere 25 minutes. Josh remembered watching him sit there, so calmly, awaiting a sentence that would undoubtedly leave him in prison for the rest of his life. It was his eyes that were burned into Josh's memory. They weren't the deranged eyes of a stereotypical sociopath. It wasn't the deranged look of a Charles Manson, nor the blank apathy of Jeffrey Dahmer. Instead, they were the eyes of a man that has spent decades fooling everyone around him, with complete confidence. The eyes held behind them a depraved agenda, an agenda with no regard for other humans, and a certain pleasure in having deceived so many for such a long period of time.

It was a case that bothered Josh for some time, but he had scarcely recalled it in the past few years. However, during his dream, this man had been acquitted and set free. In the confused course that so many dreams followed, this man had now moved to Josh's hometown but had been given immunity to any future prosecution. It had driven Josh into a fit of rage that eventually led to him waking up.

As he became oriented, the realness of the dream melted away. Still, there was something that stuck. Why was he having this dream, and why now? It was a case he hadn't thought about for several months. As reality returned to his consciousness, the events of the last week flooded back to Josh. The events of the day prior, a shift that ended at the late hour of 4 AM when he was convinced by a deputy to sleep for a few hours, sprung back into his memory. He recalled these in reverse chronological order. There was a reported burglary, a drunk driver on I-94 that he helped the State Patrol with, and a number of other calls that were all routine, as far as Josh was concerned. He was grateful for the relative peace and quiet in his county but was concerned that the mayhem across the country would seep into his own proverbial backyard.

He was about to stand up from the edge of the cot when he recalled the manner in which he started the day prior. The call from Mrs. Johnson, the house with new residents. Mitchell Jenkins. The eyes. The dream had not occurred at random, it was triggered by the visit to the rural house. Mitchell Jenkins had that same look in his eyes. It didn't make sense to Josh why or how his brain made this connection. The two men were otherwise of an entirely different appearance. *But those eyes*, Josh thought to himself. It didn't make sense, while also filling his head with a dread that was all too real.

He placed his face in his palms, rubbing his face, trying to wipe away the grogginess of the short rest and the long hours he had been enduring. He tried to return to rationality. The man had not committed a crime. It was nothing more than a hunch. No, calling it a hunch was giving himself too much credit. It was only a bad feeling, a coincidence he had fabricated within his own head. There was no crime Josh had in mind that the man could even possibly be connected to.

Due to the spreading unrest and violence, Josh knew his responsibility to the public was greater than ever before. It would make for a busy day, filled with what would hopefully be routine police work. In the past, he would find a busy day to be a welcome distraction from worries, but there was no comfort to be found this morning. As he got dressed and put on his gear, he felt compelled to act on his feelings.

"Good morning," said Sharon, as Josh walked by her desk.

"Is Carl here?" asked Josh.

"Just got here. He should be down the hall," she said.

"Thanks."

Josh was ready to go back to the Jenkins' house to put his worries to rest, but he wasn't going alone.

"Ok, let's get this straight. First, they grab Kate Larson, and then they go to St. Paul and take Marcus Avenrow, before finally going to Russel's house in Edina?" asked Dana.

"Makes sense to me," said Chris, as he stared at the laptop that had been provided to him.

The FBI database had been able to identify the woman in the video as Kate Larson, of Chicago, Illinois. However, they were able to use her phone to track her location to a site near Eau Claire, Wisconsin, on the night Russel had been captured. They also had received word that Marcus Avenrow, an executive at Russel's branch of Spencer & Creed, had gone missing as well. Dana and Chris were now working off of the assumption he had been taken by the same group of individuals as Russel and Kate.

"But what if they got to Russel and Marcus first, and then went after Kate?"

"You're right, they could have done that. And I hope that's not the case. See, we're hoping to catch them on a camera on I-94 between Eau Claire and Edina or St. Paul," said Chris, as he turned his laptop towards Dana, though her screen was also covered in traffic camera footage from the night that Russel was taken. "It doesn't matter whether they went to Marcus's place first, or Russel's, because that'd still be the most straightforward route. If they took back roads, that's not the end of the world, because we're still going to have a treasure trove of video to go through for Minneapolis, St. Paul, and surrounding areas. It'd take time, but we could figure it out. The advantage to that would be that once they leave the city, we'll have a good idea of which direction their safe house is. Minneapolis and St. Paul are surrounded by suburbs and smaller cities, and we'd have more than enough footage to narrow it down."

"And? if you're wrong?" asked Dana.

"You said so yourself they probably picked a secluded, rural location, right? There's a forest outside the window in those videos of Russel, and they don't have a single building in the shot. If they stopped at Eau Claire last, then we are going to have a hard time figuring out their location, because they could go in almost any direction and we would have no clue, unless they were stupid enough to take a major highway with cameras on it."

Chris returned his laptop to his desk, as Dana pondered what she had just heard.

"I'm going to grab some coffee down the hall, want anything?" she asked, as she began walking to the door.

The two had worked on this through the night, and daylight had begun to shine through the window several hours ago.

"Hold that thought, take a look at this," said Chris, gesturing at his screen. "This is a camera from the westbound lane."

"I don't see anything," said Dana.

"Right there, in the eastbound lane. See that? Does that look like a grey van to you?"

The image was taken at night, and the lights along the side of the highway didn't provide enough light to allow for easy identification of color.

"It's hard to say. Maybe?" replied Dana.

"Just a second," said Chris.

He toggled through other cameras along the freeway. After a few seconds of searching, he settled on a camera that focused on the eastbound lane. After a few more seconds of rolling the footage forward, the van once again appeared in the field of view. The resolution was relatively sharp, though the frame rate was well below what one would expect on an average video. The mere fact such a high-quality video had been stored within a database from such a period over 24 hours previous, was thanks to advancements in technology and investment in massive data centers by the federal government that could house the data from an ever-expanding network of cameras across the country.

"That's it, that has got to be the van," said Chris.

The large cargo van was unmarked and had Minnesota license plates. The camera, in this case, had been strategically placed so as to allow the nearby street lights to illuminate the center of the image far better than other parts. The color was still not as clear as it would have been during daylight, but was clearly a shade of grey.

"I hope you're right. It fits the description and the timeline. Can you give me the license plate off of that?" asked Dana, with excitement in her voice as she returned to her seat.

"GLC-148," replied Chris.

Dana typed this into a database search on her computer.

"Looks like it's registered to a Mitchell Jenkins, of Glencoe, Minnesota. Let me run him through a different database."

Unable to bear waiting, Chris stood up and walked around to her desk.

"Ok. It looks like he has a clean criminal record. He's lived in Minnesota his whole adult life."

Dana copied the address into a web browser. A satellite image from a mainstream web browser's map application showed the house, though it was only a small dot in the center of the image. Dana zoomed in. It was a suburban house, surrounded by multiple other houses, all with similar layouts and yards.

"Doesn't look like the house we're looking for, but since that van is going eastbound, away from Glencoe, I suppose that's not surprising," said Dana.

"What are the odds they loop back to the Glencoe area after going to Eau Claire?" asked Chris.

"That's a possibility. Even if his address doesn't match the video, a family or friend's house could be used," replied Dana.

"I'm on it."

Chris returned to his laptop. The databases were, as a whole, highly integrated with each other. He was surprised by how extensive and easy to access the information was for persons of interest. According to Dana, it had not always been so. She had also explained that, under normal circumstances, there would have been much more regulation in essentially accessing any citizen's profile they saw fit. But, a few days prior, the Bureau had released guidance, giving increased leeway for accessing information. This had been approved by a panel of judges, though the decision was not yet public. Chris was experienced in sorting through mountains of data and found this to be similarly enjoyable.

"Looks like he has a brother that lives in Des Moines," said Chris, as he flipped from tab to tab.

It was now Dana's turn to stand up and move closer to Chris's screen. The fatigue of the last 24 hours was a distant memory, as the two of them could sense that they were close to something important.

"Any family in Glencoe?" asked Dana.

"Checking now," replied Chris. "Looks like his mom still lives there. Here's the address," Chris said as he pointed to the screen.

Dana returned to her desk and typed in the address.

"No luck. Doesn't fit the house in the video."

On the screen was a satellite view of another house, this one in what appeared to be an older, suburban neighborhood.

"So, who's next?" asked Chris.

"Let's make a list. We'll want to start with family since that'll be the easiest to find. Aunts, uncles, grandparents, cousins. And then, we can move on to other possible connections. Past roommates, close ties on social media, anyone that might-"

"Hold that thought. Where's Hixton, Wisconsin?" asked Chris.

Dana knew he could search for it easily enough, but obliged.

"About forty minutes south of Eau Claire."

"So, Mitchell's mother's residence is listed as Glencoe. But she has a house in her name, with an address in Hixton, Wisconsin. Looks like it was previously in the name of her father, Ronald, but was given to her a few years ago."

"Looks like it could be a match to the house in the video. Remote location, down a country road. A small field in the backyard that stops at the edge of a forest."

"Any chance there's some major roadways between Eau Claire and Hixton?" asked Chris.

"It's right off of I-94," replied Dana.

"Alright, let's see if we catch this van on any cameras," said Chris.

"You can start on that, but I'm not wasting any more time. I'm calling the Jackson County sheriff's office and Wisconsin State Patrol."

Chapter Ten: Missteps

Russel still held some satisfaction in the fact he had enraged Mitch to the extent of his burst of anger the night before. He was not certain that the man was becoming more unhinged, but hoped that was the case. However, even if such a development could offer an opportunity for his escape, found himself becoming frustrated. The logistics of any sort of escape were difficult. On one hand, a single person escape was feasible, though risky. Rushing out the door if an opportunity presented itself, or even escaping through the second-floor window in his room if he were able to remove the steel bars, were both escape methods that had crossed his mind. There was a considerable chance that either method would lead to his death or recapture, but it would have been a risk he would be willing to take.

The problem with either of those plans was that Kate was also being held within the house, and Russel feared what would become of her if he were to escape on his own. Her location in the basement further complicated any plans involving assisting her in escaping, and this physical distance was likely intentional on the part of his captors.

The day prior, another potential opportunity for escape presented itself. While still nursing his wounds from Mitch's fit of rage, he heard someone knock on the front door of the house. He heard a voice as well, though he was unable to make out any words. At the time, he considered attempting to get the individual's attention by yelling but decided against it. He feared that if someone were to learn he and Kate were in the house, it would hasten their death, as the risk of them being discovered would outweigh the benefit of keeping them alive. He froze in that moment, and if it was an opportunity, Russel let it slip away.

The torture sessions had continued, with one to two visits from the men each day. Mitch had not been present for the single session the day prior, which Russel found to be curious, and surmised that it was likely related to his outburst of anger. The other men that replaced him in his absence appeared to struggle to muster up the same amount of anger and spite that Mitch summoned on a daily basis. They also appeared unsure of themselves at times. Up to that point, Mitch was the only one that had actually inflicted the pain on Russel. The other men that accompanied him acted as assistants to Mitch and had previously only assisted in restraining Russel and in operating the camera. The pain from the substitute men was as real as ever. The fear of the pain was still distressing to Russel.

However, despite this continued fear and pain inflicted, Russel found it to be less emotionally taxing with Mitch, the head figure, absent. It allowed Russel more mental clarity to consider his options. As he sat at the edge of his bed, his mind remained fixated on the day prior and the visitor at the front door. What were his options, should it occur again? If he were to get their attention, what were the odds that it would at least offer him an opportunity to bring the men to justice, should the noise arouse any suspicion and subsequent investigation? It even offered a sliver of hope for an escape, though Russel struggled to come up with a scenario in which a random visitor would offer assistance.

Russel stood up and walked over to the window overlooking the field. Russel decided that in all likelihood, such a scenario was unlikely to present itself again, rendering it a moot point.

Thunk

Was that a car door closing?

Russel quickly decided the noise was most likely the door of the van closing.

Knock knock knock

The knocking on the door. This was no mere coincidence. Every rational cell in his body told him that an attempt to get anyone's attention would be dangerous and futile, but he knew this had to be his opportunity.

Josh stood at the doorway to the house, awaiting a response. Beside him stood Carl Williams, a deputy in his third year of service to Jackson County. Josh had briefed him during their drive to the house. He was honest with Carl in his suspicions, as well as the fact that his suspicions were largely founded on nothing more than a gut instinct.

The two had concocted a simple ploy to gather information that involved a non-existent investigation that they would use as a pretense for asking questions, as well as potentially entering the residence. Josh knew the situation the county, state, and country were in and was willing to bend the rules somewhat, knowing that he was unlikely to draw much scrutiny considering the backdrop of current events.

The door opened.

"Officer, two visits in two days. What can I do for you?" asked Mitch.

"Yeah, sorry about that. I was hoping you could be of assistance," said Josh.

Mitch opened the door somewhat, as he continued to stand in the doorway.

"There's been a string of burglaries on a few of these back roads lately, and I just had a few questions that might help us out as we try to get to the bottom of it."

"I sure hope you're not accusing me of anything," said Mitch.

"No, it's not like that. These started several weeks ago, well before you would have been in town. Last night, there was another one about a mile down the road."

"I don't know anything about that, wish I could help," said Mitchell, with a smile on his face.

The smile sent a shiver down Josh's spine. It took every fiber of his being to not allow this emotion to show.

"Would you mind if I came in out of the cold for a minute? There's just a list of questions I'd like to go through, just for the sake of procedure."

"By all means," replied Mitch.

Carl followed Mitch and Josh into the house. Right inside of the doorway was the living room. A few family photos lined the walls, but the house's appearance was that of a house that had not been inhabited in several years. There were no newspapers, magazines, or pieces of mail sitting out. As Josh sat on the couch, he noted an old, musty scent. Carl sat beside him, and Mitch sat in a chair opposite the room.

"Can I get you anything?" asked Mitch, in his best attempt at a hospitable host.

"No, thank you. I'll try and make this quick," replied Josh.

He pulled a small, yellow notebook out from his back pocket, and a pen from inside of his winter coat. He began asking his questions he and Carl had written down on the way to the house. As a whole, they were routine questions, crafted with the intent of not arousing any suspicion to their motives.

"Ok, let's see. Last night, around 11 P.M., did you notice any suspicious activity outside? A car pulling into your driveway, or maybe driving by more slowly than usual?"

"No, I didn't notice anything like that," replied Mitch.

"How about some of the other people living here? Yesterday, you said a few of your friends were staying here with you. Do you know if they would have seen anything?"

"They didn't mention anything to me," replied Mitch.

"And where are they right now?" asked Josh.

He knew he was pushing his luck. Mitch's brow furrowed, and he adjusted his posture in his chair.

"They're upstairs. Playing a video game, I think," said Mitch.

"Would you mind getting them? Just so that we can hurry up and move on to the next house," said Josh, trying his best to appear casual in his delivery of the questions.

"Yeah, I can go get them. Hang on a second," said Mitch, appearing annoyed.

He walked up the nearby flight of stairs and disappeared around the corner.

"I don't know Josh, seems like everything is Kosher to me," said Carl.

Josh's phone rang. It was Sharon, from the office.

"Hello?" said Josh as he answered the phone.

"Josh, are you okay?" asked Sharon.

"Yeah, why?" replied Josh.

"Where are you?"

Josh looked up the stairs. Mitch had not yet returned.

"At the Jenkins house. What's up?" asked Josh, with concern in his voice matching the concern he heard in Sharon's voice.

"The Jenkins House? I need you to leave as soon as you can. We got a call from the FBI."

Josh froze. His heart began to race.

Sharon continued. "They said that Mitchell Jenkins might have some connection to those abductions that have been all over the news."

Josh could see Mitch turn the corner, and begin to walk down the stairs.

"Okay honey, thanks for the call. I'll talk to you later," said Josh, in an attempt at a calm, casual tone, while also trying to disguise the nature of the call.

"I talked to the guys," Mitch said, before pausing. He looked between the two men. "Is everything okay officers?"

Josh looked over at Carl. The man's face was pale. He returned a knowing look to Josh. He had overheard the other end of the phone call. Josh watched as Carl, in a visible and obvious manner, glanced down at Josh's right hip, where his 9mm handgun was holstered.

At that moment, a loud banging noise came from the second floor, in the direction of where Mitch had just returned.

"Help!" shouted a muffled voice.

In unison, Josh and Carl rose from the couch, as they drew their sidearm.

Because he was already standing, Mitch was able to draw his handgun first, as he lifted up the front of his T-shirt. He aimed first at Carl, who stood directly in front of himself, fifteen feet away. He fired a single shot a split second before Carl had leveled his own handgun in Mitch's direction. His aim was true, and Carl collapsed instantly, a result of a shot that entered through his forehead.

Shortly after the round left the barrel, Josh tackled Mitch, sweeping his arm that was wielding the gun safely out of his own direction but had dropped his own handgun in the process. Mitchell lay flat on his back, with Josh on top of him. The two struggled for the gun in Mitch's outstretched hand. Josh wrapped his hand around the grip, and several rounds let loose as his finger was forced into the trigger guard by Josh.

Josh propped himself up on his other elbow and delivered a headbutt to Mitch's nose. Mitch let out a groan, and Josh took the opportunity. He used his other arm that he had been propped up on, to reach across to the gun. The move simultaneously gave him control over the gun but also allowed Mitch to roll over on top of Josh. However, Mitch was not fast enough to block Josh's arm.

Josh thrust the handgun against the side of Mitch's abdomen and, without hesitation, pulled the trigger. He could see the shock on Mitch's face. Josh tried to pull the trigger again, but it had gone slack. The muzzle against Mitch's body had prevented the slide on the gun from traveling forward. This had prevented the loading of the unfired round into the chamber after the case of the already fired round had been ejected, thus preventing the gun from firing again until the malfunction was cleared. Through the adrenaline-induced numbness, he could feel the wet, warm sensation of Mitch's blood trickle onto his hand. Mitch continued to struggle despite the wound. Realizing the gun had malfunctioned, Josh turned his focus away from the gun and the hand that held it. He placed a forearm across Mitch's throat and shifted as much of his weight through it as possible. He came up on his knees, and delivered a knee to the side of Mitch's abdomen, just below his ribcage.

Josh watched as Mitch's face, which had first shown shock after being shot, transformed to rage. With Josh now holding the positional advantage, Mitch glanced up and behind Josh's head. It was not the transition to unconsciousness that Josh was hoping for; he had not restricted his breathing and blood flow long enough for that to occur. His eyes were not losing focus but instead were intently fixed on a point that was behind Josh. Josh watched a grin form on Mitch's face.

Pain ripped through Josh's body. He writhed in pain and shock as the pair of 5.56 mm rounds tore into his back. The speed of the bullets, which neared three times the speed of sound, cut through Josh's soft body armor as easily as they would bypass a heavy winter jacket. The body armor, designed to offer protection from handgun and shotgun rounds, as well as offering some protection from puncturing weapons, such as knives, was simply not designed to defeat rounds of that velocity.

Mitch rose from the position on his back and kneeled over Josh's body. Though the rounds would prove to be lethal, Josh's consciousness did not slip away until a full 15 seconds after he rolled onto his back. He lay there, gasping for breath as his lungs filled blood while also collapsing in on themselves.

Mitch coughed violently, a result of the intense pressure that was placed on his trachea. He finally regained composure, and looked at his bloody hand, a hand bloodied by the wound delivered by the sheriff. His face turned to rage, and he seized the rifle from the other man's hands, the rifle that had been used to save Mitch's life while taking that of Josh's. Unsatisfied with such an arrangement, Mitch decided it was best he was the one to ultimately end the man's life. He leveled the barrel at the officer's face.

After the long hours of work, Chris would have expected himself to be exhausted. He and Dana had been waiting for over an hour for an update from Wisconsin. Dana said that the woman she had spoken to at the Jackson County Sheriff's office seemed flustered and hung up shortly after Dana had begun explaining the situation. She called back several minutes later and told Dana that the officer had been at Mitchell Jenkins' house. She also disclosed that Wisconsin State Patrol and Jackson County officers were en route to the house.

In the meantime, he and Dana had been left with nothing to do. Instinctually, Chris kept sipping at this coffee but realized he didn't need the caffeine to stay awake. Finally, after what seemed to be an eternity, Dana's phone rang.

"Hello, this is Agent Covington."

After listening to the reply, she pulled the phone from her ear, and pressed a button, putting it in speaker mode.

"Hi Frank, thanks for the call."

Dana mouthed the words *"State Patrol"* to Chris.

"I'll give you a quick rundown. First off, thanks for the tip, I just wish it had come a little sooner."

As if on cue, Dana and Chris heard the faint blaring of a siren through the phone.

"As of right now, the house in question is in flames. We have some fire engines on site, but it looks like the house will be a total loss. The two Jackson County officers that first arrived are unaccounted for. Their squad car was found in the driveway of the house. I've been told that going in the house to search for them is unsafe at this time. The suspect or suspects are also unaccounted for. My best guess at this time given the information I have, would be that they set the house on fire before getting out of dodge."

"Were any other vehicles present when the additional officers showed up to the scene?" asked Dana.

"No. They were able to access the garage before the fire spread that far, but it was empty," said the state patrol officer.

"Sir, I have no doubt you have a busy day like the rest of us, but we have good reason to believe that these suspects are involved in the-"

"Right, the abductions and killings by the UWF. I'm aware. You're right, I am busy. The whole state is stretched thin in terms of law enforcement. But, nevermind the investigation you're conducting, these people went after one of our own. I knew Sheriff Edgerton personally, and you have my word that I will do everything in my power to catch those responsible."

Chapter Eleven: Frequency

A major initiative by the past several presidential administrations in the United States had been a modernization of the U.S. power grid. When discussing modernization of the power grid, much of the focus of the public was on the role renewable forms of energy would play in the future of U.S. power generation. Well over one trillion dollars had been invested by the federal government, with large sums also accounted for by state, municipal, and private funds. These dollars primarily went to wind and solar projects, though some were also invested in geothermal and hydroelectric projects. Modern nuclear power plants had also been planned or constructed, though they continued to be a polarizing topic for many.

However, though it was a much more popular topic among the public and a common point of emphasis for politicians, increasing the contribution of forms of renewable energy to the power grid was only part of the focus of government and private organizations. Those familiar with the industry also realized that serious investments had to be made to make the grid more reliable and efficient, regardless of the future of renewable energy. This was what many industry insiders considered true modernization of the power grid. However, though this was an important consideration, it received less attention from politicians and the public. Therefore, it received less funding. Despite this, one initiative that fell under what some considered modernization of the power grid that had been successfully implemented was a full integration of the power grids that spanned the United States.

In the past, the continental United States had been divided into three separate regions. The Eastern, Western, and Texas interconnections were, individually, closely tied networks. The three were somewhat tied to each other, though the Texas grid was only loosely connected, something that was a point of pride among many Texans familiar with the arrangement. However, following repeated failures of the Texas grid due to cold snaps, heat waves, hurricane related disruptions, and, in one instance, an acute shortage of natural gas, public and political support had increased in favor of integrating Texas with the rest of the country.

The final nail in the coffin for the segregation of the Texas grid came two years prior to this fateful day. A major U.S. news agency, using the services of an undercover reporter, published a story detailing collusion between several of the smaller energy producers to drive up electricity rates. They represented less than five percent of the power generated across the grid and would have had an insignificant effect on the electricity rates across the state. Regardless, the damage to the image of utilities had been done, and the image of the independent grid had been further tarnished. A Congressional hearing occurred and, with the support of the public and much of the Texas state legislature, the grid was connected more broadly to both the Western and Eastern Interconnections. Simultaneously, the Western and Eastern grids were more closely tied together, leaving the vast majority of the lower 48 states fully integrated.

Two years later, this integration would at first appear to be prudent, but would later be disastrous. A string of coincidences would cripple the grid across the United States, an event that would occur simultaneously to the most significant unrest and upheaval the country had experienced in its history. The cascading series of events began the moment that the global financial system began to seize up.

In essence, the market price of energy commodities, including crude oil and natural gas, were essentially frozen in time. Rudimentary trading activity continued, though it lacked the infrastructure and sophistication of energy markets, including the usually highly liquid futures markets. This had the effect of there no longer being a benchmark price on which these commodities could trade; the market price had not moved in several days and was undoubtedly incorrect. The less formal trading that occurred outside the inactive markets was relatively small and not widely reported, meaning such prices were also an unreliable indicator of what market participants felt the prices should or could be.

This was seen as an opportunity by many that simply chose to hold onto their own product, in hope of selling in a few days or weeks once markets opened, presumably at a much higher price for energy commodities. Occurring simultaneous to this, was a slow down in the delivery mechanism of these energy products. This included trains, ships, and by trailer began to grind to a halt, as payment methods began to fail, and many workers in these positions didn't report to work, and many decided to hold onto their product, rather than deliver them to refineries, power plants, or other end users.

To compound these issues, a snowstorm struck the East Coast, bringing several inches of snow from Northern Virginia to Southern Maine. This was followed by a deep freeze that extended from the plains of Oklahoma, north of the Canadian border, and East to the Atlantic Ocean. This drove up the use of natural gas and electricity. Utility companies were faced with a dilemma. There was a real risk of demand exceeding the capacity of existing power plants. Along the East Coast, where the squeeze on power was its highest, rolling blackouts had begun several days after the initial market crash. The power plants designed to respond to surges in demand for electricity, termed "Peakers", were unable to source enough natural gas and oil to run regularly. This shortage of fuels continued, as demand by consumers increased inversely to the air temperature for over one-hundred and fifty million residents. The cloud cover over much of this same region, as well as relatively low wind speeds, hampered the solar and wind fields' ability to alleviate the problem. Demand from industrial and commercial sources faltered as a result of the economic standstill, but this drop was outpaced by the increased demand among residential users.

On the evening of Mitch's escape from the authorities in Wisconsin, two unpredictable events occurred that served as a death knell for the power grid as the United States knew it. First, an angry mob stormed multiple Northeastern power plants in Maryland, Virginia, Delaware, and New York. Their anger stemmed from the utilities' decision to cut power to many of the poorest neighborhoods within many of the major cities, in order to prevent a full shutdown. However, they continued to supply power to the financial districts, hospitals, airports, and some of the nearby suburbs. These decisions were widely publicized by several politicians, with further help from some in the UWF. Social media further amplified this anger, an anger that built on the growing unrest and distrust in many communities. Next, social media further assisted their efforts by enabling widespread gatherings to protest the injustices, though many in the group sought to harness the anger. These protests rapidly devolved into full blown sieges and infiltrations of power plants and other elements of the power grid infrastructure.

Already undermanned and tied up in widespread unrest the National Guard and local law enforcement were caught off guard, and were thus unable to deploy sufficient assets in time to prevent the crowd from gaining access to the crucial contributors to the power grid.

One power plant, in particular, had an especially undesirable outcome. Unsatisfied with the explanation given by those that worked at the plant, the leader of a small group of infiltrators sought a resolution to his community's blackout. At gunpoint, he threatened one of the operators at the plant with death, should they not restore power. The operator obliged, restoring power to the portion of the grid that had been deprived. At that moment, further strain was applied to an already ailing grid.

The second event built upon the first, though at a much larger scale. Seeing an opportunity that was both rare and unlikely to be present again in the future, a state-sponsored group of operatives based in Eastern Europe, with loose links to North Korea's DPRK, as well as China's PLA, chose this moment to act. Like many foreign intelligence agencies, these operatives had long since gained access to elements of the U.S. power grid. However, with only a few exceptions, these vulnerabilities had been left unexploited. In theory, should tensions rise between the U.S. and a foreign nation, an attack on the power grid could potentially serve as a partial escalation that fell short of an act by the military. In essence, it was a card up their sleeve, not unlike a cyberattack or an attack on a country's political structure.

This state-sponsored group had established access with the SERC, an organization responsible for grid maintenance across much of the Southeast and Midwest of the United States. These operatives had been able to see the distribution of power throughout the grid since first identifying this vulnerability, though chose to only observe for a number of years. They continued this observation and were able to see in real-time the load put on the grid as the power plant that had been assaulted by protesters restored power to the areas that were previously strategically deprived of electricity.

The head of this division of the organization knew nothing of why this had been done, but knew that it was irregular; such restoration of power should not occur until the grid had a higher capacity. However, capacity was not increasing, but actually decreasing. He knew they had a narrow window in which to act. Their decision was unconventional; contrary to conventional wisdom, their goal had never been to simply shut down power to a section of the grid or to render a power plant inoperable. Such an act could easily be undone in a relatively short amount of time. Instead chose to do the opposite. They began by overriding safety mechanisms within the grid that were designed to shut down portions of the grid in the event of a rapid rise in load on the system. This was coupled by also restoring power to some areas that had their electricity cut off in order to save the rest of the grid.

The restoration of power to specific areas in the Northeast at the request of the angry crowds was followed within minutes by this hack of the SERC. This caused a cascading series of events. In short order, the load on the overall grid was felt through much of the Eastern seaboard, Midwest, and Texas. For the average customer, this was experienced as a dimming of light bulbs and some electronics not working properly. However, the implications were far more dire for power plants and their powerful, delicate generators.

The U.S. power grid was designed to operate on a specific frequency of 60 Hertz. A deviation from this frequency, if significant enough, would cause significant damage to generators and their components, ultimately causing a failure to operate. In nearly every case, fail-safe mechanisms exist to shut down generators, should the frequency deviate too far to the downside, thus sparing them this damage. However, such fail-safe mechanisms were disengaged by this rogue group in nearly 20% of the U.S. grid. What followed was catastrophic. Countless generators across the grid shut down in short order to spare them from damage, though the amount of load on the grid did not decrease, another implication of the hack on the grid. A large number of power plant generators quickly sustained damage and shut down, damage that would take weeks, if not months, to repair under normal circumstances.

At 6:34 PM, Eastern time, the United States power grid underwent a coast-to-coast shutdown. Included in this was the entirety of the Canadian power grid, which was closely tied to the U.S. grid. The only area spared north of the Mexican border was the Alaska interconnection, which operated independent of the rest of the grid. Over three hundred and fifty million individuals lost power in the span of a few seconds. Generators and batteries kicked on in limited locations, including some government buildings, hospitals, military installments, water treatment plants, schools, communication centers, and cell phone towers. But, for the vast majority of the United States and Canada, a foreboding darkness settled over the land, a darkness that had not been seen in hundreds of years in some places, since well before Europeans arrived on the continent. It was a darkness that matched the dark cloud of unrest and violence that continued to spread across the continent.

The wood stove glowed in the corner of the basement living room. On the opposite side of the room, an oil lantern sat on a shelf, casting light on Alice and her daughters. David walked into the room with an armful of wood. He added it to a pile near the wood stove, brushing some snow off of the top in the process.

"That should last the night. Are you excited to have a sleepover downstairs like we're on The Little House on the Prairie?" said David, smiling in Maya's direction.

"Ooh! I can be Laura, and Harper can be Mary!" said Maya.

"Dad, why did the power go out? Will it come back on soon?" asked Harper.

"I don't know, honey. Hopefully soon, but it might be a while. We'll try to make the best of it, though. Let's be thankful that we're warm, and that we're all together right now," answered David.

For the time being, the power outage appeared as though it would be a distraction from David and Warren's attempt at establishing a collaborative community market and security solution, as well as the question of how the Libertas organization fit into the equation. Still, David suspected that even if this power outage was short-term, future outages would be likely, and he would need to find a way to continue towards their goals regardless of this variable.

David and Alice had pulled out a futon mattress, which was now topped with a blanket and pillows. On the floor rested a mattress for the girls to sleep on. The room they were in was part of their finished basement and had sheetrock walls on all sides, but the floor was a vinyl floor that was as cold as the concrete underneath. The weather had been relatively cold for Southern Indiana over the past several weeks, and the state had received more snow in two weeks than it generally received all winter. In the last twenty-four hours, however, the cold had intensified. David's phone, which still had reception despite the power outage, notified him that the low for the night would be around zero degrees Fahrenheit. In the basement with the wood stove running, he felt confident they would be able to stay warm for the night. However, much of the rest of the house would likely freeze.

"Mommy, can we watch a movie tonight?"

"I don't know Maya, did they have TVs and movies on The Little House on the Prairie?" said Alice, with a smile.

"No... But maybe we could watch The Little House on the Prairie while we're pretending we're on the show!" said Maya with excitement in her voice.

"No, honey, the TV isn't working," said Alice.

"The power's out, Maya. None of the electronics work," said Harper.

"Why is the power out?" asked Maya, having clearly not listened to the prior conversation.

"It's a long story, girls. How about Dad tells one of his stories, instead?" replied Alice.

"Oh I don't know..." said David.

"Please!" the two girls said in unison.

"Oh, alright. Once upon a time..."

He continued, as two girls settled in for the night, and Alice rested with her head on his chest. The past week had been far from normal, but tonight felt like it was a return to normalcy in the Ruiz household, even if just for a few fleeting hours.

Chapter Twelve: Priorities

Charlotte stood at the window of the office and looked at the scene that unfolded below, as Emily sat at her desk and nervously clicked her pen. The city of Washington, D.C. sat as a dark behemoth that surrounded the capital perimeter. The office buildings that were used by the Senate and House of Representatives both still had power, which was afforded to them by generators. The Capitol Building also had power, though the dome was not lit on this night. Spotlights shined outwards from the perimeter at crowds, as soldiers and Capitol police officers stood at the ready. This unrest, which had been unceasingly present over the past week, had hit a fever pitch in the hours since the city went dark.

"This is bad, Emily," said Charlotte.

"I know, I know! Where are those helicopters at?" asked Emily rhetorically.

Thirty minutes prior, Emily had received an automated phone calls that was intended for members of Congress that were still in the D.C. perimeter. They had instructed Emily and the others to shelter in place for the time being, but that an extraction of the key elements of the U.S. government and other personnel was being planned via airlift. Evidently, they either had lost control of roadways out or else were not confident in the safety of such a route.

Charlotte could see the crowds clash with the security forces in a vicious melee, as an attempt was made to keep the crowds at bay. This occurred near their own building, though she was unable to see them from her line of sight, and could best see the crowds across the lawn of the Capitol Building that were amassed at that side of the perimeter. From the activity she could see down below in front of the Russell Senate Office Building, she suspected the situation was no better near the perimeter that extended beyond the nearby office buildings. The security forces had been largely successful thus far, but the crowd had managed to advance a few yards in the last thirty minutes. Tear gas rose from behind the battle lines on the side of the civilian crowd. Already, Charlotte had heard the crack of gunfire from the nearby perimeter and had also seen at least one muzzle flash on the opposite side.

Someone knocked at the door.

"Senator Thompkins, this is Officer Williams of the Capitol Police."

Charlotte walked to the door, unlocked it, and opened it for the man. Emily had risen from her desk, coat and briefcase in hand. The man was wielding an assault rifle and wore body armor and a helmet with a face shield.

"Come with me. You've been designated as part of the priority extraction group."

Outside, from her vantage point near the door, she saw several other senators in a small group. They walked in silence. One was looking at his phone screen. The others briefly made eye contact with Charlotte, before looking down or turning away from the door.

"Charlotte, get your coat. It's cold out," said Emily.

Before the officer said anything, Charlotte already knew she was not in the priority extraction group.

"I'm sorry ma'am, but I'm under orders. She will have to stay here until the next round of extractions."

Emily looked Charlotte in the eyes.

"Charlotte, will you be okay?"

"Don't worry about me. I'll catch the next flight," said Charlotte, with a cheerful smile on her face.

"OK. Text me if you need anything. Oh, and don't forget to grab that extra briefcase," said Emily.

She walked out the door at the prompting of the officer. She had referenced a briefcase with some files that were not overly sensitive, no doubt related to the relief bill. For a moment, Charlotte was hurt by the casual nature in which Emily had left. But, she reminded herself that it had often worked out this way. Charlotte knew the extent to which Emily could manipulate and emulate true feelings, which left Charlotte often wondering if Emily valued their friendship, or if she simply viewed Charlotte as a useful tool. She pushed such thoughts away, as they were unnecessary and distracting to her current situation.

Charlotte Yates walked to the window. Within sixty seconds of Emily's departure, she could see the transportation arrive. Further away, she could see multiple V-22 Ospreys fly in quickly, before rotating their rotors downward and making a slow descent that continued out of view of Charlotte's window, but in the direction of the front lawn of the Capitol Building and the lawn between the Capitol Building and the Washington Memorial. Soon after, she heard the approach of more rotored craft, though these were Pave Hawk helicopters. They began landing in the smaller lawns flanking the Capitol Building. The rotor wash kicked up the light, powdery snow that had recently fallen on the D.C. area.

Charlotte was hardly optimistic about the overall situation that she, Emily, and the nation found itself in. However, she still found herself marveling at the might of the U.S. Armed Forces. She and so many others had been fearful for their lives, and for legitimate reasons. But now, or at least as soon as the second round of the extraction took place, she'd be safe and better able to assist Emily with the myriad of problems that both Congress and the nation faced.

More than anything, Russel was frustrated with himself. He had an opportunity, and he hadn't taken full advantage of it. When he had called for help, one of the men in the room had left, leaving him in the room at the most favorable odds to date of overpowering or escaping the grasp of his captors. He knew that he may never be one on one with one of these men in an unrestrained state again, and he had believed at the time that he had a legitimate attempt to escape. Before he had an opportunity to either fight this man or else get out of the bedroom through the door, the man swung the side of his hand into Russel's throat. This had stunned Russel. He had lost his initiative, and the man had no difficulty in forcing Russel onto the floor on his stomach and then restraining him in that position.

Russel's throat had since recovered from the blow, but his spirits had not. He sat opposite of Kate in the back of the same vehicle that had delivered him to the house. Some of the men from the house accompanied them in the back of this van and prevented the two from talking. Russel was unsure how many of the men were present; he once again had a hood over his head that blocked nearly all outside light. He only knew Kate was in the back because he had heard one of the men instructing her where to sit. He was unable to talk to Kate because of a gag that had been placed under his hood. He was unsure about the time they had been in the back of this van. They had left the house at some point late in the morning, but without a frame of reference for time; Russel could only roughly estimate the duration of the current trip. He had noticed after his prior trip in the van that the cargo space behind the cab did not contain any windows, and thus did not allow him to even catch some sunlight under his hood. He could only see the faintest glow of a light that did not change in intensity, a light source he had decided was positioned on the roof of the cargo space.

Mitch wasn't in the van, but the men in the cab of the van occasionally had communicated with him via walkie-talkie. Early in the trip, one of the men had asked about Mitch's condition. Mitch has assured him that he was fine, and regarded the wound as only a "grazing". Russel suspected it was the result of at least one of the gunshots he had heard downstairs as he was being subdued by one of the men in his bedroom. Russel was curious as to their destination and tried to listen to their conversation to gather clues. However, the men acted as professional as ever, and they only spoke vaguely regarding their location and direction. However, more recently, communication between the vehicles had become more frequent. Russel, who had found himself nodding off at times, sensed that this may signify they were nearing their destination. This had brought him out of his drowsy state. His ears perked up further as he felt the van begin to slow.

"What's this up ahead?" asked the man inside of Russel's van.

"I don't know. A checkpoint, maybe," replied Mitch from the other end of the conversation, presumably inside of a vehicle ahead of the van.

"Looks like the local hillbillies came out to play," said the man inside of Russel's van.

One of the men in the back, near Russel, chuckled at this.

"Can it. That kind of mentality gets you killed. Stay sharp, and don't underestimate these people. Weapons at the ready, but keep them concealed. We're acting friendly, so stick to the script. I'll do the talking. If things get hairy, be ready to light them up as we drive away," replied Mitch.

Russel was surprised by his professionalism in this type of situation. It made him wonder what type of training Mitch had undergone in the past. Was this preparation the work of the UWF? Or had he served in the military? Regardless, he was cool-headed and showed no hint of the instability of which Russel had been on the receiving end of a few nights prior.

"What's the ETA?" asked Mitch.

"Twenty-five minutes," replied another voice on Mitch's end of the radio.

"Pull up on the right side of the road, and they can pull in behind us," said Mitch.

Evidently, Mitch had turned on his radio so that his end of the conversation could be heard by those in Russel's van.

"Don't do anything stupid. Remember, my rifle barks, but this knife whispers" said a man near Russel, as he brushed the blunt end of a knife along the side of Russel's neck.

Russel nodded, unable to vocalize a response because of the gag.

"Hello! What can I do for you? We're not looking for any trouble," said Mitch, whose voice had suddenly taken on an accent that was either very Minnesotan or else Canadian; Russel wasn't certain.

A reply could be heard, but the voice was muffled, and Russel couldn't decipher any words.

"Libertas, you say? No, I can't say I have heard of you. Is that Spanish, or something?"

Again, a muffled voice replied.

The two men in the back of the van with Russel and Kate could be heard adjusting their position.

Click.

To Russel, the click resonated through the back of the van. The flipped safety switch sounded exactly as it did in the movies.

"Did he say Libertas?" said a man on the opposite side of the back of the van

"The one and only. Get ready for a fight," whispered the man nearest Russel.

The man talking to Mitch finished his reply.

"Now, I know things are different now, but I still have my constitutional rights. I would prefer you not search these vehicles," said Mitch, still attempting his best "Minnesota Nice" impersonation.

The voice replied to Mitch.

"We're just passing by on our way to Southern Ohio. Good Hope, actually. It's just a little town. We have some family there. This is my brother here, and those two back there are cousins."

The voice replied once again.

"Just the four of us. But we're not traveling light. I think the writings on the wall, so we took everything that was important from our houses and from a few other family member's houses. In fact, my aunt and uncle, Rich and Anna, passed through here a few days ago, maybe you saw them."

For all his usual professionalism and cunning plans, Russel felt Mitch's story was quickly falling apart.

"Like I said, I'd really prefer we get on our way. We have a long night in front of us, and-"

"You either turn around, or else you open those doors!" said the man on the other side of the conversation, loud enough to be heard by Russel.

"Alright, if turning around is an option, then I think we'll do that," replied Mitch.

Russel could hear a hint of fear in his voice. He wondered what there was at what Russel presumed to be a checkpoint, that would cause Mitch to turn around with such little hesitation. He felt the van's transmission as it shifted into reverse, and began slowly rolling backwards while turning. It then shifted into drive and began driving away. Russel noticed that his heart had been pounding in both fear and anticipation. This took some time to subside, even as they drove away.

"That was no good. We'll find another way around," said Mitch over the radio.

"That was two against six, I think we could have taken them," said one of the men in the front of the van.

"Wasn't worth it. Besides, four vehicles blocking the road but only two manning the checkpoint doesn't add up. No need taking the risk of other militants at the treeline," said Mitch.

This was the first Russel had ever heard of Libertas. Were they Mexican, as Mitch had said? Cartels not only operating in what presumably was the Midwest but also setting up checkpoints? Regardless, it was evident that Mitch and his group were familiar with the group, despite his feigned ignorance during the interaction. Russel sensed that there was more to be said about the group and the interaction, but that some of it was not being said because of his presence. This was consistent with their communication throughout the current trip, and also while Russel was at the house. He rarely, if ever, heard them discussing business, except in vague terms that rendered the snippets of information useless.

"Okay, follow us. We have an alternate route set up. It'll add another forty minutes, but gives us a good chance of avoiding another situation like that," said Mitch over the radio, informing the men in Russel's van.

The rumble of the engine continued. Despite the recent excitement, Russel's consciousness gave way to sleep, as he nodded off.

Chapter Thirteen: Reversal

The first group of Pave Hawks and V-22 Ospreys had already departed. Charlotte watched from the window of the Senate office building as a second group landed in the same configuration as the first. Her line of sight was obscured by snow-covered trees, but they proved to be less restrictive to her line of sight than trees with a full set of leaves. From the second-story window, she could see part of the nearest helicopter's midsection. She was unsure if Emily had been included in the first flight, or would soon be boarding. However, she was more concerned about her own situation. No one had arrived at her office to notify her of her evacuation. She had a sneaking suspicion that it was either low on the list of priorities for the powers that be, or not on the list at all. She had quickly used her phone, which still had reception despite the blackout of the city, to search for the specifications of both the Pave Hawk helicopter and the V-22 Osprey. The sites she had found had stated that around twenty and thirty-two passengers could be carried on the rotored craft, respectively. She could see that a few armed soldiers, besides the flight crew, were already aboard the Pave Hawk that was landing closest to her. Worryingly, the first helicopter appeared to have only allowed around ten additional passengers to board in addition to its own crew. At this pace, she'd be fortunate to be evacuated by the morning, if at all.

Her attention shifted from the Pave Hawk helicopter nearest to her building, as she spotted a change in the corner or the perimeter nearest her building. The perimeter had extended three blocks to the east of the office building but had slowly given up one full block to the progressively advancing crowds. However, when her focus had been elsewhere, it appeared as though a large portion of the crowd had withdrawn. A few remained, screaming at the soldiers and officers, while others held signs in protest.

The street beyond the front line was largely obscured by darkness, with the exception of a few still smoldering vehicles in the far distance. Suddenly, the few protesters that remained on the road looked behind themselves, down the dark road. They scrambled out of the way as the line of soldiers and officers quickly split to either side of the road. A few soldiers that were already on the sidewalk aimed their rifles down the road and opened fire. A nearby .50 caliber machine gun that sat atop an M-ATV erupted in fire as it slung lead in the same direction as the smaller rifles.

Zero Sum

From Charlotte's perspective, a dark shape came into view, hurtling towards the line. A spotlight that had shone down to the lines between the crowd and the authorities, shifted its focus down the road. The bright light illuminated a large, eighteen-wheel tanker truck that barrelled towards the defensive forces. As soon as it was illuminated, the soldiers held their fire as they realized their mistake. Charlotte felt herself wince as she braced herself for an explosion of the gas tank, much like one would expect to see in an action movie. Instead, the truck continued at a speed of at least forty miles per hour. As the soldiers dove for cover, no doubt also expecting such an explosion, the truck slammed into the front of an M-ATV that was parked several yards behind the now dissolved line of soldiers and officers. It slammed the military vehicle backwards as the tanker truck ricocheted off the truck, still carrying momentum. However, the engine had been damaged, and the front end dragged on the ground because of the damage caused to the suspension. The truck slid to a rest, leaving a shower of sparks in its wake.

The soldiers and officers began to encircle the large truck, though they quickly realized the threat it posed. The sparks themselves failed to light the spilled diesel from the truck's gas tanks, as well as the leaking gasoline within the large tank behind the truck. However, the engine compartment had begun to burn. In the light of the surrounding lights and spotlights, Charlotte could see a dark smoke ascend from the wreckage. In short order, this flame spread to the puddle of diesel and gasoline that was slowly forming around the base of the vehicle.

Meanwhile, she watched as soldiers ushered a group of what she presumed to be members of congress to a nearby clearing in which a Pave Hawk helicopter sat, rotors still turning. Suddenly, she saw one of the men in the group, an older man that was struggling to keep pace, drop to the ground. A soldier stooped over to help him up, only to collapse onto the man's body. Through the window, the noises were subdued. However, she began to hear the crack of gunfire against the backdrop of the helicopter's rotors. She searched for its origin and spotted the muzzle flash of several rifles in the darkness that shrouded the street from which the tanker truck had originated. The gunfire started sporadically; evidently, it had caught the Capitol Police and the soldiers off guard. Charlotte could see several defenders had fallen as a result of the gunfire, while the rest scrambled for cover. One by one, the defensive forces began returning fire, as the volume of gunfire from the other end of the street increased simultaneously.

Charlotte crouched, sheltering part of her body behind the wall, but continued to watch the firefight on the street below. The defensive fighters were quickly losing ground as a result of the surprise attack. The congress members were huddled behind a vehicle a full fifty yards from the landing zone, with a small escort of soldiers offering protection. Charlotte dreaded the thought of Emily being present in the group. The crowds on other sides of the perimeter that were within view of Charlotte had begun to subside, though she could also see sporadic gunfire in those directions, though not as furious as the firefight near her building. The attackers had slowly come into the light cast by the perimeter lights. Charlotte saw men that wielded military-style rifles. They were dressed in drab colors and wore bulletproof vests that had magazines and other gear attached. Through Charlotte's political lens, they appeared no different than the far-right or libertarian, so-called militia members, that were ever-present at the rallies and protests of the last decade, during which they stood in opposition to the often progressive theme of the protests.

The soldier that had manned the .50 caliber machine gun atop the M-ATV had sat slumped over since the tanker had slammed into his vehicle, a collision that had rendered him unconscious. A second soldier climbed the side of the vehicle and began removing him from the turret, before himself being raked with several bullets from a nearby attacker. Reinforcements trickled in the direction of Charlotte's building from elsewhere around the perimeter but were scarce. Charlotte continued to see fighting elsewhere along the margins of the safe zone that were within view, though it continued to be of a lesser intensity. She noticed a pair of M-ATV speeding away from their post, not in the direction of the firefight below, but out of sight in the direction of the rest of the safe zone, a zone which included the White House and the National Mall. Charlotte could see that the attacking forces, which numbered at least 50 men, had reached the bottom of the Russell Senate Office Building. Only 50 yards stood between them and the large vehicle that the members of Congress had taken shelter behind in the middle of the lawn. Another 15 yards further was the Pave Hawk helicopter, awaiting its passengers. The other helicopter, which had landed a further one hundred yards away, had taken off shortly after the firefight had begun.

All the while, the large tanker truck sent billowing, dark smoke into the night sky, as the flames engulfed the whole of the cab and the forward half of the tank. The heat alone prevented any soldiers from standing in a large radius. The flames had spread to a nearby town car, which let out an explosion as its gas tank exploded. The scene was mayhem, and the defensive forces appeared to be on the ropes. Suddenly, in a coordinated manner, the soldiers and officers began returning fire at a brisk pace, halting their own retreat. With the addition of a few soldiers that had run across the perimeter to assist, they seized the initiative. Charlotte watched as they laid down a barrage of covering fire. The group of congress members, accompanied by a small escort, made a move for the waiting helicopter.

Within a few moments, the group had made it to the helicopter. One by one, they were ushered into the helicopter but were slowed due to the advanced age of some members of the group. The defensive forces continued their barrage and had effectively pinned down much of the attackers. However, Charlotte spotted a problem. She watched helplessly as one of the attackers climbed the side of the M-ATV. The pair of bodies, as well as the protective shield that encircled the turret, offered the man some visual cover from the advancing forces. He finished the task of maneuvering the original gunner, who had been draped on the shield of the turret, out of the way and slipped into the turret himself. Charlotte watched in horror as he turned the turret nearly a full 180 degrees and aimed the .50 caliber machine gun at the helicopter. The last of the passengers had just boarded the Pave Hawk as the machine gun came to life. She heard the bark of the turret as it hurled lead in the direction of the helicopter. There were no tracer rounds that allowed her to visualize the flight of the bullets. The rotor wash, poor lighting, and distance also did not allow her to see the rounds impact the ground in front of the helicopter, or impact the side of the cockpit window and body. However, she was able to see as the machine gun raked the inside of the helicopter that was open to the outside through the open door on the side of the helicopter.

Within seconds, several nearby soldiers opened fire on the turret. The shield protected the gunner for a few moments as he continued to fire in the direction of the helicopter. However, the top of his head was unprotected, and with the high volume of gunfire directed at him, a round finally found its home in his head. The gun went silent. In fact, the entirety of the battlefield on Charlotte's side of the perimeter went silent for a moment, with the exception of the whip of the helicopter blades. The damage had been done. Charlotte could make out the outline of several slumped bodies in the helicopter as it lifted off the ground. It did not linger, but the minigun aboard the Pave Hawk, now in a good position to safely return fire, delivered a stream of bullets in the direction of the attackers. Many of these struck the side of the tanker, spilling more fuel which quickly caught fire. The helicopter sped away, presumably in the direction of Joint Base Andrews nearly 10 miles away.

Charlotte felt a sour taste in her mouth. Her abdominal muscles tightened. She fought back the vomit that rose in her throat as the fighting below resumed. Up to that point, the fighting and death had been terrifying. However, the thought of people she knew personally, killed in such a manner, sent Charlotte into a near panic. She fought back tears at the thought that Emily could have been on that helicopter. She had no way of knowing. She pushed aside the thoughts as she struggled to remain objective and calm. The attacking forces had regained some momentum as the defenders gave up some of the ground they had fought for in futility to cover for the escape of the helicopter. Her own building was nearly surrounded by the attacking men. She realized that her evacuation was unlikely, given the circumstances. She needed to do something. Make a run for it? Hide? Call someone? Anything was an improvement over simply sitting at the window as a spectator. She began to grab her coat and the briefcase that Emily had asked her to bring with her when she heard voices in the hallway. It was too late to run.

"How long do you think the generators will last?" asked Chris.

"Not long enough. Give it up Chris. Let's call it a night for now. We can regroup tomorrow," said Dana.

Chris sighed in frustration. The trail had gone dead along with the nation's power grid. The only lead they were able to salvage was a single reported sighting by a Wisconsin State Patrol officer, an hour and a half south of the now smoldering house. Since then, the databases that the two had been relying on for traffic cameras had gone dark, along with many of the databases the FBI accessed to supplement their own data. He had been awake for over 40 hours, and he felt his mind begin to go numb. He had lost its usual sharpness. Even so, he had felt an urge to press on. But, Dana was right. They were spinning their tires, and he needed rest.

"Alright. I'm exhausted. You're probably right on this one. Where do we sleep around here?"

"That's the thing. Chris, I think it's time to get out of dodge," said Dana.

"What do you mean?"

"You already asked about how long the generators will last here. I'm sure we could get an answer from someone in the building, but I'm not sure I want to stay much longer anyways. You and I know that the power grid for essentially the entire country is down. That's knowledge that few people know right now. It hasn't been reported to the media, yet. I don't want to stick around to see what Richmond or other big cities look like when everyone else learns of this. I mean, think of how bad it is already? We're fortunate we were able to make it into the office earlier today, with how bad some of the streets were."

"I think you mean yesterday," said Chris.

The two traded an exhausted smile.

"Point being, we can still work on this remotely. I can bring my laptop. The Bureau has satellite uplinks that plug right into the side of the computer, and I'm sure we can borrow one. Any heavy research will be a bit slower, but we can still keep in contact with the rest of the agents working the other cases," said Dana.

She had been sharing their findings with the rest of those working the case. Several days into the investigation, their information was far from being the only lead. At least one safe house had been found; the hostages and captors had all been killed in a hostage situation. Much like the house in Wisconsin, any and all hardware had been destroyed before the agents entered the house. Many other agents had made significant headway, though the overall progress continues to be hampered by the combination of poor staffing, the ongoing civil unrest, and the coordinated, yet decentralized nature of the UWF.

"How is this going to work? Hole up at your place?" asked Chris.

"No. Even if this is unlike any case I've worked on in years, and despite the fact I'm not the typical, action hero, gun carrying FBI agent you see on TV, I'm still accustomed to working in the field. I think it's time for a road trip."

"To Wisconsin?"

"Possibly. I have a request I put it in. It's an interagency request for some very specific information. It'll take some time, because of the staffing shortages that exist at other government agencies. Who knows? Maybe it won't get completed at all. Unless we get some good intel on the location of these safe houses, we're going to need to get creative to find Mitchell Jenkins, along with Russell. The request is based on geolocation data. The best guess I have is to look at the data from any cell phones that Mitchell Jenkins and his accomplices may have. I'm no expert on this, but I know that government agencies can keep tabs on this. I didn't tell them how to do their job, but I essentially asked to see if there were any devices in the area around the house that have now traveled far out of that area, especially somewhere to the south."

Dana spoke as she read some reports from other agents. She looked up from her computer, having expected a reply from Chris. He sat at his desk, face down, fast asleep. They needed rest. Tomorrow, they'd need to start their trip.

Charlotte closed her eyes and tried to slow her breathing. She had seen two pairs of boots walk by the desk she was sheltering under, and had heard a third person talking from the other side of the desk. The desk in the office was large, and the space underneath was more than large enough. It allowed her to squeeze underneath while also using a briefcase and a shoe rack to block the open end of the desk. She could peer out, but would only be seen if the desk was moved or if someone deliberately looked under the desk.

She heard the men talking to each other as they walked into the office.

"We need one at this window, and another at the window in the other room," said one man, referring to the two rooms that made up Emily's office.

Charlotte heard the gunfire continue outside the window. With one of the bursts of gunfire, she heard a loud crack.

"Hang on, this office won't work. They're bulletproof windows."

Charlotte breathed a sigh of relief, remembering the safety changes made to many of the buildings in D.C. following several years of protests, riots, and on one occasion, the storming of the Capitol Building. The men walked out of the room in search of more suitable perches to join the firefight down below, as many of the stairwell windows and those in hallways were not reinforced. More men in boots came running down the hall.

One voice shouted instructions to the others. "Set up shop boys! It's time to dig in! We gave 'em hell, but there's nothing we can do out there in the open with those helicopters flying around!"

Charlotte realized that with her focus on the nearby hallway and offices, she hadn't noticed the near-continuous whirring of at least one helicopter. She could hear the chain fire from the helicopter's miniguns, sending bright flashes of light through the nearby window. She also began to hear the echo of gunfire within the building and surmised it was some of the nearby attackers shooting outside of the non-reinforced windows that had been shattered with ease. This continued for a few minutes before she heard the helicopter fly nearby and a chain of bullets released from the minigun, which then raked the side of the building. The thud of the bullets hitting the stone and reinforced glass reminded Charlotte of the sound of a woodpecker. This burst was followed by a second barrage. The string of rounds shattered a window somewhere outside of the office. She heard a man begin to scream in pain, and noticed the echo of the gunfire from nearby the office halted, though she still could faintly hear it elsewhere in the building.

Charlotte considered her position. She knew the building as well as anyone and weighed the option of trying to escape. She also knew that the fighters outside of her office were unlikely to sympathize with her, given their treatment of the members of Congress boarding the helicopter. The alternative of hiding had worked thus far, but what if these attackers were able to hold the building? She could find herself trapped for days. Her decision was quickly decided for her. She heard a group approach the office.

A voice spoke to the others. "Like I said, we'll be staging from this building as we move west and as we cross the lawn to the Capitol. This second floor will be home to any wounded that don't need to be evac'ed immediately. We'll use this floor for snipers if we can, but as you can see, many of the windows here are reinforced."

The group had stopped outside the office Charlotte was in, and she could feel the man gesturing to the nearby window which she knew was full of cracks from gunfire.

"With that being said, it is not entirely bulletproof. It will stop most small arms fire, but some higher powered rounds will penetrate. Speaking of which."

The man walked by Charlotte's desk, and she could hear him close the blinds as a precaution against any potential snipers or other adversaries with weapons capable of penetrating the glass.

"Your responsibility is to set up this half of the second floor. I want it defensible, ready to accept wounded, and realize that this will be where some of our men will be sleeping if things get too drawn out. Understood?"

She didn't hear the loud reply that would have been given if these men were from the U.S. armed forces. The man that was speaking, however, spoke with the confidence of someone that had been in the military. Maybe an NCO, Charlotte thought to herself. Regardless, the men were here to stay, and Charlotte remained trapped.

Chapter Fourteen: Objectives

The side door of the van slid open. Russell heard the two men in the back of the van exit through the door. He could feel the air from outside the van; it wasn't much cooler than room temperature. The men's footsteps walking outside the vehicles echoed in whatever building they were parked in.

"Which one of you is Mitch Jenkins?" said a woman's voice in a serious tone.

"I take it you're Carmen Perez?" replied Mitch in a friendly manner.

"Just Perez is fine. It's about time you showed up, you're forty minutes late past the ETA you gave me," she replied.

"Yeah, about that. What the hell is Libertas doing out here?" replied Mitch.

"I'd appreciate some communication next time. We run a tight ship here, you'd do well to do the same. As for Libertas, this is their home turf. This is where most of their members are from, out in rural and suburban areas," replied Perez.

"Are we going to do anything about them?"

"We? As far as I'm concerned, I'll start saying "we" when you show me that you and your crew can be relied upon when needed."

"I was under the understanding that we'd be leading in a collaborative manner," said Mitch.

Russell had nearly forgotten that Kate was sitting nearby in the back of the van, but he heard her quietly laugh at the interaction outside the van.

"I don't care what their instructions were. As far as I'm concerned, you had two people to keep track of in a house, and yet here you are, showing up on my doorstep because of some mistake you made. I don't know how it worked in Wisconsin, but here in Indiana, respect is earned," replied Perez angrily.

Russell heard Mitch whisper something to Perez.

"OpSec? Don't lecture me about OpSec. I don't care if they hear a thing, because they aren't going anywhere. The outside world is never going to hear from them again. My women, they know how to run a compound like this without making mistakes," said Perez.

Russell heard her walk closer to the van.

"We're outside Columbus, Indiana. My name is Carmen Perez. My social security number is 535-32-4534. Anything else you want to know?" she asked rhetorically to Kate and Russell. "It doesn't matter, Mitch. What matters is that we lay low, stick to the guidelines for comms, and only release info on a need-to-know basis."

The irritation in her voice was obvious. Russell also found humor in Perez berating the man, but Mitch's apparent demotion was hardly welcome, considering the man's temper when he perceived things to be not agreeable to his own liking.

"Bring these two to their cells. Mitch, you and your team can take some time to unload your supplies. Christie will show you to your rooms. We weren't expecting company, so you'll be bunking up for the time being. I want you and your team back in the garage in thirty minutes for a debrief," said Perez, flatly.

Russel heard Kate being taken out of the van. He scooted himself to the edge of the open side door. He was pulled forward as a hand gripped his wrists that were still tied behind his back. He was led in the same direction of Kate's footprints as they meandered through unseen doorways and around corners, though never going up or down any stairs. He heard Kate's footprints continue straight as he was turned to the right down a separate hallway.

"Home sweet home," said a woman's voice.

Russell felt his wrist restraints being cut. As soon as his hands were free, he felt a boot kick him squarely in the back, and he tumbled forward, face first, without enough time to catch himself. Instead, he landed on a soft surface. It was a mattress, he realized.

"Breakfast is at eight," said the woman's voice.

Russell began to remove his hood but didn't turn to face the door fast enough to catch a glimpse of the woman. The door slammed shut. Once again, Russell was alone. He knew his time was running out, and he felt more powerless than ever.

Christie Eckles was proud of what she had become a part of. Yes, the nightmares interrupted her already limited sleep, and she found herself increasingly in need of a distraction to keep her from her conflicting thoughts stemming from her actions on that first day. However, to the rest of the compound, she was a bright and dedicated addition to their ranks. Though she wasn't a planned member of Perez's group and was entirely uninvolved in the plans to take hostages, someone in the UWF had taken notice of her work in Cleveland. Part of Christie knew that she deserved this. She didn't belong on the streets, inciting riots and fighting law enforcement or other groups in hand-to-hand combat. She was cut out for more than that. She didn't want to only participate in the new future the UWF was carving out, she wanted to cement her legacy as a young leader with potential.

In keeping with that plan, Christie had been intentional with her role with the UWF. She knew that, first and foremost, she needed to show dedication. Her acts of arson and the murder of the shopkeeper, which she been candid in discussing with her leadership, had served the purpose of showing her loyalty. It was what had led to her being handed her current position in the movement. But, Christie knew that loyalty, dedication, and obedience did not make a person a good leader or a dynamic member of a group. Those were qualities she still needed to prove. The last 24 hours gave her that opportunity. First, Perez had told her and the other women in the building that they would be absorbing some other UWF members into their cell, along with two additional hostages. The second event was the power outage that occurred a few hours later in the day. These events had brought a new urgency to their mission, and the stale routine of the past few days was replaced with new challenges. Christie planned to capitalize on these challenges.

It was clear to Christie that her best bet would be to continue to align herself with Perez. Mitch may be an effective leader in his own right, but it was obvious that he was not on his own turf, and that Perez's opinion of him as a careless and ineffective leader had affected him. He was flustered and had quickly taken a more submissive role for the time being. As she led Mitch and the rest of the men to their rooms, she knew what her next plan would be.

"Here's the room. The kitchen is two doors down, on the right. We'll handle breakfast this time, but each of you will need to start chipping in around here. See you all in a few hours," said Christie, with a smile on her face that stood in stark contrast to Perez's harsh demeanor.

"It's Mitch, right?" she said to Mitch before he walked in the door.

"Yeah, that's me," he replied.

"Can I chat outside the room with you for a second?" she said, as she walked a few paces down the hall.

Mitch followed, still holding his bags at his side.

"Look, sorry about Perez. She can be a real, well, let's just say that she's very passionate about what she does. We all are passionate about what we're here for, but she expresses it a little differently than the rest of us. But I'm sure she'll warm up to you, just give it some time," said Christie.

"Thanks," replied Mitch.

"See you in the morning," said Christie, with a smile on her face as she walked away.

David was no stranger to waking up before sunrise, but he had willed himself to wake up especially early. The power outage added an unwelcome wrinkle to his already busy day. He sat at his kitchen counter and used his phone to gather information about the extent of the power outage, as he lamented the absence of his usual hot coffee to accompany his morning. David was disappointed, but not surprised, that the reports appeared to be consistent with a complete blackout across the country. No announcement by the federal government had been made, which appeared to also be dealing with its own crisis in D.C., if he was to believe some of the reports and videos on social media. Still, a multitude of state and city governments had made announcements, and social media filled in the rest of the gaps about the nationwide blackout. Mainstream media sources had rapidly synthesized the data, and many of their articles were accompanied by maps that illustrated the extent of the blackout, though they were hardly necessary, considering that the vast majority of the grid was down.

It all seemed so surreal to David; the internet, especially social media, was ablaze with absolute and total carnage to an extent he had never witnessed. Much of the country was on the brink of anarchy or else had already entered into such a state. Parts of the federal government were literally under siege. Despite that, here he was, using his phone and accessing websites and social media platforms as if nothing had happened. He knew that, if the blackout persisted, that wouldn't be the case for long. The generators powering cell towers, news agencies, internet servers, and data centers would all eventually run out of fuel. With it would disappear a large portion of the North American internet, leaving the rest of the world to fill the void. David had charged a portable external battery in his truck overnight, enabling him to charge his phone as he sat at the counter. That would have to work for now, but even his phone would soon become less useful, once the local cell towers went offline. Only those near working cell towers or those with satellite internet would retain access to the internet.

Among his first tasks for the day would be to start his generator. He had decided he would need to ration the remaining gasoline, and that the generator would only run for a short time each day. This would enable him to run his water well pump, cool the fridge and freezer, charge any needed devices or batteries, run the furnace for a short period of time, and even brew a pot of coffee. It would be less than ideal, and would only be a stop-gap measure, but would limit their use of firewood, maximize their ability to use what was left in the refrigerator, and perhaps most importantly, retain some sense of normalcy. Part of David knew that the normalcy of the past would be replaced by a new normal, but he also knew that his family, himself included, would struggle with the transition.

While the generator ran, he had his usual farm-related tasks to finish before talking with Warren. The plan for setting up a marketplace for barter between the locals had thus far been a major success. David wasn't aware of any trades that had taken place, which wasn't unexpected, because they had scheduled a meeting for the following morning among those that had signed up, a meeting that would help orient others to the process and to set some ground rules. David felt that enough individuals had shown interest that they might be able to create something that resembled a legitimate market. However, he had run into some roadblocks on the plans for security for surrounding communities. Specifically, many of those that David had talked to cited the presence of Libertas as a reason they could not commit to such a proposal. Many felt that the security network would be redundant, or worse, could appear antagonistic towards the militia group. David and Warren understood these concerns but were themselves concerned about aligning themselves with the group. They only had limited knowledge of their motivations and knew that the organization was at least partly aligned with a specific political ideology.

All of this, and more, would make for a busy day, a day in which he'd need to spend a large portion of the day away from home. He found himself longing to spend more time with his family on days like these, but he also knew that he was doing what was best for Alice and the girls, the community, and the farm. Before heading out the door, David said a short prayer. He asked for wisdom and discernment; he prayed for the well-being of his family. Finally, he prayed a prayer of gratitude for the ways God had blessed him, despite the circumstances he was faced with. David put on his boots and a heavy coat and walked out the door to face the day.

Chapter Fifteen: Sacred

Charlotte instinctively shook herself awake in response to the familiar vibration of her phone. Her surroundings, however, were not familiar, at least at first. Her first thought, besides a brief sense of panic stemming from a fear of oversleeping through an alarm, was a sore hip she was laying on. In fact, her whole body was aching. She tried to stretch out her legs and straighten her back, but was unable. Suddenly, she transitioned from a semi-conscious state to a full awareness of her surroundings and circumstances. The helicopters, the gunshots, the men in the Russell Senate Office Building, and the desk that she was curled up underneath. She realized that she must have fallen asleep during a short lull in the gunfire and chaos. The gunfire did continue, however, and she could hear the echo of gunshots originating from her own building. Voices, too, the same voices from the men she had heard before. It was still dark out, but she could see a hint of dawn with the small field of view she had of the window.

She quickly repositioned herself underneath the desk and reached to the top of the desk where the phone still buzzed. She couldn't risk the men hearing the noise. In all reality, she had entirely forgotten about the phone until it had awoken her. In a state of shock and panic, she had forgotten that the phone sat only inches away on the surface of the desk. The phone stopped buzzing as she withdrew once again under the desk, and she repositioned the briefcase to conceal herself. The phone showed multiple missed messages and phone calls from Emily. Charlotte was relieved to see that Emily was alive; she hadn't fallen victim to the barrage of gunfire from the turret that was directed at the helicopter. She had also received multiple notifications from a news app on her phone, one of which was reporting on the situation she found herself in the midst of, something the media had termed "The Siege of D.C.", while others reported on a widespread blackout, the ongoing unrest, and painted a dire picture of the state of the nation.

The phone gave Charlotte some hope of reaching someone that could offer her some help. Emily herself held a significant amount of sway within U.S. politics; maybe she could use that influence to put a rescue operation in motion, Charlotte thought to herself. Worryingly, however, was the fact that the phone was only at 3% power. It would only last a matter of minutes.

Emily, glad you're OK. Still at the office, hiding. They took control of the building. Any chance you can help?

She hit send. 2%. She turned down the brightness and turned off the screen. What else could she do? No one was in a better position to help than Emily. 911 was obviously out of the question. No other contact from Capitol Hill would yield any assistance. Her phone buzzed.

I wish I could, Charlotte. They're already fighting, but they're stretched so thin already. I'm thinking they might give up on it soon.

Charlotte's heart sank. There would be no rescue, no offensive, at least in time to save her. The cavalry wouldn't arrive. No, that's not right, she thought to herself. The cavalry had already arrived, and they left with the high-value persons, leaving the rest behind. She knew that if, for example, Emily and a few other high-ranking members of congress were in her position, the response would be far different.

She was disappointed that Emily wouldn't so much as try to convince some top brass to mount a rescue operation, but she knew what Emily said was true; the military and Capitol police were stretched too thin. She was thankful, too, that Emily had told her that information. She knew that, even though they were both using supposedly secure lines, it was a piece of intel that Emily could lose her job for sharing with Charlotte, given the circumstances. Of course, given the circumstances, it was unlikely that anyone would go after her for it, let alone discover the disclosure of information.

Thanks for the heads up.

Unsure of what else to add, she sent the message. What else was she supposed to say? See you soon? Sorry, I don't think I'll be able to make it to work tomorrow? A few moments later, her phone died. There was a charger, halfway across the room, and she was fairly certain the building still had power, but she deemed it to not be worth the risk. She still could hear the gunfire down the hallway; also, on occasion, she'd hear footsteps in the hallway outside of the office.

"Sniper!" shouted a man in the hallway. Charlotte heard footsteps in the hallway as the men scattered from wherever they had been positioned.

"Hold on, Jeremy, we're going to get you some help," said a voice, as Charlotte heard two pairs of boots enter the room.

Inches away, she heard one of the men sit down and prop himself up against the desk. He was breathing heavily and groaning in pain.

"It's going to be OK. You're going to make it, Jeremy," said the voice.

She heard the snip of scissors as they cut away from clothing.

"How does it look?" asked the injured man, as he struggled to vocalize words between heavy breaths.

"Good. Looks good Jeremy," said the man.

His voice had begun to crack as if he was holding back tears.

"You sure?"

The other man paused before replying. Charlotte could hear him begin to choke up with tears as he spoke, "Yeah. We'll get someone to fix you up in no time."

She heard footsteps moving away from the desk.

"Wait," the dying man gasped as the other man walked away.

The footsteps paused for a second. A heavy pause filled the air before the footsteps continued out into the hallway. The man continued to breathe heavily, and a deep gurgling noise began with each inhalation. He groaned in pain. It was a pain that likely emanated more from the realization and knowledge of his fate, than the gunshot wound. The gurgling increased with each breath. She heard him adjust his position as if he tried to stand, but ended up slumped against the desk once more. A moment later, the groaning and gurgling stopped. The man was still.

Chapter Sixteen: Schemes

David stood in his driveway as Warren pulled up in his pickup truck. He gestured for David to get in through the passenger door. David couldn't blame him for not wanting to step out into the cold, morning air. Warren had a warm smile on his face as David sat down.

"Surprised?" asked Warren.

"Not in the slightest. Didn't I predict this a few days ago?"

"I do recall something being said along those lines. Although, I think you were giving it a few more weeks before it'd happen; you doubted me when I said it could happen sooner than one might expect," replied Warren, with a smile on his face.

"I said no such thing," said David, returning the smile.

He enjoyed this banter that he was able to share with Warren over the past few days.

"Who's on the list today?" asked David.

"We're starting out south of Columbus," said Warren, as he handed David a map that was accompanied by a list of addresses and names.

"Let's see, it looks like a Richard Ortiz is first, then Michael and Laura O'Neil, and then Trent's Sand & Gravel," said David, reading off of the list.

"Any of those ring a bell?" asked Warren.

"I think I've seen the Trent's dump trucks around. Never worked with them, though."

David and Warren had continued to focus their efforts on those most able to meaningfully contribute to the planned market. This included anyone that would be able to provide products or materials needed by the other participants. The first two on the list appeared to be family run farms, not unlike Warren and David's farms. Trent's Sand & Gravel was a locally owned business. David didn't anticipate those services to necessarily be in high demand, but the use of a dump truck could come in handy to a farmer or other member of the market.

In all reality, David and Warren didn't want to make it a market of membership. Ideally, it'd be open to anyone, including businesses, city governments, and private citizens. Out of practicality, they had limited their list to those that would most benefit and be able to contribute in a significant way.

Zero Sum

The two drove in silence for a few minutes as David studied the map and the names further down on the list. Satisfied with the work that was lined up for them to complete, he put the map and list down.

"How long do you think it'll last?" asked David.

"What's that?"

"The power outage. If it's not local, but national..." said David, as his voice trailed off.

"Hard to say. In ideal circumstances, I'd guess anywhere from a few days to a few weeks. Depends on the damage that was done."

"But these aren't ideal circumstances," replied David.

"That's the thing. It's no longer a matter of fixing what's broken, it's a matter of getting those parts, making sure the power plant operators are available to do repair work, and that oil and gas keep flowing in the meantime. Add to that any damage done to power lines or transfer stations, and it's a tall order."

"And, they need to coordinate that work across the whole country," said David, finishing his thought.

"Right. If the blackout was more of a stand-alone event, let's say from a solar flare or a cyber attack, then the government might be in a better place to respond. In that situation, their first steps would be to maintain order and to get to work on getting the grid online. The difference is that they lost order days ago, and losing the grid makes it that much more difficult to restore law and order," replied Warren.

"Thank the Lord that it's already almost February. I couldn't imagine what we'd do if this was November, having the winter ahead of us."

"Be thankful you don't live way up in Michigan or Minnesota. Winter still lasts another few months up there," replied Warren.

"How are you on gas?" asked David.

"15 gallons last time I checked, plus whatever is left in the truck and the tractors."

"Hm. I'm down to a 5 gallon can, plus the truck, car, and tractor," replied David.

"I'm hoping we can secure some sort of consistent supply from this market. I don't know where it'd come from, maybe a different community city, someone that needs what we have. There's too many people around here that need that gas. Quite a few that'll need diesel, come springtime."

Warren had explained a few days prior that his own generator ran on natural gas, something that Warren had a large tank full of since it was what he used to heat his home. This put him in a better position than David, as well as many others in the community, that were more reliant on gasoline. The high demand for gasoline in the spring was a reference to the farmers that had fields to till and plant, a process that required the use of machinery that was by and large powered by diesel engines, though many engines involved in the process also needed gasoline.

"Michael and Laura O'Neil are first up. Looks like they live up here on the right," said David, recalling it from memory from the map.

It had become routine to David. These meetings sometimes only took a minute or two, other times they were invited in for coffee, which they felt they couldn't turn down if they wanted to have a chance of persuading others to get on board with their plan. The truck turned into the driveway and parked in front of the garage.

"Let's do this," said Warren, as he opened his door, and climbed out of the cab.

The group that Christie belonged to had chosen an old, abandoned business as their location to keep the hostages. The building had a steel roof and steel siding and was painted a light brown color. It had been a fabrication shop, many years ago, but had sat abandoned near the edge of the town of Columbus, before it was purchased by an associate of the UWF a few months prior. It had a large room in one wing with two garage-style doors, though could easily fit 6 large vehicles the size of the transport vans, though only housed 2. There was a front lobby that was connected to several offices; there were rooms designed for meetings, electronics and communication equipment, a common area for leisure time, and a room that had been fitted with kitchen appliances. A few other offices and storage rooms served as bedrooms for the UWF members. A second large room, identical to the makeshift garage, had been modified to house several smaller rooms that would serve as the cells for the captives. Originally, the building only housed 2 prisoners, though it had been constructed with a total of 5 cells. The building was one of several across the country that could serve as overflow for other UWF groups that had been compromised or were otherwise unable to remain in their original location. Thus, it had not been at full capacity prior to the arrival of Mitch's group and technically could still house one more prisoner.

"Follow me Mitch. I'll show you the ropes," said Christie, as she walked down the hallway.

The morning meeting with the newly absorbed UWF cell had just concluded. Christie sensed tensions were lower between Mitch and Perez, though that was only the case because Mitch had appeared to make the decision to submit to her authority over those in the compound, including himself. His body language, however, alluded to his continued frustrations.

The other men that had arrived had been allowed to go to their rooms and sleep, with some delegated to nighttime guard duty. Mitch, however, had been instructed to follow Christie for the next few hours in order to become oriented to daytime duties in the compound. Christie knew this amounted to a punishment for Mitch; the fatigue of the preceding day and night was evident on his face.

"So, I'm sure a lot of the procedures are universal from one compound to the next, or at least that's what I was told. Still, there's a few unique aspects to this place. In this room right here is Mark Hill. An executive from a bank in Cleveland. You'll see him in a few minutes. He's a bit older, in his 60s I think. He's broken, his spirit, I mean. He misses his family, his wife, mostly. A bit of a wet blanket, to tell the truth.

"Then, there's Kyle, Kyle Leland. He was a hedge fund guy from down south of here. Louisville, I think. He's still pretty angry about all of this. But believe me, I've looked the guy up on social media; he's absolute trash. He deserves every bit of what's given to him. Not that Mark doesn't, but you know what I mean. Any questions so far?" asked Christie.

She had intentionally maintained her overly cheerful demeanor from the previous night. Mitch, still processing the information, nodded his head without a word and maintained an otherwise blank expression. She realized she might be overdoing it with the cheerfulness; maybe some empathy was the way to go in her pursuit of gaining his trust.

Christie turned, and looked Mitch in the eyes, "I talked to Evan, and he told me what happened," said Christie, referencing one of the men from Mitch's group.

"He did?" replied Mitch, caught off guard.

"I know Perez isn't going to believe you, or him, but I do. I don't know how that cop found you, but I guarantee it wasn't something you did. Those men respect you. They know this isn't your fault."

"Yep," replied Mitch, showing some irritation.

"Look, I know it can feel like I'm one of the bad guys, but I'm not. I'm on your side. I'm on Perez's side too, but she and I, well, we have a different philosophy on leadership."

She could see she was getting through to Mitch. He was no longer returning the eye contact, but staring off into the distance, as if considering the words she was saying.

"I won't push the issue anymore, for now, I just wanted you to know-"

"I can't tell you how much work I've put in to be where I'm at, to be in a position where I feel like I'm making a difference," he said, as turned to her and looked her in the eyes. "I'm not one to buy into the feel-good message of making the world a better place. I signed up to lead my own group because I wanted to make them pay for what they did to me. I've been hellbent on that for years now. For Perez to accuse me of carelessness, for her to not so much as acknowledge what I've done..." said Mitch, with an angry passion in his voice.

Christie didn't know the backstory but could tell that there was more than met the eye in Mitch's psyche. Something had happened in his past that was a motivator for his current life. Though it was not what drove herself forward, Christie knew revenge could be a strong source of motivation. Originally, the sense of community and purpose was what led her to join the UWF. That still was the case, to an extent, but she found herself motivated more by power, prestige, and recognition. A motive of revenge was a strong motive, but it also clouded judgment. She found herself better able to make progress towards her goals when able to calmly and deliberately make decisions. This contrast between herself and Mitch would be used to her advantage.

"I get it Mitch. Bide your time, things will change. Who knows, maybe you'll be in Perez's position in a week's time," said Christie.

Mitch didn't say anything, but smiled, considering what she had said. He thought she was on his side. He was exactly where Christie wanted him.

Dana tossed the keys to Chris.

"You're driving."

"I'm driving? It's your car," replied Chris, as he opened the driver's door and entered the car.

"I know, but I need to keep my eyes on the computer. I want every bit of intel we can get, especially if that GPS data doesn't come back. Besides, I don't trust you to be the navigator," said Dana, with a wry smile.

"Fair enough," said Chris, returning the smile. "Where to first?"

"I'll let you know what turns to make. We'll pick our way through mostly county roads or back roads. I'd prefer to stay off the highway. We'll shoot to make it somewhere south of Chicago. I think that'll be a good place that might be at the center of a radius I'd expect them to be inside of."

"Might be?" asked Chris.

"It's no different than in the investment world. This is a game of probabilities. We know they headed south, at least as far south as close to the Wisconsin-Illinois border. Personally, I don't expect them to be going as far south as, say, Tennessee or Arkansas. And if they do go that far south, we'll need to figure out something for gas."

Dana had been able to secure some extra gas from the Kentucky State Patrol. Evidently, someone from the Wisconsin State Patrol had contacts in Kentucky and had pulled some strings. The car already had a full tank, as well as 2 5-gallon cans in the trunk. A refill of the tank and the 2 cans in Kentucky would give them the range to make it some distance into the Midwest. The biggest risk they faced would be getting bogged down on back roads. Taking the route that was longer and slower was already going to add a significant amount of miles and time to the trip, and unforeseen obstacles could further hinder their movement west.

Chris began driving down the road as Dana intermittently called out directions.

"So, here's my big question. Let's say we go out west, we get some good intel, and we know where they are. Then what?" asked Chris.

"Ideally, we get some help. Local police, state police, maybe more agents from the Bureau."

"Ideally? Are you insinuating that there's a less than ideal scenario in which we take care of it ourselves?"

"Well, no-"

"Hang on, do you have a gun?" asked Chris.

"What do you mean, do I have a gun?"

"I mean, I know you don't usually work cases like this, so you don't seem like the type to carry a gun with you everywhere."

"You're right, I don't usually have a gun," said Dana, with a small smile.

"But do you have one now?" asked Chris, persistently.

"Maybe."

"Maybe?"

"You're not going to let this go are you?"

"I think I have a right to know, that's all."

A pause followed. Chris was curious; he was not accustomed to being around guns. He had only fired a gun a few times in his lifetime. Generally, he'd feel uneasy about the presence of a gun in his close proximity. However, given the circumstances, he hoped that Dana had a gun with her and that she knew how to use it.

Chris looked over at her expectantly, not giving up on his line of questioning.

"Clearly, we can't move forward until I give an answer," said Dana.

"Clearly."

"I grabbed my own handgun from my house a few days ago."

"I knew it! Do you know how to use it?" asked Chris.

"Do I know how to use it? Of course I do! Why else would I have it? It's been a few months since I've had a chance to go to the range, but yeah, I know how to use it," said Dana, amused by his questions.

"Do you plan on using it?"

"I'd prefer not. But, you know the old saying."

"I don't," said Chris, genuinely unsure of what she meant.

"Better to have a gun and not need it, than need a gun and not have it. Take a right up ahead, by the way."

Chris turned onto a county road. It would be one of many otherwise obscure roads that they would traverse today in their trip westward. He knew that for Dana, this was a pursuit of justice in the name of duty. For him, however, it was more about a sense of adventure, intrigue, and a desire to help his friend and colleague. It was not a path Chris had foreseen himself following. However, in his mind, this was something he was fully invested in. A portfolio invested in a single asset was rarely a good strategy in the world of wealth management, and likewise, he was the type to always prefer a multitude of options in life. This situation, however, was different. He was fully committed and could see no other way forward, except down the road that he followed.

Charlotte had seen more death in the last 12 hours than she had in the rest of her life, up to that point. However, it was the death that she could not see, but only hear, that affected her the most. She found herself sobbing following the man's death. There was no sympathy for his cause, but she did feel an immense amount of sympathy for the circumstances of his death. The rational side of her brain told her that his death was no different than the scores of U.S. soldiers of Capitol Police that had died. Little separated his death from the death of those members of Congress that had been mowed down while boarding the helicopter. Yet, those deaths felt less real than the death of Jeremy. No amount of rationality could make her forget the sound of that man's death.

She had spent the last several hours in the same position under the desk. Shortly after the man died, she felt a warm wetness along the side of her thigh. She realized quickly that it was his blood. She now sat in a puddle that was a mixture of his blood and her own urine. She was embarrassed by this but knew that she could wait no longer, and could not risk leaving her cover to go to the nearby bathroom. That risk, however, was waning. The footsteps in the hallway outside were less frequent. Gunshots could be heard coming from a nearby window on occasion, but only occurred once every few minutes. She guessed that this was a sniper, similar to the one that had taken the life of the man leaning against the desk. The gunfire continued outside, though the gunshots were more distant. The U.S. military had not retaken this building; evidently, the attacking forces had gained considerable ground. This was consistent with what Emily had told Charlotte before the phone died.

Despite the emotional shock, Charlotte's mind was still working to find a solution to her predicament. Given the decreased activity, at least on the 2nd floor, she had decided she needed to escape. Eventually, a more detailed search of the building would take place. It undoubtedly held some classified papers and electronics, and Charlotte would likely be found during such a search. Her first course of action would be to take advantage of the low amount of activity on the second floor, in order to set up her escape.

She began by moving the flimsy barricade she had erected by the underside of the desk. As she maneuvered her way out, pain shot through her joints. She had been in a small, confined space for hours and took a minute to stretch her back and legs. As she stood up, she could see the door to the hallway. It was mostly closed, meaning she could only see a small sliver of the hallway, and they could only see a small portion of the office. In a crouched position, she turned the corner of the desk. The man sat there, motionless. He looked to be in his 30s; a bearded man. His chest wound, having been exposed by the other man, was a dark red, almost black color. Blood stained his chest and had run down to the floor. He had no rifle to match the magazines that were in pouches on his waist but did have a handgun holstered on his right hip. Charlotte made a mental note of that.

She walked silently into Emily's office, which did not have access to the hallway. She grabbed a change of clothes that Emily kept in a desk; the senator occasionally would jog when the weather permitted, though she had not done so over the past 6 months. She changed into the sweatpants and light sweatshirt and laced up the running shoes. The shoes were somewhat tight, but the clothes otherwise fit well. She peered out the window; the windows were filled with bullet impacts, which made it difficult to look out of much of the window. She crouched down to a small, relatively clear area of the window that sat a few feet above the floor.

The appearance of the landscape around the Capitol Building matched the incessant fighting she had heard through the night and could still hear during the day. Many of the trees on the lawn were mangled; the smoldering remains of the tanker truck remained below the window. The carcass of a helicopter sat far across the lawn. She could see movement around the Capitol Building. Upon further inspection, she could see many other attackers down below, most of which walked close to the buildings, trees, or burnt-out vehicles so as to stay behind cover. They were not actively fighting; it appeared most of the action was far across the lawn and on the opposite side of the Capitol Building.

Charlotte suspected her best option would be to head northeast. In that direction, she would primarily find residential parts of the city. However, she'd first have to escape the immediate vicinity of the Russell Senate Office Building. Of course, Charlotte reminded herself, her first obstacle would be escaping the building itself. She walked back in the direction of the office and desk she had hidden under, taking care to walk as quietly as possible. She considered covering the dead man's body, out of respect, but decided not to, as it may arouse suspicion.

Charlotte grabbed the man's handgun from his holster. She inspected the firearm, first to ensure there was no blood on the grip, and then to familiarize herself with the weapon. Unfortunately, the extent of Charlotte's knowledge of handguns was what she had gleaned from movies. Holding the gun in her right hand, she attempted to find the safety. There was no lever above the grip that was indicated as the safety, which was unexpected. She did, however, find a small button on the grip. Unsure of its function, but suspecting it was the safety, she depressed the button. In an instant, the magazine dropped from the grip.

Clack!

The magazine noisily landed on the floor. For a moment, she simply stared at the handgun in her hand and the magazine on the floor. Her body, no longer frozen by shock, went into action. She grabbed the magazine and returned to her hiding spot under the desk. Her heart pounded in expectation of someone entering through the doorway and finding her. She wasn't sure if she waited 2 minutes or 10. After some time, she heard the nearby shooter fire his rifle out the window. This was comforting to Charlotte; the sniper was the only nearby person she was aware of, and he either had not heard the noise or else had decided not to investigate.

She slowly crept out from under the desk. The door had not been disturbed and remained barely open. Charlotte was left with a dilemma. She had begun to suspect that this handgun must not have a safety lever but was unsure of how to test this theory. She contemplated leaving the handgun altogether but decided to test the theory. Before inserting the magazine, she pulled back the slide. This took a considerable amount of hand strength, but she was able to pull it back far enough for the gun to eject the round in the chamber. It popped out the top, and Charlotte positioned her foot under the falling round in order to break its fall. She picked it up off the floor and placed it next to the magazine on the desk.

Now certain the handgun was not loaded, she pointed it at the ground. She winced, as she pulled the trigger.

Click.

She breathed a sigh of relief. She inserted the loose round into the magazine and then inserted the magazine into the grip. She felt clumsy handling the weapon and entirely unsure of her abilities, but decided a weapon was better than no weapon.

Next, she knew she needed a plan. The entire layout of the Russell Senate Office Building was an irregular, four-sided shape with a courtyard in the center. A long hallway stretched along all four sides of this building. The sound of the sniper came from down the hallway to the left of the office Charlotte occupied; that made sense to Charlotte because that was the direction of the rotunda, a large, circular, open area at the corner of the building. It would have 2nd story windows with a good view of the Capitol Building and surrounding roads and lawns. In short, it seemed like a good place for what she presumed was a sniper. To the right of the door, the hallway stretched to the other corner of the building, before continuing after a turn to the left.

She slowly opened the door and peered down the hallway to the left, then the right. To the right, at the end of the hallway, she could see movement; the hallways were darker than usual, but a figure could be seen at the corner of the hallway, silhouetted by the light coming in from the window. She ducked back into the room.

The figure was around 50 yards away; she hoped they had not spotted her. Charlotte considered her options. Fighting her way out of the building, either covertly or otherwise, was out of the question. Waiting and hiding in place carried its own risk, especially as these attackers became occupiers. She reminded herself that exiting the building was only half of the battle. She still would need to make it to safe territory, which could be as far as half a mile to a full mile to the northeast. Sneaking out of the building and across that distance outside would be nearly impossible, at least during the day.

Charlotte drew on her experience. She was a mere aide to Emily, but they both knew that Charlotte was a skilled strategist. She had always been one to think outside the box, and an idea suddenly sprang to mind. In her personal life, Charlotte had never been a risk-taker. Professionally, she allowed Emily to be the one taking those risks. But, for her plan to work, she would need to take what could be the biggest risk of her life.

Chapter Seventeen: Fury

David and Warren walked out of Trent's Sand & Gravel. It had been a productive meeting, and the owner had agreed to join the growing community based market. The gate to the property was closed when the two men had first arrived, but Trent had opened the gate upon their arrival. Their truck remained parked outside of this perimeter on the side of the road.

"I'm telling you, those trucks could come in handy to someone. Imagine you're a corn farmer trying to bring your harvest to a city, or maybe delivering a load of feed," said David, as they walked out the front door of the office.

"I hope we're not getting ahead of ourselves," said Warren.

"What do you mean?" asked David, taken aback by the doubt Warren expressed.

"I don't know. Can we really make this work? And what if-," Warren stopped mid-sentence.

"What if what?" asked David, looking down at the list as they walked to the gate.

"Do you see that?" asked Warren, in a hushed, intense tone.

David looked up. Warren had stopped and was looking beyond the gate and across the road. At first, David didn't see anything out of the ordinary. Then, he saw movement. A figure was running towards the road and in the direction of David and Warren. As the figure came into focus, David could see it was a man. He was wearing a t-shirt and sweatpants, did not have any socks on, and stumbled as he ran. David also noticed he kept looking over his shoulder as he ran in the direction of a large, steel-sided building that sat opposite Trent's Sand & Gravel. The man had not yet spotted David and Warren and continued to be fixated on the building that lay behind him.

Warren began walking again, this time more briskly than before.

"Stay low, David," said Warren.

The two reached the gate and slipped through the door on the side that the owner had left open for their visit. They stood behind Warren's truck, which mostly blocked them from his line of sight, but allowed them to continue watching the man. He had tripped, but recovered, and was now running again. David couldn't get over the fact that he wasn't wearing shoes, despite the time of year. He was running from something.

"Hey! Need some help?!" yelled David, as he stepped out from behind the truck.

The man looked at David. His face was at first filled with fear, but then showed a sense of relief. He began weakly jogging across the road. David started walking out to meet him.

"Thank you, thank you, thank you!" said the man.

"What happened to your shoes? What are you running from?" asked David, as the two men met in the middle of the road.

"Not now, we need to go," said the man.

He started jogging once more towards the truck, pulling David along with him. David grabbed his shoulder firmly and pulled him back.

"Hold on! Before we get in that truck, we need some answers."

"You don't understand, I-"

"David, get down!"

David instinctively ducked at the command and turned to look at Warren. His eyes were focused in the direction of the steel-sided building across the road. David spun his head around as he heard the crack of a gunshot. He had not seen who fired the shot in the split second he had been looking in that direction, and he ran for cover behind the pickup truck. When he arrived, he found Warren also taking cover, handgun already drawn.

"Who was that?!" asked David.

"I don't know, but I think they're after our new friend," replied Warren.

David realized he had let go of the man when he ducked, and subsequently left him out in the road. He peered out from behind the truck, looking around the tailgate area. The man was crouched in the road, with an arm bracing the right side of his chest. Further away, in front of the large building, was another figure that was wielding a rifle. He wasn't sure why, but the lone figure hadn't fired another round after the initial shot. In fact, it almost appeared that they were not aiming at the man, but actually manipulating the controls of the rifle. David knew they had to act.

"Warren, give me the keys."

Warren shot David a look of concern.

"Let's get out of here, David," replied Warren.

"He needs our help," said David, with urgency in his voice.

"Help!" said the man in the road, as if on cue.

Warren hesitated, then pulled the keys from his pocket.

"Stay behind cover, and help him in the back seat of the cab," ordered David.

David opened the passenger door, climbed in, quickly maneuvered himself over the center console and into the driver's seat. He started up the truck. He made a sharp, 180-degree turn that placed the truck in the road and shielded the man from the direction of the building. He didn't distract himself by looking at Warren and the man to his left; instead, he kept his eyes fixed on the building that was no more than 100 yards away. It was evident the lone figure was having difficulty with the rifle. David couldn't help but think that this was a gift from God, but it was not a gift he intended to squander. The door to the back seat in the cab opened. At the same time, the front door to the steel-sided building opened up. Two figures emerged, each holding rifles. The original shooter yelled something and gestured in the direction of the pickup truck.

"Warren, we have company!" shouted David, as the two figures raised their rifles in the direction of the truck.

The man, still able to stand, climbed up into the back row of seats and slid over to make room for Warren. Warren climbed up, using the step on the side of the truck. He closed his door as the shooting began.

"GO!" said Warren.

David could hear the crack of gunfire outside, muffled by the closed doors and windows of the truck. Suddenly, one of those windows shattered. As David smashed the gas pedal, he heard the metallic thuds of additional rounds striking the truck. Another round shattered the back window and left a hole in the front windshield, a hole that was surrounded by fragmented glass, though the front windshield remained otherwise intact.

"Warren, are you OK?" asked David once they were out of sight of the building.

"Yeah, I'm OK."

"What about him?" asked David.

The man tried to sit up but was in considerable pain. David adjusted the rearview mirror and could see he was bleeding profusely from his wound. Warren leaned over to assist, not taking the valuable time to reply to David's question. He saw Warren bend over, and emerge with a first aid kit. He had told David in the past that he kept these around, but David had no idea that he had kept one in the truck. He heard Warren unzipping the kit, which was contained in a large, fabric pouch. David had slowed to a more reasonable pace as he watched the scene in the back seat. Warren grabbed a pair of large scissors and began cutting away at the man's shirt around his shoulder. It revealed a large wound, 2 inches wide and 1 inch tall, just below the man's collarbone. Warren continued cutting and inspected the back of the shoulder.

"What's your name?" asked Warren, trying to distract the man from the intense pain and fear he was experiencing.

"They got my leg, too," said the man, in between strained breaths.

"Right through the door," said Warren, almost too quietly for David to hear.

David turned to look and could see a large, crimson spot on the man's grey sweatpants. Warren got to work again, this time pulling a tourniquet from the pack. The man was of little assistance in applying the band, and Warren had to lift his thigh to slip it around. He pulled it tight as the man screamed in pain.

"I know it's tight, but it'll slow the bleeding," said Warren.

David watched in the mirror as he went back to work on the wound in the top of the right side of his chest. He grabbed gauze and packed it around the front exit wound, which was the man's worst wound. He watched as Warren pulled a flat, clear, plastic square from a plastic package. He went to work, starting with the wound on the back of the chest that was out of sight of David. The man had leaned forward to allow this, but Warren had to push the man back into an upright seated position. His head flopped to the side as he sat up. The man's eyes were closed.

Warren looked forward as if hoping David was nearing a hospital. In reality, the two knew that there was no hospital near enough to help. The closest, in Columbus, had closed 2 days prior, according to a nurse's husband they had visited the day before. Warren, with a look of both desperation and resignation, went back to work, applying even more gauze to the gaping wound on the front. David watched as he checked the man's pulse at his wrist, and then put his ear in front of the man's mouth. Warren rested the man's head against the door, and looked forward, meeting David's eyes in the mirror. He shook his head, ever so slightly.

Warren, for all his know-how and experience, was at his core a gentle man. David could see tears begin to well up in his eyes, which brought David tears as well. David was in shock and was also deeply affected by the stranger's sudden, violent death. However, it was Warren's sorrow that brought David a sense of deep sadness that acknowledged the sacred nature of life. David drove the truck down the road, eventually looping back to his house. Not a word was spoken between the two along the way. The flow of blood onto the back seat came to a halt, but David's blood began to boil.

To the untrained eye, it would appear Perez had calmed down after her sustained outburst of anger. Two broken shelves, a shattered window, and a bloody fist later, Christie knew that the anger was far from quenched; she simply had gained her composure.

"Christie, start from the top again," said Perez.

"Look, I-"

"I've heard enough out of your mouth, Mitch," said Perez, cutting off Mitch mid-sentence.

She turned again to face Christie but kept her eyes on Mitch for an extra few seconds.

"I showed him the procedure for 3 of the cells, and we went to Kyle's last. I was there for the whole thing but walked away at the very end after we had left the room. I must have walked away, trusting he'd lock the door correctly," answered Christie.

She had no difficulty telling Perez this because it was the truth. What she didn't mention was that she had quickly looped back, unlocked the door, and left it slightly ajar, before again looping back, thus giving Mitch the impression that she hadn't set foot in the cell area again after initially leaving. In reality, if he had a better understanding of the layout of the compound, he would see that, based on the time they were separated and the distance she'd need to cover, it was a possibility that Christie had been responsible for allowing the man to escape. Of course, Christie had correctly guessed he would not make such a connection, let alone an accusation directed at her. Additionally, she knew that even if he were to make an accusation, Perez would be unlikely to side with Mitch, given his recent track record of what she viewed as a pattern of recklessness and carelessness. This latest perceived failure on the part of Mitch would be another addition to that track record.

"I'm telling you, I locked that door. I swear I did," pleaded Mitch.

"I don't care if you were tired from the lack of sleep, or if this is your first day here and you're learning the ropes, I expect professionalism and accountability, especially from someone that was a cell leader. You've shown yourself to be incapable of embodying those qualities," said Perez, holding back her anger as she stared down Mitch.

"I-"

"Heidi, take him to his room. We'll talk later, once I clean up this mess," replied Perez.

Mitch, with a sullen look on his face, followed the woman out of the room. After they had left, and the door was closed, Perez turned to Christie, the only other person that remained in the room.

"Perez, I take full responsibility for this. I should have verified that he locked the door. For that, I'm sorry," said Christie, doing her best to show humility in hopes of gaining Perez's favor.

"I know what you did," replied Perez.

"It's a mistake that I won't make again."

"No, Christie, I know what you did. It was no mistake. You intentionally unlocked that door. You wanted Kyle to escape from his cell, and you wanted to pin it on Mitch," said Perez.

Christie shook her head slightly. It was all she could do, unable to voice a response.

"I'm not upset."

"What?"

"It was a calculated risk you took. You knew the chance of him escaping successfully was slim, to none. You knew Heidi was on watch, and you knew she was an excellent shot," replied Perez.

Christie, first having been caught off guard by Perez knowing she was responsible for the failed escape attempt, was caught even more wrongfooted by the lack of admonishment.

"So, you're OK with this?" asked Christie.

"No. What you did was a calculated risk. Kyle died, but these hostages will have soon outlived their usefulness anyways, especially with how everything seems to be falling apart. It was a low-risk decision; he was unlikely to go through the door that led to the rest of the compound, and instead choose the door that leads to the side exit. You're thinking like I would have."

"I'm confused," said Christie.

"You asked if I'm OK with what you did. I'm not OK with you making a decision like that, without consulting me first. You're young, you're new here, you didn't train with the rest of us. If you want to be one of us, you can't be a lone wolf," said Perez, forming a welcoming smile that was unfamiliar to Christie. "Thank you for helping take care of Mitch. He's dead weight. The rest of his crew, they'll work out fine here, but there can't be any question about who's in charge."

Christie returned the smile.

"Now, do me a favor and get Heidi and Evan in here. I want to debrief those two. From what I could see, the shot she landed was a good one. I hope it was only Kyle's corpse that escaped, I don't want to have to deal with any loose ends, including whoever it was in that pickup truck that drove off," said Perez.

"Thank you, Perez," said Christie, as she walked out of the room.

Chapter Eighteen: Contingencies

"Stop! I said stop! Drop the phone, and put your hands up!"

Charlotte complied with the instructions, dropping the phone on the marble floor that she stood on. She didn't say a word as she raised her hands above her head. The man, with the rifle pointed in her direction, approached her with a confused expression on his face. As he neared her, she could see him transition to a more relaxed posture.

"What are you doing here?" he said, in a calmer tone than before.

"I'm sorry! I'm only here to take pictures and videos," replied Charlotte, in a pitiful tone.

"Who do you work for?" the man asked, suspicious of her motives.

"No one, I work alone. Well, I work for the Smithsonian as a tour guide, but I don't think they'll be opening up anytime soon!" said Charlotte, as she let out a nervous laugh.

"So, you're filming us for the Smithsonian?" asked the man.

"No, not really. I mean, I'd love it if my work made it in there one day! I'm trying to document what's going on here. This is historic, and I want to be the first to document it, and I want to get as close as possible to the action," said Charlotte.

She could tell he was buying the story. He lacked the more formal and authoritative nature of someone that had been in the military, at least as an officer. He acted as though he himself was unsure of his authority over the halls he now patrolled. She also reminded herself that the best and brightest of this group would be fighting or in charge. It was the people you didn't have confidence in either of those roles, that you assigned to guard an occupied piece of territory.

"Huh. Never thought about that. I guess this is historic. Still, you shouldn't be here."

"Wait, before we go, could you do me a favor? I have all this footage and what not, but I don't have a single account from a veteran from the Battle of D.C. Would you do the honors?" asked Charlotte.

The man gladly obliged, and the two went into a nearby office for the next 15 minutes for Charlotte to conduct her interview. It was entirely unnecessary, but Charlotte knew it would help sell the story of her identity to any other members of this group. As she had suspected, this man was not heavily involved in the actual battle. He was part of a reserve force, a reserve force that was now fighting the southwest, further along the National Mall, as the forces pushed across the Potomac towards the Pentagon. He evidently had been left behind. He didn't explain why that was the case, but Charlotte drew her own conclusion that either he was ill-trained, or else lacked the abilities to be trusted in such a role.

The man, whose name she learned was Richard, told of his own personal story over the past 2 weeks, including the imploding economy and the simultaneous societal collapse. Richard, a 33-year old TV repairman, had joined a group several years prior, a militia that he referred to as the KLG. The KLG was a smaller militia that had collaborated with many larger groups, including Libertas, the 1776ers, and other larger, nationwide militias that had seen their ranks swell in past years, and together had coordinated the attack on D.C. Charlotte was surprised by what appeared to be a sophisticated communication network and effective command structure, no doubt a result of the high ratio of current and former members of the military and law enforcement.

The operation, which had thus far been a wildly successful operation for the militias, had been planned to counter UWF elements in the area that many militia leaders suspected were working together with the U.S. military. In fact, Richard told of a command structure that was believed a vast majority of Congress and the White House were UWF and communist sympathizers. There were, however, some elements of the U.S. government that Richard referred to as "loyalists". These were members of congress and other officials that were loyal to the Constitution and the American people, according to his own definition and criteria of loyalty. He named a few members of congress, requiring Charlotte to suppress her disgust. Many of the individuals, who viewed themselves as champions of personal liberties and the Constitution, were longtime political enemies of Emily.

Richard finished by sharing some key details of the attack on the Capitol, including the use of a fuel tanker truck, infiltration via the underground D.C. Metro lines, and two smaller diversionary attacks on both Joint Base Andrews and nearby Fort Detrick in Maryland, in order to further stretch the limited resources of the U.S. government. Richard stated that, according to his leadership, much of the remaining U.S. forces on the D.C. side of the Potomac River were surrounded, and the rest were retreating across the river.

This gave Charlotte a more complete picture of the last 24 hours, but it also meant she was unlikely to locate friendly U.S forces on this side of the river. Her hope would have to rest in maintaining a low profile, or else the sanctuary of the locals.

"Richard, I really appreciate you taking the time to do this. This is a moment in history that will be remembered for generations to come, but you'll be the first to have given a first-hand account," said Charlotte, trying to find a balance in her tone without sounding too patronizing.

"Glad I could help," said Richard, as he stood from the table and gestured to the exit of the room.

"Say, would you be able to do me one more favor?" asked Charlotte.

"What's that?"

"I really would appreciate an escort out of harm's way."

"I just got off the phone with the State Patrol. They said they don't have the resources to deal with it right now and to report the crime to the local police department and deliver the body to the nearest morgue," said David.

David had already called the Columbus Police Department, who stated the crime occurred out of city limits and referred David to the Bartholomew County Sheriff's Office. They had been noncommittal to the emergency, stating that their drastically reduced police force was occupied by a half dozen other deaths, and countless other assaults, acts of arson, and theft. David was told that a unit would be dispatched within the next 24 hours. Dissatisfied with the long timeline, David hoped he would have better luck with the State Patrol, though they were evidently unable to assist any sooner than the Sheriff's Office.

Warren closed his eyes, as he thought hard about the situation. It was evident to David that his friend was deeply shaken by what had happened. His thoughts were undoubtedly clouded by the emotions of having a man die before your eyes in such an act of violence. It was a side of Warren that was unfamiliar to David, though he noted that Warren still retained the same gentleness and restraint that had marked his life as long as David had known him.

The two stood on the porch outside of Warren's house. The man lay on the cold wood of the porch, face up, with a sheet covering his entire body, with the exception of one arm that hung out to the side, leaving the hand, wrist, and half of the forearm exposed to the frosty air. David had told Alice what had happened and decided to bring the body to Warren's house so as to spare his daughters the trauma.

Warren opened his eyes and stared at the body that lay before him.

"Wait a second," said Warren.

He bent down and grasped the man's hand and wrist that extended out from under the sheet.

"David, what does this look like to you?" said Warren, holding up the hand.

"Hm. Looks like what they'd call ligature marks. From a rope, maybe? Or something similar." replied David.

Warren continued to examine the wrist, then pulled the other hand out. It contained identical red marks that wrapped around the wrist. To David, the marks looked as though the restraints used were either too tight, or else this man had been struggling against the restraints. Warren said nothing, as he pulled up the sheet, uncovering the man from his feet. David was puzzled. Warren then pulled up the man's blood-soaked shirt to the level of just below his shoulder.

"Warren, what are you-"

David's question was cut off by a disturbing answer. Besides the obvious gaping wound, the man's torso contained a myriad of wounds, all in different stages of healing. In some places, bruises could be seen. Along his left rib cage, there were wounds that David instantly recognized as being caused by hot iron.

"They branded him?" asked David rhetorically and with disgust.

Warren pulled down the shirt, and returned the sheet to its position over the corpse, this time taking care to also cover the hands and wrists.

"I've seen enough," said Warren.

"What do you think happened to him?"

"Something dark; something unspeakable. David, we can meet with the deputies tomorrow. Maybe, they'll have more information on what's going on. But, I have my doubts."

David slowly nodded, trying to comprehend what he meant.

"David, something evil is happening in that building, in our very own community. I don't know what, but I do know that it's time we come up with a contingency."

"What do you mean?"

A grim look formed on Warren's face. "You and I, we're in over our heads. It's time we get some help, and I'm not talking about the Sheriff."

Russel's sense of hopelessness and fear of an impending end to his captivity that would come by way of death loomed over his day. He had barely touched his breakfast, trying his very best to conceive a way out of this situation while also coming to terms with his own mortality. Escaping the house had seemed hopeless enough, especially if rescuing Kate was part of that plan. Now, in a new building with no sense of the routine, little knowledge of his captors, and an ever-shortening timeline, he felt that it was not so much a dead end, as it was a path that could not start in the first place.

Much like the house he had been in before, this building followed a schedule of regular checks on himself and other prisoners. The heightened state of fear and anxiety had briefly given way to sleep in the mid-morning, before being interrupted by one of these checks. He had been awoken by Mitch, who was accompanied by another woman. He was relieved that there was no torture session this morning, nor had there been one since he had arrived.

It was about 15 minutes later that he heard the gunshots. The first gunshot sent a chill down his spine. He imagined the captors going room to room, delivering a fatal gunshot to the heads of the undetermined number of hostages. The rapid succession of shots that fired put these fears to rest, especially once he realized they sounded as though they were exterior to the building.

Russel couldn't help but get the sense that trouble followed him everywhere he went. First, there was the gunfight on the first floor of the house. It was hard for him to realize that those events, including leaving that house, had taken place barely 24 hours ago. In less than 12 hours at this new building, he was already hearing gunshots, gunshots that he hoped were simply routine target practice, though part of him knew that was not the case. Additionally, he reminded himself, he was unfortunate enough to have been targeted to be abducted in the first place.

He had not been visited since the gunshots occurred. He had no exterior window in this room, but his internal clock told him that this was well past his usual lunchtime, not that he was overly hungry. He walked about his room. He knew it was cliché, but when working for his financial firm, he often did his best thinking while walking, whether it was a long walk outside, or within his own office.

He paused as he heard footsteps approach down the hall. He heard two female voices conversing. He couldn't make out the words initially, but it became clearer as he put his ear to the minuscule space between the door and the frame.

"I wouldn't be surprised if Perez put him out of his misery. We did fine before he was here, and we'll do fine without him."

Russel again felt a wave of doom sweep over his mind at these words.

The other voice responded, "I would do it for her, but I know that the rest of his crew wouldn't put up with that. I don't know, maybe we ship him off to some other compound, make him someone else's problem."

Russel breathed a sigh of relief at this, realizing that they must be referring to Mitch or someone in his group. He had caught a whiff of this animosity when they had first arrived but was unsure why it had seemed to grow since the early hours of the morning.

"I wonder who it was that picked up Kyle," said the first voice.

The two had been walking closer to Russel's room but had now seemed to stop walking.

"Who knows. I'm not too worried about it. I put a round through his chest; I could see blood pool on his shirt almost right away. I'm still pissed my gun jammed so I couldn't take out the other two," said the first voice.

"Those two guys said they put a dozen rounds into the truck, maybe they got them."

The voices paused and shared a laugh.

"Somehow, I doubt that," said the first voice, laughing.

"I'm not gonna lie, I was hoping to put Kyle out of his misery myself," said the other woman.

"A couple more days, and I would have been fighting you for that privilege."

The footsteps resumed, walking away from Russel's door. He heard a lock on another door open, though it was some distance from his own. Muffled voices, quieted by the distance, proceeded. He stepped away from the door; he didn't want to bring any undue suspicion or discipline on himself, were he to be caught eavesdropping.

Russel replayed the conversation in his head. It answered the question of the gunfire from earlier in the day. That, however, was not what caught Russel's attention.

A couple more days and I would have been fighting you for that privilege.

What did that mean? Was Russel jumping to conclusions by assuming it referenced his own expiration date? Or had he just discovered the timeline for his own demise? It was a possibility that he had been forced to come to terms with. Russel took a deep breath and confronted the fear that sat in front of him. He knew his death was likely, but Russel resolved that it was a death that would occur on his terms.

Chapter Nineteen: Familiar

After a brief moment of consideration, Richard had gladly agreed to escort Charlotte a short distance behind the active forces in the region of the Capitol Building and National Mall. Charlotte requested to be brought to the northeast, though she was informed that no other direction was feasible. Much of the staging for the sizable attack force was to the east. Union Station, a key military objective despite the loss of power, was to the north, and fighting continued in every other direction.

Charlotte walked alongside Richard down the sidewalk, not far from the Russell Senate Office Building. She could see the now captured Capitol Police Headquarters that had been given up to the crowds hours prior to the actual assault, in hopes of appeasing the masses and concentrating friendly forces. Charlotte considered walking with her phone out, pretending to document the scores of militia members around her, but decided against it, in hopes of not drawing attention to herself.

Charlotte was surprised to see a man in a suit, walking alongside a pair of militia members donned in drab colors and bulletproof vests and wielding rifles. He walked with the confidence of a comrade, not a captive. The group was walking on the opposite side of the street and in the opposite direction. As they neared, she kept her eyes on the man in the center, but his face was obscured as he talked to the man on his right.

As he turned his head to his left, a shiver went down Charlotte's spine. She recognized the man. His name was Edward Mills. Edward was a former congressional aide that worked as a lobbyist for the past several years. The two rarely conversed anymore; he worked for the interests of select corporations and generally catered to the members of Congress on the opposite side of the aisle. In fact, she despised the man, and he had regularly made it clear that he reciprocated those feelings towards both Charlotte and Emily.

As Edward turned his head and glanced across the street, his eyes locked on her eyes. What had been a smiling face as he conversed with the men beside him, turned into a face that, at first, displayed confusion. Charlotte imagined that, despite the fact they were in the same area they regularly worked, the sensation they both felt was that of a person meeting a friend or acquaintance, by pure chance, when traveling halfway across the world. The confusion on his face quickly turned to a scowl, as he turned and began to walk briskly in the direction of Charlotte.

"Richard, what is that over there?" said Charlotte, pointing across the road, though not in the exact direction of Edward.

"What's what?" replied Richard, as he looked in vain for whatever Charlotte was referencing.

In an instant, Charlotte broke off to the right and climbed over a short fence that bordered a parking lot full of abandoned vehicles, taking advantage of the short-lived and improvised distraction.

"Hey! Stop her!" shouted Edward, as she began to weave between vehicles in the lot.

She could hear Richard briefly protest Edward's demand before his voice was out of earshot. Edward's shouts, however, continued. She found cover behind some vehicles that stood at least 6 feet high but didn't stop running. As the shouts continued, she could spot several other men near the Capitol Police Headquarters begin running in her direction. She weaved through the parking lot and sprinted across a nearby street. Briefly glancing back, she could see the militia members were still in hot pursuit.

She ran to the front of a church whose entrance was opposite the parking lot, but decided against attempting to hide inside, and instead turned the corner to the left, and continued down the sidewalk. A long sidewalk stretched in front of her as she ran. For a brief moment, Charlotte was out of sight of her pursuers, but would quickly be spotted once more when they rounded the corner. To her left was an open gate and a path that led behind the church. Without hesitation, she took the path.

Charlotte's lungs burned with the sudden exertion and the chilly winter air. She pushed through this, fueled by adrenaline and an understanding that she needed to run until she knew she was safe to stop. Partway down the path, she spotted a wooden fence. With all of her might, she pulled herself over the fence. Surprised by her sudden feat of strength, she did not anticipate the descent. She landed hard on her feet before tumbling forward and breaking her fall with her arms. Her hands stung from the impact on the cold pavement. She paused for a moment, recovering from the fall and listening for the pursuit of the men.

She heard nothing. Charlotte was thankful for the heavy foot traffic that accompanied the urban warfare that had scarred this part of the city in the past 12 hours. It made her own footprints in the slushy snow simply another pair of ill-defined footprints. On her side of the fence was a small alley that served as the home for a number of dumpsters and a row of cars. The alley extended across the street, leading to what appeared to be a small parking lot. Charlotte crouched, with the fence on one side, and the back of a car on the other side, concealing herself from the road. She heard running footsteps and hid herself entirely behind the car, as one of the militia members ran down the street.

She breathed deeply, taking care to not make too much noise. She heard more footsteps, this time on the other side of the fence. One of the militia members evidently had decided to investigate behind the church. She held her breath. A pair of hands grasped the top of the fence. Charlotte scrambled from where she crouched and maneuvered to the side of the car, placing herself between the car and the nearby multi-story residential building. The cover was less than ideal, but it was the best she could do, given the few seconds she had to find concealment.

Her body begged for oxygen, but she did her best to keep her breaths shallow and infrequent. She could not see the man but heard him walking in the direction of the car. She faced the car but didn't dare try and sneak a glance at the man. Charlotte was about to be discovered. She knew that her attempts would end in vain, and she would be treated to fate as terrible as those members of Congress boarding the helicopter that had been gunned down in an instant.

The man's steps neared the car. Charlotte was frozen in fear, knowing escape was futile at this point. Suddenly, she heard a noise behind her. Another set of footprints were closing in on her from behind, and this second person had undoubtedly already spotted her. Charlotte held her breath in fearful anticipation and turned to face her approaching demise.

Chapter Twenty: Help

"Mason, I'm not asking that you solve this problem for us. All I'm asking is that you take this into consideration. That man, I don't care what happened to him, he didn't deserve what happened to him. Normal people, they go to the authorities when trouble comes their way, whether that's the police or people like yourself. They were hiding that man, and I've got a bad feeling they're hiding a lot more in that building," said Warren, with passion in his voice.

"Hmm," said Mason Jennings, as he rubbed his rugged, auburn beard and considered the matter.

After telling a brief synopsis of their story over the phone, no persuasion had been necessary to convince Mason Jennings to meet with David and Warren. He had, however, requested they meet at a neutral location of his choosing, in this case, the parking lot of a car repair shop that had been abandoned a number of years prior. He also requested they bring the body along for proof of their claims.

Mason, the local leader of Libertas for the surrounding half-dozen counties, was a man no older than 30. He carried with him an aura of authority and confidence, though still managed to retain the amiability of a Midwesterner. David wondered to himself whether Mason was a veteran of the military, but was unsure. Beside him, stood another man and woman that he had introduced as the head of Libertas in Bartholomew County. David recognized their faces, but couldn't recall their names. He continued to be surprised at their level of organization and the number of individuals that were affiliated with the militia in the surrounding towns and countryside.

Mason had been clear from the beginning that his interests corresponded with those of Libertas. Their interests, he explained, included the well-being of the communities they served. But, the safety of his own men and women and their families, as well as the restoration and preservation of constitutional rule of law, were among Libertas' highest priorities.

"And you said that you already got ahold of the sheriff?" replied Mason.

"Yeah. He said they would come to check out the body and talk to us, probably sometime tomorrow," answered David.

"As far as the sheriff and the local police are concerned, this meeting right here never took place. I don't want to butt heads with them, and helping out with this, well, they might not agree with our methods."

"So you'll help us?" replied Warren.

Mason looked at the man and woman that stood beside him. They returned looks of subdued approval.

"Maybe. I'm going to have a few of my people recon the place. You know, drive by, maybe fly a drone overhead to get a feel for what's going on. I agree with you. If there's something unsavory happening on that property, I want to get rid of it. I don't care if it's the drug trade, human trafficking, or even just some idiots from one of those big cities that decided to hole up in that place, I want them out."

David could see a small smile form on Warren's face.

"Like I said though, we're not going to knock on their door and ask them to come out. That's how the sheriff might do things, but I'm not about my guys being in that kind of a situation. We go with a clear objective of eliminating any threats. And, that's if we decide to go ahead with this."

"How do we know if-"

"I have your number, I'll let you know. Meet with whoever comes from the sheriff's department. Tell them what happened. They don't have the men and women to spare on something as risky as this, especially with how they do things."

"Look, we really appreciate this," said David.

"One more thing," said Mason, talking past David's thanks. "With you bringing this to us, we expect some skin in the game."

"What do you mean by that?" asked Warren.

"The both of you, you'll be helping out with this operation if we go ahead with it. Now, I'm not stupid. I won't make you rush through any doors. Unless you've had training like my own people, you'd probably end up getting yourselves killed, and some of my own men and women too. But, I see you're both carrying a sidearm."

David and Warren looked at each other, surprised by the comment. They did both have a handgun; Warren had loaned an additional handgun to David following their rescue of the escaped prisoner, but they had been careful to conceal them in their waistband and out of sight.

"I hope you know how to use those. And if you do, I hope you know how to use a rifle as well."

The two returned a nod.

"Good. You'll both be coming along."

"Here you go. I wish I could get you something hot, but, well, I'm sure you know why that's a problem right now."

Charlotte accepted the bowl of cereal and milk and began eating as she spoke between bites, mouth still full of food. She didn't realize how hungry she had been until he had offered her food.

"Thank you. I can't tell you how thankful I am," said Charlotte, taking a break for another bite.

The man sat opposite Charlotte and watched her eat with a smile on his face.

"You never answered my question. Why'd you do it?" asked Charlotte.

"You know, I've been thinking about that too. The last few days, I've been asking myself why I hadn't left yet. Everyone else in this building either left days ago or scattered as soon as the shooting started. I thought about doing the same. If I could get over to Virginia, I have a few family members that live over there that would have let me stay with them. Still, something kept me here. Something inside me told me that I had to stay.

"Honestly, I was terrified for a while. I watched dozens of armed men and women stream past the building heading for the Capitol, just minutes before it all started. And the shooting, well, that's still going on. For a while, it was right outside the building. At least, that's what it sounded like. I've lived here for 2 years. I thought this was as close as it gets to the center of democracy and civility. But to see this, it's unreal. It's like I'm living in some kind of a movie. Probably sort of like how people felt in New York City on 9/11, or do you remember how weird it felt at the beginning of the COVID pandemic before anyone was sure what was going on?" asked the young man rhetorically, as he ran his hand through his hair and stared off into the distance as if he was rewatching the events of the past few days.

Charlotte watched him talk, having already nearly finished the bowl of cereal. He was a young man, college-aged, guessed Charlotte. He was talking rapidly, and fidgeted some as he spoke, though now seemed distracted by his own thoughts.

He turned to Charlotte again. "You know, I probably saved your life out there, telling that guy that I saw you running down the street. The least you could do is tell me your name."

"Charlotte."

"Charlotte? Nice to meet you, I'm Virat. It's Indian if you couldn't tell," said Virat in a decidedly American accent as he gestured to his complexion. "Most people just call me Vir, if that's easier for you."

"Nice to meet you, Vir."

Charlotte leaned back in her seat, and the two sat for a moment in a prolonged, awkward silence.

"So, what do we do now?"

"What do you mean?" asked Charlotte.

"I don't know. I feel like I was meant to stay here for some reason, and that reason must have been to help you. But, now I've helped you, so there must be something else we need to do. Sorry, I don't mean to say we, maybe you have somewhere you need to go, or maybe you don't want to stay, which is fine, it's just that-"

"Mind if I hang out here for a bit?" said Charlotte, with a smile on her face in an attempt to ease his nervousness.

"Yeah, that's fine too! You can crash on the couch if you'd like. Plenty of food in the cabinets. Sort of. I haven't gone shopping in a while. Still lots of cereal, but I think that was the last of the milk."

"Vir, relax. I owe you one, and I won't forget that. I'll try and be the best guest I can be."

He smiled, as he took her bowl from the table to bring it to the kitchen sink.

"I've gotta ask, Vir. You're young, how in the world can you afford a place like this? Make it big buying one of those cryptocurrencies? Maybe a famous, what do they call them, influencer, on some social media platform?" asked Charlotte, trying to lighten the mood.

He finished bringing the bowl to the sink and returned to the table.

"No. I'm a college student, actually. At Georgetown."

Charlotte returned a puzzled look, knowing that this made his ability to afford such a location, only blocks from the Capitol Building, even more unlikely.

Vir looked down at the table. "I guess you could say that I'm one of those rich kids. My father started as a software engineer, and started his own company based around a product he created, that he sold for, well, a lot of money."

"Where do your parents live?" asked Charlotte.

"Out west, in California."

"Have you been able to-"

"Talk to them? Until a few days ago, I could. My phone still works, even with the power out, but they aren't answering anymore. Not returning my texts, either," said Vir, somberly.

"Maybe they lost power, and their phones aren't working."

"Yeah, maybe. I don't know, I've been reading whatever news stories they're still publishing online. They live outside of San Fran. It's... It's not a good place to be right now."

Another long silence filled the room. Distant, sporadic gunfire could still be heard.

"What are you going to college for?" asked Charlotte, trying to change the subject.

"I thought it was the right choice at the time. Better to go to college, and make a name for myself, than live off a trust fund for the rest of my life," said Vir, still sounding distant. "Wait, you mean what I go to college for." Vir smiled at himself. "I want to be a doctor, a cardiologist, actually. I was planning on applying for med school within a month or two from now. Then again, maybe I'll take a gap year before med school."

The two chuckled at the joke that made light of the way in which the world had fallen apart lately.

"Why a cardiologist?" asked Charlotte.

"I'm not sure, actually. People ask me that all the time. Sometimes I tell them it's because I want to help people, which isn't a lie. I like the idea of helping people. Other times, I tell them it's because I like the challenge. Also, not a lie. But to be honest, it's sort of something that felt right. I mean, at this point, I could easily change my mind and become some other kind of MD. Maybe I won't make the cut, and I'll have to settle for being a family doc, or something like that. Not that there's anything wrong with that, but I would feel like I'm settling, I guess."

Charlotte nodded, rubbing her face and yawning simultaneously, something that Vir noticed.

Charlotte smiled a weary smile. "Sorry, I'm not bored, I just didn't get much sleep last night."

"Y'know, you never told what it was you were doing down here, and what you did to get the attention of those militia members."

Charlotte took her turn looking off into the distance. "Where do I begin?"

"I don't like it, David."

"I don't like it either, Alice. There's part of me that wishes I could look the other way and pretend we never had seen a thing."

Alice furrowed her brow.

"I know you're not that kind of man."

David pulled her closer into his arms, as they stood beside the kitchen counter.

"Alice, I promise you that I will be safe. Mason said himself that they don't want me killed. They're only having Warren and I drive the vehicles down the road a bit, and then not get any closer than a few hundred yards."

"Unless you need to," said Alice, finishing the thought.

"Well, yes. But they're practically professionals. They'll have the element of surprise."

"I'm not changing your mind, am I?" said Alice, with a thin smile.

David sighed, returning the smile. "I suppose not. To be honest, I want to get this over with and put it behind us. I mean, I'm falling behind on my to-do list for the farm. We're all adjusting to this new life, now without electricity most of the time. That's what I want to focus on. I know I'm not some kind of special forces operative, saving the world one bullet at a time."

"Believe me, I know you're not. I haven't forgotten the time you tried fighting that guy at that bar, all those years ago," said Alice, with a broadening smile.

She had recalled a time, years ago, when David was soundly beaten in a brief and altogether one-sided fight. It had been an attempt by David to stand up for Alice, though they had only recently met at the time.

"Hey, just don't forget that me losing that fight was what won you over."

"It was cute how brave you were, even if you couldn't fight," said Alice.

"I'm not a fighter. Neither is Warren. If I have it my way, I won't have to pull the trigger on that rifle tomorrow night," replied David in a more serious tone, gesturing to the closet that contained the rifle.

Alice didn't have words to reply at the thought of David in harm's way and instead laid her head on his shoulder. David meant every word he said. He didn't want to get hurt, or worse, over something like this. He knew he wasn't a fighter, even if his aim with his rifle had improved; the false alarm the other day with the Libertas members had been a stark reminder that he was mentally unprepared for a life or death situation. For that reason, he was dedicated to keeping his word that he would be as removed as possible from any possible confrontation. Alice and the girls were depending on him.

"When I saw him, it was like my heart stopped. Then, he looked at me, and I knew immediately that he recognized me. So, I took off running. I didn't want to wait and find out what they were going to do to me, someone from the other side of the aisle. That led me to right outside here," said Charlotte, gesturing to the front door of his apartment.

"Charlotte, you're kind of a badass," said Vir.

139

He had scarcely said a word for the last ten minutes as she recounted her experiences over the last 24 hours. As Charlotte reflected on what had transpired, she found herself still in shock of all that had happened in less than a day's time.

"So, wait, you said you were able to get ahold of Emily, the senator. And you charged your phone before sneaking out of that place. Have you texted her yet? Maybe time to give her a call?"

"No, I guess I haven't talked to her yet," said Charlotte, as she shook her head.

The thought had crossed her mind, but she had decided against it. Why she decided against it, was another question altogether. She understood Emily's inability to help her when she was in the senate building; the seemingly false empathy that was transmitted through the text messages stung, but Charlotte was accustomed to this behavior. She knew that Emily, like so many powerful and successful individuals, often had difficulty themselves in discerning between genuine and half-hearted emotions towards others, especially their subordinates.

This, however, was not the reason she had not yet contacted Emily. No, it was something else altogether. Part of her had begun to resent Emily; in truth, she had begun to resent herself. In her time under that desk, the same desk she had worked at for years, she had been given time to reflect on what had become of the country. Once the fear of death or capture had at least partially subsided, she once again found herself trying to come to terms with the role she played in a series of events that had entirely spiraled out of control. For some time, she tried to rationalize the goals of her own party and the clandestine plans of the UWF. At other times, she tried to shift her own guilt onto Emily. Evidently, her conscience was not satisfied by these solutions to her culpability.

"Charlotte."

Charlotte blinked a few times and looked up at Vir.

"You OK?" asked Vir.

"Yeah, sorry. Were you asking me something?"

"Oh, nothing. I was just asking if you had any idea what set this all off. I mean, it's like one day there's a market crash, and the next day, everyone went crazy," remarked Vir, unknowingly prodding Charlotte as she ruminated on her growing sense of guilt.

"Good question," said Charlotte, shutting down such thoughts. "Vir, I hope I'm not imposing on staying here tonight."

"No, not at all! To be honest, I was getting kind of lonely."

Charlotte smiled but was interrupted before she could say any more.

"And I don't mean that in a creepy way. I just mean that it's been a while since I've talked to anyone, besides my parents. And that goes for before all this started," said Vir, with a nervous smile. "I'll grab a blanket for you; you can take the couch if you'd like."

"That'd be great," said Charlotte as Vir walked out of the room and down a short hallway.

Emily's way of seeing others as nothing more than an asset or an enemy had rubbed off on Charlotte, and she found herself at first seeing Vir as nothing more than a useful character in her own story of overcoming the odds and escaping from an ending that would undoubtedly be unpleasant. However, she had begun to see him as more than that. His transparency was disarming and his authenticity was refreshing. Maybe, she thought, it was nothing more than the lack of sleep and considerable stress she had experienced. A separate part of her desired to revolt against what she had become.

"This is the best I could do," said Vir, reemerging with arms full with a thick blanket and a pair of pillows.

"I think that will be just fine," said Charlotte, grabbing the blanket from his arms and spreading it on the couch.

"It got chilly last night with the power out," warned Vir, as he turned to walk back to his bedroom.

"Hey Vir?" called Charlotte.

"Yeah?"

"Thank you."

Chapter Twenty One: Warnings

Christie had been hiding her fatigue from the 36 hours she had gone without sleep; not only did she not want to show weakness, but also knew that there were many others in the compound that also had gone without sleep the night prior. As she woke up in the morning, it was as if she had just fallen asleep. The night had flown by, with only fleeting, vague dreams, and no recollection of having woken up at any point in the night. Feeling well-rested, she still carried some grogginess with her as she went to the early morning meeting, a meeting that overlapped the sleep schedules of those that were awake during the day and those that were awake at night.

Christie arrived as several others were filtering into the meeting room. As was usually the case, Perez stood at the front of the room. She was the type to have woken up several hours earlier than necessary, and it showed. Many of those present were yawning, and only those that were finishing their overnight shift appeared amenable to conversation. Christie was still relatively new to the highly structured schedule of this compound but had learned that the original members of this group had lived at this compound for several weeks prior to their first assignment, which consisted of the abduction of the two financial executives. They had been given time to rehearse and learn their responsibilities, both in relation to the mission and in maintaining security and order in the compound. Christie had not been afforded this advantage but was pleased with how well she was integrating into the group of women. She already felt a sense of belonging, at least among Perez and her group.

"Alright everyone, take a seat," said Perez.

The door closed behind the last to enter, and each person found a seat. Christie was surprised to see Mitch present at the meeting.

"Yesterday was a long day. The good news is that we have one less mouth to feed."

This elicited a few chuckles from those that were more awake and alert at the early hour.

"The bad news is that we have a bit of a loose end from the incident yesterday. As of this hour, we have no information on where Kyle Leland's body is at this time. I've checked the spot outside myself. We can thank Heidi for a well-placed shot; with how much blood he lost in a matter of seconds, I doubt he lasted long. Still, it's not clear if he

Matthew J O'Connor

was able to tell any meaningful information to the two men in the truck. We need to work on the assumption that at least some information was shared with them. Additionally, the man that works across the road at the gravel pit is not there today; we need to assume he witnessed the incident as well. Both of these possibilities constitute a compromise of our location, identity, and other key details, but they do not constitute an immediate security threat."

Christie hadn't considered this possibility. Her unease appeared to be shared by others in the room. The grogginess of those beginning their day and those ending their night had been suddenly replaced with attentiveness.

"I think we should consider ourselves compromised at this time. I've forwarded this up the chain; they have not made a decision as of yet, but I do anticipate phase one of our operation will be wrapping up shortly, with the added complication that we will need to relocate in the near future."

Perez paused, allowing the statement to sink in. Phase one referred to the psychological warfare operation that consisted of a wide array of actions, though the most pertinent part to this compound was the hostage-taking and torture that Perez and Mitch's groups had participated in. For other cells, it consisted of fomenting civil unrest, sabotage, intelligence gathering, and a host of other missions.

"Until that time comes, there will be a few changes to procedure around here. First, with the new additions here from Wisconsin, we will be doubling the amount of security around the clock, both inside the building and watching the perimeter. Second, I'll be briefing each of you individually on your role should we need to pack up and go. I want to be able to leave at a moment's notice. Finally, we'll be reviewing security in the cell block following the breach in protocol yesterday."

Perez's gaze met Mitch's eyes as she said this. He avoided eye contact, but his discomfort was evident.

"You're dismissed," said Perez, concluding the meeting.

Chris gasped as he opened his eyes. His dream, a dark and confusing place, gave way to the sunny world that lay beyond the car that had served as his bedroom for the night. He realized that a hand tugging on his shoulder was what had awoken him.

"Chris, wake up," said Dana in a rough voice that matched the fact that she had recently woken up as well.

A laptop sat on her lap with the screen on. Unlike his own seat, her seat was no longer in the reclined position and was also free of blankets; he was still bundled within them. The windows were wet on the inside from hours of humid breath through the night, though the condensation had turned to frost in the corners of the windows. Chris sat up in his chair and rubbed his face, trying to usher in wakefulness.

"What is it?" asked Chris.

"We have a response from the team working on that location data."

"And?"

"It looks promising. Check this out."

143

Dana opened a window on her laptop screen. It displayed a map made up of satellite pictures, similar to the one they had used to locate the first hideout Mitchell Jenkins had utilized. In the middle of the screen was a red pin, signifying the GPS coordinates that had been entered into the system. Dana zoomed in on the target, showing an aerial view of a large building.

"I looked into it, it sounds like this place has been abandoned for a few years."

"Where is it?" asked Chris.

"Columbus."

"Ohio?"

"Indiana, actually," replied Dana.

"Hm. I'm not familiar. How far out is it?"

"3 or 4 hours if we're going to avoid Indianapolis and some of the other big cities."

"So, what's the deal? I assume we won't be mopping up. It's only our job to find them, right?" asked Chris.

"Right. I've communicated this to the Bureau and the State Patrol, without responses from either. But, it's early in the morning, and we have plenty of time for them to get back to us."

Chris grew weary at the thought of another few hours of driving. His body ached from the uncomfortable positions forced on him by the chair that reclined but did not go entirely flat. His mind was drained by the constant stress. Still, he was grateful that Dana had offered to drive the next leg of the trip.

Appearing to see the weariness, Dana offered encouragement. "Chris, we almost got them last time. They won't get away this time around."

Chris pulled the blankets off himself, throwing them on the floor of the back of the car. He took the laptop from Dana, placing it on his own lap.

"Alright," said Chris as he yawned. "Let's do this."

Dana grinned as she inserted the keys into the ignition.

"Hey, Dana?" asked Chris

"Yeah?"

"I know it's the end of the world as we know it and all that, but do you think we could find somewhere to get some coffee? Or else, I'll be showing up to Mitchell Jenkins' place and asking him myself."

Charlotte surprised herself by sleeping in far later than she had in a number of years. It was the knocking on the door to Vir's apartment that had pulled her from her slumber. She heard Vir talking to someone on the other side of the threshold, before hearing the door close.

"Rise and shine," said Vir as he returned from the doorway and into the living room.

Charlotte could see he was already dressed for the day and appearing as alert as Charlotte generally would be at this hour.

"Who was that at the door?" asked Charlotte, skipping any morning pleasantries.

"That was a militia member," said Vir, with a smile on his face.

144

"A what? What did he want?" asked Charlotte, as she sat up on the couch.

"Supplies. He didn't really say what supplies. He was checking to see if the other apartments are occupied."

"Vir, what if he saw me?!" exclaimed Charlotte, standing up from the couch in exasperation.

"I wasn't going to not answer the door. He might have kicked it down if he thought no one was home. Besides, even if he did come in, it's not like your face is on the side of milk cartons. He would've just thought you were my girlfriend or something."

Charlotte returned a look of frustration.

"No, I didn't mean it like that, I-"

"It's fine, Vir. I know you didn't mean it like that," replied Charlotte, in a less harsh tone.

"Don't you think we'll be safe here?" asked Vir.

"I don't know, Vir. I don't think much of the political class or other wealthier residents are still here in D.C. Most of them left days ago. The police and military are gone from this side of the river. That leaves the militias, maybe on both sides, and a city of a few million that are running out of food and water, and now without power in the middle of winter."

Vir nodded. Charlotte could tell by his expression that this was not something he had fully considered. A look of worry overtook his face. Charlotte sympathized with Vir and felt her previous frustration subside.

"Do you think we should leave?" said Vir, with apprehension in his voice.

"Vir, you told me yesterday that you stayed when everyone else in the building left because there was something inside of you that told you to stay."

"Yeah, maybe. Or, maybe I was too worried to leave."

"I don't think so, Vir. You saved my life. Those things don't happen for no reason other than pure chance."

Charlotte could see his expression change at this. She wasn't sure she believed what she was saying; part of her wondered if she was lying to Vir and herself and that this was nothing more than the manipulation she had become so skilled in while working for Emily. What she did know is that she had already made the decision for herself. She needed to leave. Part of her cared for Vir as another human being in harm's way. Another part of her knew she might have a better time escaping The Beltway to the west if he was with her.

"I don't know, Charlotte."

"You're worried."

"Paralyzed, is more like it," said Vir, looking down.

Charlotte had noticed from the beginning that Vir was a nervous person. This description of himself, of being paralyzed by his own fear, was consistent with his earlier behavior. Whether it was the tense way in which he talked or his frequent concern that he had somehow offended Charlotte, she saw a pattern of behavior that told the story of a young man plagued by some unknown fear or doubt.

Charlotte spent the next several minutes trying to empathize with Vir. She had little to no experience with such counseling and had never personally experienced anxiety to as great of an extent as Vir. However, she did her best to relate her experience in the Russell

Senate Office Building to Vir's current fears. In her eyes, it was a stretch. Nearly any person unaccustomed to such experiences would have been afraid in her situation. She recalled vividly her sensation of being paralyzed by fear while concealing herself under the desk. She concluded by explaining that it was rational decision making and the courage to act that had ultimately allowed for her to escape from the building. Vir did not speak for the entirety of this time, as he stared off in the distance, though Charlotte knew he was listening to every word she spoke.

"Can I tell you something personal, Charlotte?" said Vir as he moved aside the blanket on the couch and sat down.

"Of course, Vir," replied Charlotte, sitting next to him on the couch.

"I haven't left this apartment since before Christmas. After the stress of final exams, the whole semester, actually, I couldn't take it anymore. I ordered all of my groceries to be delivered here. I was planning to go out west to see my parents over the holidays but told them I had an important project I was working on that I needed to finish over the winter break. Classes started a week before all of this started, but-"

"You didn't go?" interrupted Charlotte.

Vir nodded, staring at the floor. She clasped his nearest hand between her own two hands. Vir looked into Charlotte's eyes and returned the warm smile she was sending in his direction. The two sat beside each other in silence for a long moment. It was not romanticism that Charlotte was trying to convey in the gesture, and she was confident Vir perceived this. Instead, it was simply the love between two fellow humans, both placed in an extraordinarily difficult situation, with Charlotte helping Vir as best she could to take the next step. However, she found herself less concerned about that next step. No doubt, she still knew leaving the city should and would continue to be a high priority. However, at that moment, it was Vir that was the highest priority. The young man, 10 years her junior, needed her at that moment. Just as he had been at the entrance to the building at the perfect time to misdirect the militia member and save Charlotte from an unspeakable fate, Charlotte was seated on a couch beside Vir, to help him out of a dark place that rivaled the desk she had been under only 24 hours prior. She could see a lone tear roll down his cheek. To her surprise, she felt another tear escape her own eye.

Chapter Twenty Two: Preparation

The barn that David and Warren stood inside of was a familiar sight to David. He had often driven down this road, always passing the barn that was painted in the ubiquitous red color. In many ways, the design of the barn, which was constructed at least 50 years prior, was outdated. The wooden structures had slowly given way to their metal counterparts, constructed from steel members and covered with sheet metal, as had been the case with both Warren and David's farms. However, barns such as this prairie style barn, with a round, arching roof, were still common throughout the midwest, and they still were serviceable for holding smaller numbers of animals than the larger farms owned, could store hay within the hayloft and made for a handy space for other tools and machinery, such as a tractor or ATVs. In other cases, they had been repurposed into bed and breakfasts, restaurants, venues to house weddings, and other creative ideas pioneered out of either convenience or else with an intention to preserve the endangered species of the American Barn.

Despite the antiquated appearance, David had discovered that this barn, like so many others, had also been repurposed. The interior had been updated considerably, with a significant amount of work done to preserve or replace any aging pieces of lumber. It no longer served as a barn in the traditional sense, instead serving as an armory of sorts for Libertas. On the ground level was a veritable stockpile of everything a moderately sized militia would need to operate. The firearms and ammo, which were at the far end of the bottom level, caught David's eye initially. However, he quickly realized that the armament was only a small portion of what had been purchased and stored over the years.

One side of the barn was entirely dedicated to food, with shelf after shelf of canned goods, large, airtight plastic containers labeled according to their contents, and dozens of large buckets of self-described survival food. Also in plain sight were a bank of handheld radios, multiple jugs of motor oil, at least 20 pairs of boots, drab-colored fatigues, and much more. David had only begun to peruse the stockpile when Mason Jennings, local leader of Libertas, entered through the side door of the barn.

"David, Warren, follow me," said Mason, gesturing to a staircase that had also been added to the interior of the barn, opposite the ladder that had originally been the only means of accessing the second floor.

David had seen several other Libertas members, including the two that had escorted him into the barn from the perimeter of the property, a perimeter which was defended by at least a few militia members that David could see, and potentially more that had intentionally made themselves difficult to spot. David and Warren followed Mason up the stairs. The second level of the barn was spacious, with the arching, wooden roof above, and a wooden floor separating the top floor from the ground floor. Large fluorescent lights had been installed below the roof, illuminating the spacious room. Several tables and chairs had been arranged to face the far end of the barn. A large projector shone onto the far wall, which had been painted white to fulfill such a purpose.

"Have a seat, ladies and gentleman," called out Mason.

The Libertas members numbered 14 individuals; 11 men and 3 women. David and Warren took a seat beside each other and near the back of the series of tables. Mason took his position in front of the wall and below the projected screen several feet above his head. Beside him sat one of the Libertas members, armed with a laptop that was linked to the projector.

"Many of you are familiar with the circumstances of tonight's operation. Some of you are not. For that reason, I'll start from the beginning. Let me introduce each of you to David Ruiz and Warren Carlyle," said Mason, gesturing to the two who sat behind nearly everyone else in the room. "Yesterday morning, David and Warren were visiting with a local business owner, Trent Sanderson, owner of Trent's Sand & Gravel."

The projector, which had already shown an overhead view of the nearby geography using satellite images available from a popular search engine, zoomed in on the immediate area in question. Using a long, pointed stick, Mason indicated on the projector the location of Trent's Sand & Gravel.

"While returning to their vehicle, the two men spotted a third man running in their direction. He was not wearing shoes, socks, or a jacket, and was in obvious distress. Before David and Warren were able to render assistance, the man in question was struck by a bullet fired from this location," said Mason, indicating the building on the map.

"Evidently, the rifle malfunctioned, giving the two men time to get this third man into their vehicle. Additional individuals appeared from within this building and began firing on their vehicle as they drove away. Shortly after, the man died of his wounds."

The projector flipped to a front facing image of the deceased man. His eyes were closed, and his pale skin was a stark contrast to the dark crimson wound on his right shoulder and chest.

"Upon further examination, there is reason to believe this man was being held captive and possibly the victim of torture."

The projector cycled through several images, including the marks left by the wrist restraints and the burn marks on the man's back.

"Libertas was contacted regarding this killing, largely due to what appears to be an unwillingness or inability to handle the situation by law enforcement. My men and women with the local police departments and the State Patrol have confirmed this to me, citing a lack of resources and a desire to spare these resources from high threat operations for the time being. If I have it my way, there won't be a threat once the sun rises tomorrow."

This statement drew a few rowdy cheers from the militia members and a grin from Warren.

"Reconnaissance on this location concluded late this morning. Intel gathered on the ground and via drone footage indicate very little activity outside of this building," said Mason, as the projector flipped to images taken from a variety of angles, most of which were from the air, though two were evidently taken from a vehicle as it drove by the building. "If it weren't for us catching someone stepping out to service the generator, it'd look entirely abandoned."

The image cycled to a young woman that appeared to be in the process of filling the gas tank of a generator.

"The thermal imaging of the building, however, tells a different story."

The image flipped once more, this time to a shot of the building and the surrounding landscape in black, white, and shades of grey. The surrounding landscape, as well as some parts of the building's exterior, were dark grey or black. However, some white spots were visible, including around vents, windows, doors, and some portions of the roof.

"I would anticipate much of the building to be occupied, given this intel, as well as the account of at least three individuals firing at the vehicle as it fled."

Mason continued, explaining the operation in detail. The operation would consist of 2 teams of 4 and a third team of 3. The two larger teams would hit the building from the side facing the road, as well as from the side opposite the road. The third team, a team of 3, would enter through the side of the building that, according to Mason, was most likely to contain any additional hostages. He had been clear from the beginning that this was designed to be a hostage rescue operation, though the objective of eliminating any hostile forces would remain regardless of the presence or absence of prisoners. Two additional individuals, which had been designated as marksmen, would approach on the road, offering assistance as needed, eliminating any fleeing threats, and providing covering fire for the vehicles used for extraction, should it be necessary.

The three remaining individuals, consisting of David, Warren, and a militia member, would be responsible for extraction via a trio of large vans. Once the compound was breached, the three men in their respective vehicles would approach to within 100 yards of the compound and remain on standby. On instruction, they would approach the building, picking up the militia members and any freed prisoners, before then picking up the two aforementioned marksmen that would still potentially be further down the road.

The operation was set to be carried out that very night; Mason had explained that he was concerned about giving those within the building too much time to prepare or flee. It was mid-afternoon, giving the group approximately 8 hours before leaving the armory, and another hour before they would all be in position, giving them ample time to review the plan in more detail.

On the whole, David felt entirely out of place. The men and women in the room, some of which had likely previously served in the armed forces or law enforcement, appeared confident in their role. David and Warren had come to learn that routine training, which was referenced repeatedly during the review of the planned operation, had fostered this confidence. This was training that had been carried out over a number of years and involved a variety of situations, including the scenario they found themselves in.

Despite this high level of readiness, David did have some concerns. The first concern involved the short time period in which this operation was being carried out. The intel they had gathered, while valuable, was still only a brief snapshot of whatever may be happening within or around the targeted building. His second concern was, naturally, for his own wellbeing. He was assured that extraction would likely be occurring following a successful operation. Furthermore, the transportation they would be using, which consisted of large transport vans, were purpose-built for the militia and were equipped with run-flat tires, armored doors, and bullet-resistant glass. Even so, he did not like the possibility of being shot at again, barely 24 hours after the first occurrence in his lifetime. The third concern emerged near the end of the initial presentation of the plan by Mason, prior to more specific briefing that was to be provided to each member of the team.

"So, to answer your question Aden, the planned entrance will be through the doors. We can anticipate the doors to be moderately reinforced at most. We'll focus on ballistic and explosive breaching as our best options, to be decided upon once nearing the objective. Any other questions?"

David looked around the room.

"Is there any truth to the rumors about this site?" asked a young woman.

Mason didn't verbally respond, instead tilting his head while awaiting further clarification of the intent of the question.

"There's been some talk of this being a UWF compound," said a man sitting beside the woman.

Mason nodded as he slowly paced across the room, making eye contact with the far wall. "There's no definitive intel that suggests UWF is operating in this area," said Mason, before pausing. "We've had some reports dating back several months of that being a possibility. Leadership, including myself, believe that the evidence shows it is a possibility UWF is present in the area, and that this may be one of their compounds. If that's the case, our hope would be to gather some form of intel, electronic or otherwise. With that being said, we're not going to let that alter our planning in this mission."

David was taken aback by the statement. It was not a possibility he had considered, and it made him question Mason's motives for helping him with this operation. Was it purely out of a concern for safety for the community, or was there a political motivation? Did it matter? Additionally, the possibility of trained individuals, potentially with capabilities similar to Libertas, being present in that building sent a chill down his spine. Warren sent him a similarly concerned look.

Mason interrupted the concern that filled David's mind. "If that's all, let's break off into each specific team to be briefed on your individual role."

"Take a left up ahead. It'll be on your left, about 2 miles down the road. It looks like it's opposite a gravel pit or something like that."

The two sat in silence for a few more moments.

"Are you going to slow down or take pictures?" asked Chris.

"No, no I am not," said Dana, with a small grin on her face. "This government car sticks out like a sore thumb as it is. I don't know what they have outside the building. Guards? Cameras? No, I'd prefer to drive by as fast as we can without drawing any undue attention."

"Remind me why we're driving by it at all. We've been on the phone all day with the FBI, the state patrol, the county sheriff. Why can't we let them take care of it?"

"They are the ones that will take care of it. But, I don't know. I feel like we've done all this work, I at least want to see it for myself. Besides, they've spent the whole day running us in circles about this. At some point…"

"What do you mean 'at some point'?" asked Chris.

"Maybe we'll have to be the ones to do it," said Dana as she smiled, knowing the thought of something like that, a task so poorly matched for his skill set, made Chris squirm.

"I'll pass."

"There it is," said Dana.

She drove by at 5 miles an hour over the speed limit. She looked with her eyes at the building but kept her head facing forward. Chris, on the other hand, stared at the building as they rapidly drove by.

"Huh. That's it. Looks pretty nondescript to me," said Chris.

"It looks like the perfect place to hide. Not quite in the middle of nowhere, wide fields on every side of the building, a big garage for the vans they use."

Locating the building, which was the culmination of days of long hours of work, lucky breaks, and the death of a police officer, was a relief for Chris, despite its underwhelming exterior. Dana continued down the road for several more miles, before turning into the parking lot of an old gas station that appeared to have been closed for months, if not years. Beside the gas station was a car wash that Dana parked the car beside. It gave a decent view of the road, but also partially hid the car from the view of traffic in either direction.

"What do we do now?" asked Dana.

Chris was caught off-guard, as he usually found himself to be the one offering up such questions.

"Time to wait?" answered Chris, with a question.

"I think you're right."

Chapter Twenty Three: Disembark

"Charlotte!"

Charlotte ran around the corner, answering both the gunshot and Vir's exclamation.

"Vir, what happened?!"

"It was an accident!"

At Vir's feet lay a body, awkwardly slumped in the doorway. A crimson splatter could be seen against the wall, mixed with small bits of flesh and bone that belonged to the now-deceased man. The man's face was a grotesque display of death. One eye stared forward, lifelessly, as it bulged from the orbit. The other eye was missing, along with large portions of the skull.

"What'd you do?!" said Charlotte, eyes fixed on the body.

"I, I don't know how it happened. He said he was coming to take my stuff. I was afraid he would find you. He pointed a gun at me, and I tried to push it away, and then..." replied Vir, animated from the shock of it all.

Having first been focused on the gory scene, Charlotte hadn't realized that a handgun lay on the ground beside the man. She quickly realized that the man was dressed in a similar manner to the numerous militia members.

"Vir, I think we should go."

Vir didn't respond, instead staring at the lifeless body as he stood with hands on his knees. He was breathing heavily.

"Vir!" shouted Charlotte.

Her attempt to get his attention was successful.

"What?" muttered Vir.

"Vir, we need to leave," said Charlotte, already making a move to the coat rack to grab his coat.

Vir stood more upright. He took a series of deep breaths as he ran his hands through his hair. Charlotte could see and hear him mutter something to himself. She couldn't make out what he said but seemed to be trying to calm himself.

"You're right. We need to leave."

Still dazed, he grabbed the coat and put it on. Charlotte followed suit, having found another coat of Vir's that appeared more than warm enough for the temperatures outside that were hovering below freezing. It was oversized, but that wasn't a bad thing when warmth was the objective, rather than aesthetics. Charlotte quickly donned and tied her shoes. When she looked up, Vir was nowhere to be seen.

"Vir, where'd you go?"

He returned around the corner with a backpack.

"Sorry, I had to grab this first."

"What's in it?" asked Charlotte.

"A few things I put together. I'll show you later," said Vir, still visibly shaken, despite his presence of mind to grab the bag before leaving.

The two began out the door of Vir's apartment. Though it was unspoken between the two in the brief span of time, both knew leaving was necessary. Charlotte was unsure of who may have been near enough to hear the gunshot and had no desire to shelter in place, waiting for someone else to find the man.

"Wait," said Vir, halting outside his door but still within the building.

"What?"

Without a word, he turned the corner in the direction of his apartment. He returned moments later, backpack unslung as he zipped the main compartment closed. Charlotte gave him a puzzled look.

"The gun," said Vir, as they continued to the ground-level entrance in the otherwise fairly small apartment building.

"Do you know how to use it?"

"Sure. My dad had one just like it. We'd go to the range sometimes; he taught me how to shoot it," said Vir, in a surprisingly confident tone.

Charlotte was surprised and didn't have a reply to this bit of information. It seemed counter to the facets of Vir's personality she had yet seen, and thus counter to the picture she had constructed of Vir up to that point. She paused, realizing that there was more than met the eye. The change in his demeanor and how quickly he had switched gears from shock to action surprised her. As the two stepped out of the door into the chilly evening air, Charlotte realized that Vir may not be the liability she had once thought him to be.

As he climbed into the driver seat of the armored van assigned to him, David felt altogether uncomfortable and out of place. As part of the operation, the militia had provided him with an armored vest. It was heavy and cumbersome, though not overly heavy when walking. However, when sitting in the van, his back rested uncomfortably against the steel plate. It forced him further forward in the seat as well. The vest contained a radio and a trio of magazine pouches that each carried a 30-round magazine filled with 5.56 mm ammunition to feed his rifle, though David prayed silently that he would not need to fire a single round.

His van would carry Mason, Mason's team, and an additional team member that had arrived partway through the briefing in the barn. This woman, however, was unarmed.

Instead, she carried a duffel bag that contained a drone. Mason had previously explained that this drone would be flown overhead during the mission, providing real-time intel to the pilot, Rachel was her name, who would, in turn, pass the information along to the team via radio.

"David, you alright?" said Mason.

"Yeah. Just a little nervous, that's all," said David.

The question from Mason added to his anxiety about the night. Mason went on to explain to David that he had nothing to be concerned about. They had the element of surprise, and the benefit of the night, which did assuage his fears to some extent.

"Mason, I appreciate what you're doing for Warren and I. Part of me still wonders if this is something that could be better handled by law enforcement, but I also know that things don't work like they did a few weeks ago."

"No, no they do not," replied Mason.

Mason's radio, which was wired into a headset, came alive. "Transport Echo departing, en route to objective, ETA 45 minutes, over."

"Copy that, this is Bravo team leader. Transport Echo, Foxtrot, Golf, all departing for objective for drop off 2 klicks to the north," replied Mason.

A few additional replies came over the line to acknowledge the plans, as all 3 transport vans departed the farm. The 3 transport vans had been designated as such in order to delineate themselves from the 3 teams infiltrating the location, designated Alpha, Bravo, Charlie, and the 4th team, Delta, that would provide fire from a distance, unless required within the building. The final entity designated a call sign was Rachel, the drone operator. She had earned the designation Overwatch.

David followed the taillights ahead as his own headlights illuminated the rear of the lead vehicle with lights that would be turned off upon approach to the building. The night was otherwise calm. A thin layer of snow, some of which had been melted by the heat of the sun, still covered the familiar landscape. David placed his hand on the rifle by his side, both comforted by its presence and troubled by its necessity. Not a voice was heard in the van as it rolled down the road, each individual anticipating the night's danger. The clock within the van read 12:07 AM.

Chapter Twenty Four: Convergence

An alarm blared through the building, waking Christie from a fitful sleep. She sat up in bed immediately. The clock on her desk read 12:45 AM. Knowing that the alarm was significant, but unsure why, she scrambled to get dressed. Her roommate was on night watch and was thus unable to fill her in on what to do in such a situation. No doubt, it would have been explained in detail to Christie had she been present for the training. She, of course, had not been present, instead being a late addition to the compound's membership.

She opened the door to the hallway. A man, one of the additions from the Wisconsin group as it had been called more recently, removing any reference to Mitch's leadership, jogged down the hallway away from her room and in the direction of the meeting room. Christie followed. She arrived to find she had been the last to arrive, though the night watch was not present. Her concerns about being late were relieved, as she could see each person present appeared to have only recently arrived. They did not sit in the chairs, instead standing in a large group.

Seeing Christie arrive, Perez began. "Listen up! We're leaving tonight. I have on good authority from a source of our's inside of the militia group known as Libertas that an operation is imminent in the area. It's not clear where this will be occurring, but the source provided details that all but confirm that we're the target.

"I want to be in the vans and driving out those doors within 20 minutes. The prisoners will not be joining us. Destroy the communication equipment and hard drives. Understood?"

The room voiced an affirmative. Though Christie was evidently not familiar with every bit of procedure within the compound, she had been instructed in her duties in such a scenario. She, along with Heidi, had been tasked with dispatching the remaining 3 prisoners. Had they been ordered to bring the prisoners along, additional time and individuals would be provided to assist with the task.

She walked with Heidi to the armory in order to grab the rifles they would use to eliminate the prisoners. She had not looked forward to carrying out this task. Though she

155

was more comfortable with killing after murdering the store owner, the event still caused her discomfort whenever the memory streamed across her consciousness, though she was sure to silence such thoughts whenever they appeared. Of course, such thoughts and memories were much more difficult to suppress when she was asleep.

"Ok, let's do this together so we don't screw it up," said Heidi. "We'll start with Mark, then the new guy, then the woman."

"Russell and Kate?"

"Sure. You'll open the door, I'll shoot. Easy peasy," said Heidi.

As she inserted a magazine into the AR-15's mag well, Christie knew that dispatching the three prisoners may be considered easy kills, and knew she was physically capable of the act, but found her palms sweating and heart pounding nonetheless, as doubt chipped away at her confidence and conscience.

Chris zipped up his pants, having relieved himself some distance away from the car and gas station. It was a clear night, and he noticed for the first time just how clear the night sky had become in the preceding few days as a majority of the nation's cities and lights had gone dark. For the first time since his childhood, he could clearly make out the Milky Way, a broad swath of stars that stretched across the sky. He also noticed the silence of the night. There were no jets buzzing across the sky. No trains could be heard steaming down the track.

As he listened to the silence, a silence amplified by the snow that covered the ground, he realized that, for the first time since leaving the relative warmth of the car to relieve himself, he could hear a vehicle on the road. He looked down the road as he hugged the side of the car wash. The faint glow of headlights shown through the darkness. He crouched, slipping behind the corner of the car wash, depriving the approaching vehicle of a line of sight in his direction as they approached.

The sound of the engine grew louder, and Chris realized that he could hear more than one. The lights lit up the road as 3 large vans passed in front of the gas station and car wash. As they passed, Chris slipped fully behind the car wash once more. They were going relatively slow. He realized they were driving in the direction of the building that he and Dana had spent the preceding days locating.

Surely, Chris thought to himself, there was no relation. If anything, it was likely just a small caravan, no doubt escaping Indianapolis, Cincinnati, or some other nearby metropolis. Even so, the thought lingered. Mitch and his crew had migrated from Wisconsin to this location. What if others had chosen to do the same? What if those were vans bringing in resources? What if their purpose was to transport the prisoners and UWF members to some other location, rendering he and Dana's work useless, and essentially sentencing Russell and Katherine to death, or worse? What were the odds that a caravan of vehicles would all be similar models? As the tail lights dimmed in the distance, he jogged the few meters back to the car.

Chris opened her door, interrupting Dana's newly found sleep. "Dana, I need you outside."

Chapter Twenty Five: Action

Russel, having been awoken by the blaring alarm at least ten minutes prior, sat at the edge of his bed. He was unsure of the cause of the alarm. For all he knew, the alarm had been set off by a smoke detector that had been triggered by someone's careless cooking. He considered laying back down but decided he would wait instead. In the last few days, it seemed as though the days stretched on. He found himself fatigued, despite the adequate sleep and seeming reprieve from the once regular beatings and torture. The prospect of death, more than fear, despair, or anger, dominated his thoughts this night. He knew it was near. He still hung onto a sense of resolve; whatever method of murder planned, he still fully planned to resist, even escape, if able. Escaping his room and avoiding such an attempt on his life still crossed his mind, though he knew he was not skilled in such methods, and no feasible options had presented themselves.

As he sat at the edge of the bed, face in his hands, he heard footsteps in the hallway, along with hushed voices. This did not draw unusual attention, as such patrols were regular at all hours of the day. What did draw his attention, however, was the sound of a nearby room being unlocked. Both within the first house, as well as his brief stay at this facility, such intrusions on the prisoners' sleep was unusual. Still, Russel thought to himself, this was a new facility. Perhaps that was the norm here. His mind also considered the possibility of a late-night torture session, a prospect that filled Russel with a sense of weariness and dread.

Crack!

The unmistakable noise of a gunshot reverberated through the building. Before Russel could stand up, it was followed by a trio of additional gunshots. Unlike the gunfire he had heard outside on the previous day, this gunfire has undoubtedly originated from within the walls of the building.

"Shit! Heidi, that was loud! I can't hear a thing!" Yelled a female voice in the hallway with a raised voice indicative of the damage sustained to her hearing.

"Huh? I think he's dead!" replied another voice at a similar level of decibels to the first voice.

Russel knew instantly what fate lay in store for himself. Unless, of course, he could alter such a fate. Already standing, he turned to his bed and, in a split second, considered his options. Without much thought or goal in mind, other than to delay and disrupt the inevitable, he grabbed a pillow and stood on the bed. He looked to the ceiling, an 8-foot ceiling, on which was a lone light bulb. It was a light that, unlike the lights at the house he had been held at originally, never turned off at night, save for the brief interruption of electricity 2 days prior, an interruption that Russel had not been present for.

Though Russel's hasty plan was to do nothing more than delay and disrupt, he had conceived of a few actions that would assist him to that end in the short time he had been in this building. The first was to disrupt these lights. There was no switch inside the room. It wasn't clear where the switch was; potentially directly outside the room, or else at a more central location. Regardless, it was inaccessible to Russel. The light, however, was accessible and easily within his reach when standing on the bed.

Russel used the sheet from his bed to protect his hands from injury as he swung a pillow at the light. Despite advancements in lightbulb technology over the years, they remained fragile objects, and his captors had not protected the fitting. This was an oversight on their part, an oversight that Russel took advantage of swiftly. The bulb shattered with a single swing of the pillow, plunging the windowless room into darkness, save for the sliver of light that shone under the door.

Next, he grabbed the blanket on the bed. Ideally, he'd be able to push the steel-framed bed against the door, but the door did not swing inwards, and the bed was secured to the floor. He brought the blanket with him into the corner of the room adjacent to the door that was positioned in the middle of the wall. He kept it bundled up in his arms as he waited.

The voices outside continued to talk loudly. "Let's get the guy next," said a voice.

Russel, unsure if other male prisoners were present but fairly certain there were no others, breathed a sigh of relief that they would spare Kate for the time being. He heard the lock and door handle being manipulated, and the door was opened a scant 6 inches, before being closed again.

He heard a hushed voice and was unable to discern what was said.

"Christie, I can't hear you," said another voice, loudly.

"Why are the lights off?" said the first voice, raising her voice in order to be heard.

"I don't know, try the switch."

In the silence and with hearing that had not been damaged by the noise that was dampened by the walls of his room, Russel heard a light switch outside.

"Why isn't it working?" said the first voice.

A split second later, the sound of gunfire thundered. Russel watched as small holes appeared in the wall, allowing small slivers of light into the room. The holes traveled across the wall, starting at the far end and moving towards Russel in the span of a few seconds. He first hugged the corner, but then dove to the floor in a prone position as bullets, speeding at over twice the speed of sound, poked holes in the wall he had been standing behind seconds before.

The crack of the gunfire paused for a matter of seconds, before continuing for what felt like an eternity to Russel. Still, every round was aimed at least 3 feet over the ground, and only struck the bed or the far wall. Russel's ears rang from the repetitive gunfire, gunfire that rang much louder than the first shots in the hallway.

Unsure if more shots would be fired in the room and with his hearing impaired, Russel rose to his knees and hands. The door opened as a barrel appeared in the doorway. Russel, realizing this was his final chance, grabbed the bundled blanket that was laid beside himself. He grabbed it and threw it in the direction of the opposite wall, streaking across the view of the woman in the doorway. As Russel had hoped, the barrel followed the blanket. Russel was crouched now, and took advantage of the distraction, thrusting himself in the direction of the profiled figure in the doorway.

"This is Bravo team leader. Anyone else hear that? Possible gunfire within the target building, over," said Mason over the radio on a channel open to all team members.

"Roger, sounded like a few dozen shots, over," responded another team leader.

"Any chance they have a firing range inside? Late-night target practice?" chimed in a third voice.

"Overwatch here, no targets outside the building at this time."

"Roger, this is Bravo team leader. Proceed to objective with caution."

David viewed the building from a distance. In the darkness of the night, he was unable to visualize the drone overhead, as well as any team members, with the exception of the two other vans and the two sharpshooters that were crouched halfway between him and the building. He had not heard the gunfire the others had reported as he sat in the van with his driver's side door open and rifle at his side.

"This is Alpha team, charges are set, over."

"Charlie team here, finishing up with charges now, over."

"Bravo team still on approach, stand by," responded Mason, whose team had the furthest distance to traverse to their entrance, first looping at a distance from the building before then approaching more directly to their point of entry.

"This is Charlie, more gunfire inside."

Christie stood face to face with the prisoner. No doubt weakened by his imprisonment, he was evenly matched with her own strength that was greater than some her age but still disadvantaged by her lesser muscle mass. Despite the struggle, Christie's thoughts were still thoughts of disappointment. She had hesitated when Russel had struggled with Heidi for her gun, choosing only to fire as he had begun to gain control of the rifle. In the close quarters and with her heart pounding, 3 of her shots had missed Russel. The other two struck Heidi. The first hit her in the shoulder, while the second pierced her back just below the ribcage. At that, Heidi dropped to the floor.

The hostage had wasted no time in turning his attention to Heidi's killer, but had slipped in the small, but growing, amount of blood that was on the tile floor. It had given her a moment to recover, a moment she could have used to put distance between Russel and herself, place a series of shots in his chest, or both. Instead, she stood in shock of her poor marksmanship that had likely killed her newfound comrade, allowing him to cover the short distance and begin the struggle for her own weapon.

Knowing she was possibly outmatched and devoid of the brief advantage she had held, Christie feared for her own life. Despite the fear, she showed a brief moment of presence of mind. With her hand still on the handgrip of the rifle, she extended her index finger and depressed the tab that was forward of the trigger guard on the AR-15 rifle. To her satisfaction, the magazine clattered to the floor. Though the barrel was pointed at the wall, she pulled the trigger, firing the lone round that remained within the weapon. In quick succession, Christie surrendered the weapon and ran down the hallway in the direction of the other wing of the building.

"I don't know Chris. Like you said, maybe it was just a caravan from one of the cities, maybe even Columbus."

"Still, isn't there something we can do?" responded Chris.

"Like what? Let's pretend it was one of the other UWF vans. That'd make sense since you said they all were similar to the one that Mitchell Jenkins had used. That makes me want to stay away from the building even-"

She stopped mid-sentence, her speech halted by a quiet, yet perceptible boom from the direction of the UWF compound.

There was no sound over the channel following the countdown, a countdown that was followed by the synchronized explosion of the breaching charges that had been placed on all 3 doors into the building, with the exception of the large, metal garage doors. The silence continued for a number of seconds but was then interrupted by the pop of gunfire within the building, a noise that was audible to David thanks to the now unhinged doors.

"This is Overwatch, good breaches by all 3 teams."

"This is Charlie, one hostage identified, one tango already down."

Another voice erupted over the channel, with gunfire audible over the line. "Alpha team, we have a casualty here! Pinned down just inside the doorway."

David recalled that the Alpha team had breached near what was once the lobby of the building.

"Charlie team, 2 hostages secured now. Third hostage is deceased."

David continued to hear the faint pop of gunfire within the building.

"This is Bravo. 1 tango eliminated, proceeding to your location, Alpha."

Christie had started in the direction of the other wing to seek safety. That had quickly changed as a loud explosion had been followed by gunfire. Still, she knew that seeking the safety of the others was preferable to a man that was behind her, a man that now wielded a rifle.

She closed the door behind her as she traversed into the wing ahead and locked the door to ensure the escaped prisoner could not reach her easily. Gunfire sounded down the hall. Rather than running directly to the danger, Christie turned into the garage, a decision made out of not only fear but also pragmatism, given her current lack of weaponry. Two individuals, a man from the Wisconsin group and a woman from her own building were loading up two of the vans.

One woman stopped what she was doing as Christie appeared in the doorway. "Christie, we're getting out of here! Go tell the others!"

"But I don't have a gun," objected Christie.

"I don't care, go!" Shouted the woman from a place of fear and urgency.

Christie turned around and continued in the direction of the gunfire. At a T-shaped fork in the hallway, she realized that gunfire was coming from both directions. Unsure in which direction there were friendlies, she opted not to turn the corner.

"The vans are ready! Let's go!" shouted Christie to whoever was listening.

"Roger! Let's get out!" replied the easily identified voice of Perez.

As Christie backed down the hallway, once more in the direction of the garage, she watched as her team turned the corner. The friendly figures appeared from both directions of the T-shaped fork. She counted 6 in total. The group continued in a near sprint towards the garage, knowing the straight stretch of hallway left them exposed to the intruder's gunfire once they were able to turn the corner as well.

Of the group, Christie reached the garage first. She turned as the others streamed in, rounded out by Mitch. He took the opportunity to lean around the corner, firing several rounds down the hallway as the others ran to the side door in the vans, dividing themselves roughly evenly between the two vehicles. Christie followed Perez into a van and slid the door shut behind her.

Both vans were positioned to exit the garages in a forward manner, negating the need for a slow exit in reverse. One of the drivers had already clicked the button on the visor of the van, and the large doors opened as the last door on the second van slammed shut.

"This is Overwatch. Two vans leaving the building and… heading in the direction of Delta and the transports."

"Overwatch, take cover. Delta, engage targets but stay off the road. Transports, do not block their escape. We have the objective and there's no need to risk yourselves," replied Bravo Team leader, Mason Jennings.

"Delta engaging," said another voice.

David, now sitting in the van, could see the two vans driving down the road in his direction. Bullseye-shaped cracks spread across the lead van's windshield, but none hit in the location necessary to disable the driver. Suddenly, the side door of both vans slid open, and David could see the flash of gunfire as the vans closed on the static position of the two sharpshooters. The two sharpshooters, who were already standing halfway to the bottom of the ditch that paralleled the road, quickly halted their fire and took cover at the bottom of the ditch.

The gunfire was almost immediately redirected to the trio of vans, of which David's was the nearest to the compound and thus nearest to the fleeing vehicles. David had not considered the possibility of receiving gunfire in this scenario, instead having been consumed with watching the brief firefight ahead and with concern for Delta Team. A string of bullets impacted his windshield, each making a loud popping noise and leaving bullseye-shaped craters on the glass. One round struck directly in front of David's face, but, like the other rounds, did not penetrate the glass.

Before David had the opportunity to duck the incoming rounds, the pair of vans had already sped past his idling van, leaving only the reflection of their tail lights as they continued into the darkness of the night.

Chapter Twenty Six: Escape

"Do you hear that?"

The two slipped around the corner upon spotting the approaching headlights. Soon, the engines could be heard. They were not the roar of a muscle car, but Chris could tell by the rapid growth of the light cast by the headlights and the pitch of the engine tone, that they were driving quickly.

Oh, hell no, Chris thought to himself. It was the sight of the two vans that elicited this response. More specifically, the appearance of the second van was all too familiar to Chris.

"Is that the-"

Dana didn't finish her question. There was no point. She knew the answer, and Chris evidently knew it as well. He made a dash to the car. Dana tried to follow, but Chris sat in the driver's seat and slammed the door shut. Before she had a chance to protest, she heard the unmistakable noise of the doors locking in unison.

Chris glanced out the driver's side window at Dana. With the limited time he had to catch the escaping vans, a facial expression was all he could communicate to Dana. It was an expression that told of the obligation he felt he had, an obligation both to rescue his friend, and to stop those that had hurt, possibly murdered, Russel and many others. Sensing there was nothing she could do to change his mind, Dana returned an expression of understanding. The engine came to life, and Chris was gone in an instant.

As Christie joined the rest of the van's occupants in silence, she was doubly relieved. Not only had she escaped a sure death at the hands of the intruders, but the silence that filled the van spared her from any questions that could uncover the truth about her failure to dispatch two of the prisoners, as well as Heidi's demise. Her van was a mix of the Wisconsin and Indiana crews. She was pleased to see Perez in her own van.

Rather than mourn the loss of those that had not escaped, she instead spent her time conceiving of a response to any queries that would absolve her of responsibility for the prisoner's survival and Heidi's death. Perez was not entirely intolerant of failure; she had shown some level of mercy to Mitch in what others had perceived as a failure on his behalf in the escape of the first prisoner. Other cell leaders, Christie had been told, were not so kind.

Regardless, it was not only about her own survival. She sought to spare her own pride and to preserve her own possibilities of ascent within the UWF to a position of leadership. Christie, though ambitious, was naive to the positive aspects of a failure that one took responsibility for, rather than trying to save face. She was unaware that Perez herself had experienced many such failures in her life, and had learned quickly that taking responsibility and learning from such mistakes yielded both character development and trust from leadership.

Her thoughts were interrupted. Perez, who sat in the passenger seat beside the driver, broke the silence as she spoke with the driver. It was not a hushed tone, though Christie could not comprehend the words over the drone of the engine. Perez and the driver both began looking in their side mirrors. Christie craned her head in an attempt to look out the driver's side mirror, first spotting the bright lights of the trailing van. The driver's head blocked the mirror from Christie's line of sight for a moment as he tried to improve his vantage point of something behind the van.

His head moved, allowing Christie to see out the mirror once more. It was faint, but she could now see what the topic of their conversation was. It was a second pair of headlights.

Chris' only plan was simple. There was no backup plan, no contingency. The car was his only weapon, knowing that Dana had kept her handgun on her hip for much of the preceding days. The second van that had driven by was the van that he was all too familiar with, the van he had spent hours searching for on traffic camera feeds, the van that had carried Russel and Kate to the Wisconsin house, and then to this nondescript building in Indiana.

He had to guess what direction the vans had taken at a T-shaped intersection not far from the gas station he and Dana had been positioned behind. He chose to turn right. Speeding down the country road, Chris watched the speedometer near 90 MPH, knowing that if he had chosen incorrectly, his opportunity to stop the van would vanish.

But, he had not chosen incorrectly. The red taillights were visible ahead, glowing in stark contrast to the dark night. For some time, the lights continued to grow ahead of him. He could tell he was easily outpacing the vans. Then, it appeared they had increased their pace. Chris demanded more from the car, knowing it to be capable of higher speeds, certainly higher than those of a transport van. It responded, not with the eagerness of a sports car, but in a steady manner and with a certain smoothness.

The lights ahead began growing once more. He was gaining ground. Suddenly, the back door of the van opened. A dark figure could be seen in the glow cast by Chris' headlights. He could see the glint of something in the light. He wasn't sure if the light had caught something metallic or glass, but it didn't matter. He knew what the figure in the back of the van wielded.

The next several seconds seem to move in slow motion. The man opened fire on Chris' car, but only managed to fire a handful of rounds, all of which struck either the hood or the windshield, but not Chris' body. The man was thrown off balance as the van, which had been travelling at nearly 90 MPH, aggressively braked in an attempt to accommodate a curve in the road for which the recommended speed was closer to half the speed at which the van had been traveling. The sudden deceleration, coupled with the lateral shift in the van as it negotiated the turn, disturbed the man's balance and sent him falling backwards into the interior of the van. The rear door slammed shut as a result of its own inertia.

Chris had not anticipated this turn in the road. Though his own vehicle was more nimble, he did not have the same time to react to the braking van and the winding pavement. In order to avoid the van, Chris cut to the inside of the corner. Two wheels rode on the shoulder, and two on the gravel on the side of the road. The van had not anticipated this move. The driver cut to the inside of the corner, putting himself directly in front of Chris' rapidly closing car.

Chris' car slammed into the rear corner of the van. The impact, combined with the inertia of the van that was resisting the turn and the already top-heavy nature of the vehicle, lifted the two wheels that had been hugging the inside of the corner off of the road. The van rolled onto its side and slid off of the road in a shower of sparks. Chris, who had not had the presence of mind to restrain himself with his seat belt before beginning his pursuit, was thrown forward in his seat but was quickly halted by the deployment of the airbag. The car still carried a considerable amount of speed following the impact with the van. It followed the van off of the road to the outside of the curve, and both vehicles fell down a steep embankment that led to a ditch a full 20 feet below. There they lay, as the lead van escaped into the night.

Mark Williamson found pride in his participation in the night's assault on the compound. He was not the least bit disappointed in his assignment to drive the third van, designated Transport Golf. He was a father to two teenage boys and had every intention of returning home. His membership in Libertas, which dated back several years, was borne out of a desire to protect those two boys from what he could see was an increasingly dangerous world.

When this desire to protect and safeguard began to include things such as self-defense and weapons, he soon realized that safety could be found in numbers. This initiative of Mark's began as what amounted to a community based safety network that consisted of his own family, as well as a number of other households that were in direct vicinity to his own. However, this small-scale community-based approach quickly died with the rise of militant groups across the country, each of which was aligned with their own individual political ideologies. Many of his neighbors that had committed to the community based approach changed their mind, instead joining the growing militias that often had been founded with the intention of countering similar groups of contrasting political ideologies.

Mark soon followed suit, joining one of the larger national militias, Libertas. In the preceding days to the assault on the compound, the utility of such an organization was demonstrated in Southern Indiana, and Mark felt his sons were safer because of it. He knew he had made the right choice for himself and his family. It was a large part of why he felt compelled to volunteer for what others might deem vigilante justice, but what he considered to be a necessary act in order to preserve law and order within the community.

Mark had considered this a successful mission. Over the radio, he had learned of the success in rescuing two hostages, hostages that they were not sure were present in this building only an hour before. He also had learned of the third hostage that had been killed, as well as at least one death of a Libertas member.

Before he had an opportunity to process what had happened, Mason had ordered him to pick up team Delta, consisting of the two marksmen, and pursue the fleeing vans. The intent of this was not to disable the vehicles or to eliminate the hostiles, but instead to ensure they left the surrounding communities, and possibly to give other Libertas forces in the area a chance to finish what Mason's team had started. He had obeyed this order, knowing such a pursuit was a relatively low-risk proposition.

Like Chris, Mark Williamson had also opted to turn right at the T-junction. The road he drove on had many other, smaller roads that branched off, but none were major enough to persuade him from continuing on his current path, deeming that searching the countless country roads and dead ends would be fruitless. Instead, he continued down the state highway, deeming it to be the most likely route that the fleeing vans would take.

His radio contact with the rest of the group had been lost some time ago. The need to communicate more than 1 to 2 miles had not been anticipated. The local militia had the communication equipment necessary to communicate beyond that range, but it was determined to be unnecessary for the current mission and was instead in use by other members across the state for communication during the ongoing chaos.

"Hold on, what's this?" said Mark in a volume loud enough for his two passengers to hear from the back of the van.

The two leaned forward, peering between the driver and passenger seat. The van slowed, stopping on the shoulder opposite the disturbed brush on the side of a curve in the road. Though the snow was relatively shallow, it too had been disturbed. The three men exited the van to see what lay at the bottom of the embankment.

It took a full 30 seconds for Chris to become cognitively aware of his surroundings, and another 30 seconds to recall what had put him in this situation. His head ached; it had a feeling reminiscent of a time he had been jumped a few blocks away from a Philadelphia bar, an assault that had left him unconscious and $45 poorer. Waking up, which had already been expected to be unpleasant due to the hangover, had been exacerbated by what a physician had defined as a concussion.

He tasted blood in his mouth and realized blood was running across, not down, his face. He turned to his left to see the ground underneath the shattered passenger window. With the realization of his orientation came a painful sensation of the seat belt digging into his waist and the right side of his neck. The slow process of Chris regaining consciousness was suddenly sped up by a specific odor. Smoke. Chris knew he had been in an accident, and he could now smell smoke. That information alone was enough to tell him that he needed to exit his car as soon as possible.

He braced himself against the center console with his legs and the steering wheel with his left arm as his right arm disengaged the seat belt lock. His attempt to hold himself in place was not adequate, and gravity pulled him downwards. He pushed against the floor of the car, allowing him to then pull his legs out from under the steering wheel. He pushed up from the center console, pushing his head up through the shattered driver's side window. He contemplated pushing open the door but could feel the heat of the fire as his head emerged from the car. He instead chose to proceed through the shattered window.

Not wasting any time, Chris pulled himself from the wrecked government-issue sedan, sustaining some shallow lacerations to his arm and thigh from the glass that remained on the lower margin of the driver's side window, but ignored the pain. Chris knew that the injuries were a small price to pay to escape the danger of the growing fire that he could feel radiating on his skin. He lowered himself to the ground from the car that he could now see was laying on its side at the bottom of a ravine that ran beside the road.

Chris put a short distance between himself and the two wrecked vehicles. The fire, which appeared to have started from the van, was a bright yellow-orange and put off an acrid, black smoke. He could feel the heat once again as the fire intensified. The bright fire burned in stark contrast to the surrounding wintry landscape.

The human eye, already poorly calibrated for nighttime vision, is rendered nearly useless in a dark environment once exposed to bright light and takes several minutes to regain any ability to see in low-light situations. In his confused state, and with a sense of relief of having been spared from the crash that appeared to have been fatal for those in the van, Chris took no notice of this loss of vision in the dark spaces that surrounded the crashed vehicles. He did not see the shadowy figure that emerged from the far side of the van. Though the fire cast some light equally in each direction, the position of the fire between Chris and the figure obscured his ability to discern its presence. Likewise, he did not see the figure continue to move as Chris began climbing up the embankment, using his feet and hands to fight against the slippery snow.

A shot rang out. Simultaneously, Chris' right shoulder exploded in pain. His arm immediately gave out, and his other limbs followed suit as he laid on his stomach and began sliding down the hill. He tried to grab the shoulder with his opposite arm but suddenly felt weak, too weak to roll himself onto his side. Within seconds, his world began to grow cold. The darkness of the night began to transition to a darkness that more closely resembled the shade one experienced when their eyes are closed, complete with bluish and red splotches of color that replaced the stars of the night sky. As consciousness slipped from Chris' grasp, two additional gunshots rang out. This briefly restored some of Chris' alertness, but it too escaped, as he drifted off into the night.

Chapter Twenty Seven: Farm

Thirst. Chris was walking through his office, seeing the familiar faces of his coworkers, asking each if they had a glass of water. Each one frustratingly replied with a shake of their head. He made his way to the break room and reached into the cabinet to grab a coffee mug. He filled it with water and brought the mug to his lips. As he gulped down the water, he felt the mug grow lighter in his hand, but there was no moisture transferred to his parched mouth and throat. He repeated the process, filling the mug again with water, and was met with similar results. He threw the mug across the room, shouting in the process.

"Chris," said a voice to his side.

He looked to see a man, he didn't recognize the face, tugging at his arm. He pulled his arm away, still frustrated by his thirst that had not been quenched.

"Chris, it's me."

He looked again. The face was still unfamiliar. But the voice, it meant something to Chris. He was confused why this man beside him had such a feminine voice that didn't match his generic but decidedly male appearance.

"Chris, wake up."

Chris pulled his arm away once more, this time realizing he was not in an office, but lying supine in a bed. He opened his eyes and was met with a bright and unfamiliar ceiling. At his left side, however, was a familiar face that matched the voice he had heard. He tried to say her name, but his mouth, which had been open while he lay unconscious, was too dry. Closed his mouth and tried to moisten his tongue and throat, with limited success.

"Hang on, let's get you sitting up a little more," said Dana, seeing his frustration.

She propped some pillows under his head and shoulders. This elicited a groan from Chris as he became aware of the wound on his right shoulder. Dana then grabbed a glass of water with a straw that sat on the nightstand and brought it to Chris' lips. He sipped at first but quickened his pace. She gently pulled it away after he had downed half the glass; something told her a full glass of water might not be the best to consume at that pace and after his length of unconsciousness.

"Where am I?" asked Chris, his voice still raspy despite the drink.

"A house, in Indiana still."

"Indiana? Why-"

Chris' face shifted from confusion to contemplation, as he recalled the events of the days leading up to his last memories. *What are my last memories?* He remembered the drive nearly halfway across the country. A gas station, the snow on the ground. A van. A crash. Gunfire.

"Did we?"

"Yes. Everyone in that van was not as lucky as yourself," said Dana, knowing the intent of his question.

"Mitchell Jenkins?"

"Dead. He was the one that put you out of commission."

"Then, how?"

"It's a long story. Let's just say we had some help," said Dana, once again deciphering his short question.

Chris leaned back into his pillow with a thin grin on his face, a grin of satisfaction. It quickly disappeared. He lifted his head once more, this time with an expression that neared panic.

"Is Russel OK?" Chris asked with apprehension

Dana cocked her head in the direction of the bedroom door, which was halfway open. "Why don't you ask him yourself?" she said with a raised voice.

After a moment, Russel walked into the room. His face beamed, and Chris returned the smile. He walked to the other side of the bed. The two had locked eyes, but neither spoke for a full 15 seconds. Finally, Russel gave Chris a hug, taking care not to put pressure on his shoulder.

"We, we got you out, didn't we?"

"No, actually."

Chris looked at Dana, face filled with confusion.

"In due time, Chris. There's plenty to fill you in on, and a few people you need to meet. For now, rest up. The world's still a broken place."

"It needs a healthy Chris Jenkins," added Russel.

Chris wanted to say more but felt even more fatigued than he likely sounded and appeared to Russel and Dana. Somehow, the banter that he often engaged in with Russel, and more recently with Dana, seemed out of place. Maybe, it was the mortality that he had suddenly become so aware of. Maybe, it was the mental fog he still felt tugging at his consciousness. Regardless, Chris was more than willing to accept Dana's delay in answering his questions. He remained awake for a few more minutes but soon felt sleepiness tugging at his mind. He deferred to his mind and body's insistence on more rest and nodded off with Russel and Dana at his side.

"Girls, 20 more minutes! Then the generator is going off until bedtime!" yelled David down the basement steps.

Zero Sum

The two girls were watching a cartoon movie on a DVD. The younger one was still not clear on the details of how a movie could be on a disc, but David couldn't bring himself to ask her how all manners of videos, music, and more could be transmitted through the invisible signals and through a virtual world known as the internet. For the time being, he was content with them having some sense of normalcy, though he wondered how much longer it could be sustained.

The operation had taken place a full 40 hours prior. David had every intention to return to the far tamer lifestyle at home after what had been a dangerous mission. It had not taken long, through talking with Warren and others, to learn that David had been fired upon, though she had taken the information far better than he had expected.

His plans to return to his normal routine, a routine that was in fact a far cry from what had been his normal only weeks ago, had been upended for the time being. The house had four guests, including one that had already required multiple visits from a local veterinarian. Evidently, the vet had turned out to be a suitable replacement for an MD, given the circumstances, and David had recently learned that Chris had emerged from his semi-conscious state, which was undoubtedly a good sign. In the absence of a nurse, the man's friend, Dana, was serving as his caretaker. The other two guests, Russel and Kate, were themselves still being nursed back to health after having spent a significant time in confinement while also sustaining a substantial amount of physical damage, a result of the torture sessions they had undergone. The two had scarcely spent more than a few waking moments apart; their budding romance reminded David of his own courtship of Alice so many years prior.

David had spoken with both Dana and Russel but still struggled to wrap his brain around the sequence of events that had begun as quite unfortunate, but had then finished in such a serendipitous manner. David knew that this was not a matter of chance, but rather part of a larger plan that had been set in motion by his Creator.

The death of the 4th captive, along with the 2 Libertas members, still weighed heavily on David's conscience. He asked himself if there was anything he could have done differently. Would the local police department have fared any better? Would the murdered hostage have survived? Would all 3 have been released, or even used as a bargaining chip for some other prisoners or piece of political agenda? Of course, David knew the most likely answer to these questions was a resounding "No".

Regardless, the nagging uncertainty reminded David that he knew that he was not cut out for such business. The entire operation still felt as though it was a blur, not unlike a dream that was more surreal than normal, and left a lasting impression into the following day. The difference, however, was that the memories didn't fade as a dream often does. Instead, it had cemented itself in his mind. The sound of the explosions as the building was breached, the *thunk* of bullets as they struck his windshield, the frenzied trip following the 3rd van that had found an unidentified hostage that they later discovered was not at all a hostage, but in fact a consultant with the FBI and a friend to one of the hostages.

These memories, though not nearly as traumatic as so many that had served in foreign conflicts or domestically as law enforcement, still elicited a fear within David. His first instinct had been to shun the idea of violence, to commit himself to being a man of peace for the duration of the ongoing crisis. It was, in fact, Alice and his daughters that had

170

changed his mind. Though he did not desire to seek violence, it had been sleeping in the basement with his wife beside him and the daughters on the floor, beside the wood stove, that reminded him he had something to fight for. Always a man to contend for his faith, David had glimpsed what he considered evil, evil that could harm and kill with no regard for human life. He knew the UWF were far from being the only individuals capable of such an ideology. History was rife with examples of dehumanization that inevitably led to a host of tragic outcomes, whether it be civil war, genocide, or others. He knew it was likely that groups aligned with Libertas, even some members of Libertas, were capable of such depravity. When politics were removed from the occasion, the country was still likely filled with escaped convicts, cartel members, human traffickers, drug dealers, crooked cops, rogue elements of the military, and more. Aside from more organized groups, there were countless individuals who, if given the chance, would gladly murder, rape, and plunder their way through life if they stood to gain. That was the world that Maya and Harper needed shielding from. Though Alice was quite capable in her own right, he still felt a call to protect her too from these evils.

David was not a warrior. It had never been in his blood. However, the world had changed; was it time that he changed as well? Perhaps, he was not one to charge into battle and to seek out war. But violence to protect, that was a different matter altogether. David was many things. He was a husband, a father, a farmer, a man of God, and a peacemaker. Now, for the sake of his family, it was time to be a guardian.

Epilogue

Charlotte followed Vir down an alley and used a large dumpster as concealment. The two didn't dare peer around the corner of the dumpster to watch as the handful of men ran by the entrance to the alleyway. They breathed a shared sigh of relief as the voices and their footsteps carried off down the street.

Something tugged at Charlotte's mind. It was too easy, too similar to how it was done in the movies, in which the protagonist would hide out of sight as the villains naively strolled by. In fact, she had needed the help of Vir a few nights prior to prevent such a villain from locating her outside of his apartment building. Could she count on such luck to favor her twice in a single week?

She peered around the corner. The coast was clear. The two waited another 20 seconds, before coming out from behind the dumpster. The moment they emerged, a third figure appeared at the entrance to the alley. The man did not have a gun, instead wielding a knife. However, he did have his voice, and as he looked at Charlotte and Vir, his sinister grin hinted at his intentions. He turned his head, preparing to summon the other individuals that had been pursuing Vir and Charlotte.

Their journey out of the D.C. area had been eventful, but relatively peaceful once they had escaped the area in which the militia groups had set up camp. The two had deemed a route to the northwest to be the wisest and had managed to make it to Frederick, Maryland. However, they soon realized that this desire to escape an urban area was a sentiment shared by many. Much of the East Coast of the United States, from D.C. to Boston, was a conglomerate of urban and suburban areas, particularly along the Interstate 95 corridor. In all, it was home to tens of millions of Americans, many of which now lived without power, running water, and effective law enforcement, and were running low on food and fuel. A sizable minority of those individuals, like their predecessors so many generations ago, had decided already that, perhaps, they would find better fortune out west. This migration had taken Vir and Charlotte by surprise. Others had seen it as an opportunity to take full advantage of, including the man that stood before them.

172

Charlotte looked at Vir. His face told of the same fear that now filled Charlotte. His hand reached to the small of his back and emerged with a handgun. He leveled it at the man, knowing that the handgun's report would be as likely to draw the attention of the others as the man's voice, but also more likely to elicit fear. Vir thumbed the safety into the off position and fired.

Made in the USA
Monee, IL
20 October 2021

80480091R00104